Kiss Her Goodbye

Kiss Her Goodbye

A MIKE HAMMER NOVEL

by **Mickey Spillane**
and **Max Allan Collins**

AN OTTO PENZLER BOOK
MARINER BOOKS
HOUGHTON MIFFLIN HARCOURT
BOSTON   NEW YORK

First Mariner Books edition 2012

Copyright © 2011 by Mickey Spillane Publishing LLC

www.hmhbooks.com

Library of Congress Cataloging-in-Publication Data
Spillane, Mickey, 1918–2006.
Kiss her goodbye : a Mike Hammer novel / by Mickey Spillane and Max Allan Collins.
p. cm.
ISBN 978-0-15-101460-6   ISBN 978-0-547-54120-4 (pbk.)
1. Hammer, Mike (Fictitious character)—Fiction. 2. Private investigators—New York (State)—New York—Fiction. 3. New York (N.Y.)—Fiction.
I. Collins, Max Allan. II. Title.
PS3537.P652K57 2011
813'.54—dc22   2010025839

Book design by Brian Moore

Printed in the United States of America

DOC 10 9 8 7 6 5 4 3 2 1

For Stacy Keach,
the Hammer of a generation

Coauthor's Note

In the week prior to Mickey Spillane's death, he told his wife, Jane, "When I'm gone, there's going to be a treasure hunt around here. Take everything you find and give it to Max—he'll know what to do." No greater honor could ever be paid me.

Half a dozen substantial Mike Hammer manuscripts were found in the "treasure hunt," frequently including plot notes, rough outlines, and even drafts of final chapters. These lost Hammer novels spanned Mickey's career, from the late '40s through the mid-'60s and up to *The Goliath Bone,* which he was working on at the time of his passing.

The unfinished manuscript for this novel, found on a desk in one of Mickey's three offices at his South Carolina home, included plot and character notes, as well as a shorter false start.

The theme of an older, ailing Mike Hammer returning to New York and finding it (and himself) changed was important to Mickey, and he revisited it in *Black Alley* (1996). But nowhere did he explore it with more passion than in the two partial manuscripts that I combined, shaped, and expanded into *Kiss Her Goodbye*—the "lost" '70s Mike Hammer, written as it was between *Survival . . . Zero!* (1970) and *The Killing Man* (1989).

M. A. C.

Kiss Her Goodbye

Chapter 1

I DIDN'T WANT to come back to New York.

Nothing was there for me anymore. After a year, I almost had the city out of my system. No nostalgia, no sense of loss, no reluctance at having abandoned a place that had been so much a part of my life.

All I felt was annoyance at having to return to a town I had flushed away in one wild firefight — a firefight that nobody but me remembered.

Even before I'd left, so-called progress had squeezed out the great old neighborhood spots, leaving sad relics behind that had become sophisticated corrals for the idiotic "in" crowd. When they tore down the old Blue Ribbon Restaurant on West Forty-fourth Street, it was the beginning of the end. Why the hell ever go back?

Only a call from Pat Chambers could have changed my

mind—the captain of Homicide who had hounded and helped me over a bloodstained career that had made the tabloids thrive and the Powers That Be apoplectic.

Pat's voice had been friendly, but not questioning, almost as if he understood why I chose to disappear, and that it was all right with him.

The Ocean View Motel had two floors of rooms and half a dozen cabins. I had one of the latter and was in the midst of an afternoon nap when the phone rang. It didn't surprise me he'd got the number somehow. Nobody had been informed of where I was because I wanted nobody to know, not even my best friend, which is what Pat was.

But a good New York cop can find anybody, if he wants to badly enough.

"Mike, Bill Doolan is dead. They're having services for him tomorrow night at eight at McCormick's Funeral Home."

It was as if a year hadn't passed at all.

"What happened?" I asked him.

"He shot himself."

"*Not* Doolan."

"*Yes* Doolan."

". . . You sure?"

"I'm sure." He knew I wouldn't question him any further, so added, "He was dying of cancer. The big-pain part was coming up just ahead, and he decided to bypass it."

Outside palm trees riffled in the wind. Beyond, blue endless ocean rippled under a butterscotch sun. No palms in Manhattan. The ocean there was endless, too, only gray, and the sun was blotted out by skyscraper tombstones.

"There's an afternoon flight out of here tomorrow around three," I said with a sigh. "I should get in about supper time."

"Cutting it a little close."

"Don't want a minute more in that town than I have to."

"So when did you start to hate New York?"

"When the medic yanked me out of a nice warm womb," I said, "and slapped my tiny ass."

"And you been trying to find your way back into one ever since."

"No shit." I paused, trying to fit details of the city back in my mind. "The Pub still open?"

"Still open."

"Get a reservation."

"Nothing changes with you."

"Yeah?"

"Still telling me what to do."

"So do it," I said, and hung up, and for a minute just lay there. Finally, I said, *"Damn,"* and hauled my behind off the bed.

The soft-pac suitcase was still in a corner of the closet and it didn't take me more than five minutes to lay out what I needed. One thing good about late spring—it packed easily. The three medicine vials went into a side pocket with the worn address book and I zipped the bag shut.

When I looked at myself in the mirror, I could only shake my head. It had been twelve months since I had worn a tie, and my suit jacket was loose around my waist, but dropping eighteen pounds will do that. There was no flab at all now, which was good, but the minimal exercise I was allowed hadn't done much for muscle tissue.

I knelt to get the oiled and loaded .45 and its shoulder rig out of the box under the closet floorboard, but then stood up quickly, like I'd almost touched something hot. The old days were gone now and it could stay where it was.

The weather forecast said it was raining in New York, so I packed the trench coat and got my hat out of the plastic bag, the last of God knew how many Stetson porkpies I'd bought over the years — a nice new feel to the gray felt. I snapped the brim into place, rolling the edge until I had it just right — that was one thing I still had. Nobody could wear hats anymore, but I had that down.

Then I took the porkpie off and carried it in my hand. Down here among the sun and palms and sand, a felt hat was a little too much.

Bag in my left hand, hat in my right, I walked over to the main building and called Marty out of the pool, where he was clowning around with two well-tanned beauties, a blonde and brunette, who spent the weekends working as mates on a headboat out of Key West.

The big ex-Marine motel manager with the white crewcut and dark tan stood there dripping, looking at me in my city clothes as he held back a grin in that well-grooved, blue-eyed face.

"Where are you going?" He nodded toward the bikinis. "There's one for you. Betty or Veronica. Take your pick."

"Not in the mood."

He grunted a laugh. "Still carrying the torch for that secretary of yours?"

I gave a look that said cool it.

Then I said, "I'll be gone a few days."

"I had a feeling," he said. He seemed to be considering bringing up the subject of my secretary again, but apparently thought better of it.

Good call.

"Tomorrow the doc will be stopping by," I said. "Just tell him I feel fine, that I'll be taking it easy, and not to have a cow over it."

A frown flashed across Marty's face. "He's gonna be pissed off, pal . . . and you know how he gets."

4

I nodded toward the pool. "Loan him your extra girl . . . Look, man, I'm going to a funeral. It's an old, old friend, and something I have to do."

He nodded. No grin. Eyes slitted. "One question, Mike."

"Yeah?"

"You gonna *attend* a funeral or are you gonna *cause* one?"

I just looked at him.

"Damnit, Mike, I'm serious . . ."

I waved it off. "No action this time, Marty. Strictly a pall-bearer."

"Yeah, but whose?" His shrug was one of resignation. "Okay, I guess I'll believe you. You been here a year and haven't killed any-body yet, and that must be a record." A sigh accompanied a second shrug. "Shit, I'll just keep your cabin locked up and hope you don't come back in a body bag. What about your car?"

"I'll leave it at the airport."

"Any idea when you'll be heading back?"

"Like I said—a few days. I'll call ahead of time. When Buzz comes in tonight, cancel that fishing trip."

"Sure thing." He let a long moment go by, then asked me with a frown, "Who knew where to get a hold of you down here?"

"I told you before, Marty—I left word with nobody. But the caller was a cop. He's a damn good friend and probably knew where I was all along."

"Really?"

"Really. Probably tracked me right from the beginning, which would've been hard but not impossible. I wasn't in good enough shape to lay a decent cover down."

His eyes widened. "But if your cop pal could find you, so could somebody *else* . . ."

I waved that off, too. "Forget it. Nobody's on my tail. I am very old news."

5

"Mike . . ."

"I told you before, Marty—they went down, I went down. It's all evened out. Nobody wants to start that crap all over again. Like Capone said, 'It ain't good business.'"

"Do I need to take on extra security precautions down here?"

"No. I won't be hiding in New York. If somebody wants to settle a score, that's where they'll do it. Anybody who wants to find me? Can."

But Marty looked worried. His war was a long time ago, and he was used to a life of sun and fun and boats and bikinis.

"They might follow you back, Mike, before settling that score. In Manhattan, you'll have your cop buddies around you. They're all badges and guns, and who the hell wants to take on that combo?"

"Marty, you got one hell of an imagination. It's not like I registered here under my own name."

"Bullshit. Do me one favor—when you're finished burying your friend, and whoever else the fuck you bury—sneak back down here, really make it on the sly, okay? Bullets flying might discourage return visits by guests."

"Pal, I'm an old pro at that sort of stuff. Now get back in the pool and play with your pussycats."

He grinned and waved goodbye and jumped back in the pool. Those two dolls together didn't add up to his age, but he was a bigger kid than they ever were. Still, he'd got me thinking.

So I went back to the cabin, got the .45 and speed rig out of their hiding place, and stuffed the holstered gun in the soft-pac between my underwear and shirts.

When you went to Florida, you took your fishing rod. For Manhattan, a rod of a different kind was called for.

I picked up the Piedmont flight at Key West and watched as the Florida Keys passed by under the wing. This time of year, traffic was light. The winter tourists had packed their gear and made the yearly trek north to escape the clean heat and humidity of summer to broil in their own sweat and the clamminess of those big cities where the graffiti grew.

At Miami I got a direct flight to New York and watched the ocean with its little toy boats until the coastline came into view again with its cities that thickened the farther north we got. At one time I would have felt like I was coming back to something alive, something vital, and would have had a drink in anticipation of hitting the Big Apple.

But it wasn't like that at all. At dusk from fifteen thousand feet, it was all fireflies and Christmas tree bulbs, winking and blinking; wormy lines of a million car lights on endless paths to nowhere, just keeping that big octopus down there in motion.

We landed at LaGuardia and I took my damn time getting down to the baggage claim. I didn't want that hot spot behind my ribs to begin kicking up again. When I had my bag, I walked out to the taxi stand, my fellow passengers long gone, and after a thirty-second wait got into a taxi and told the guy to take me to the Pub on East Fifty-seventh Street.

Now it was the city's turn to pass in review and it did a lousy job. Nothing had changed. No sudden sense of déjà vu—the smells were the same, the noise still grating, the people out there looking and waiting but never seeing anything at all. If they did, they sure as hell didn't let anyone know about it.

Going over the Fifty-ninth Street Bridge, the sounds and smells brought the city up closer and I was almost ready to crawl back into it by the time my cab turned off the East Side Highway. A few drops of rain splattered on the cab's windshield and I put my hat on. Up here it didn't feel out of place.

At the curb in front of the Pub, I passed a twenty and a five over the seat and told the driver to keep the change. For a second I caught his eye in the rearview mirror, a bald black guy with a graying beard that had a big blossoming smile in its midst as he said, "You been away, Mike?"

That's New York. The first native you see puts a finger right on you, as if he were your best buddy, and it almost makes you want to revamp your negative thinking.

I grinned back at him. "Why, you miss me?"

"Never see you at the jazz clubs anymore."

"I had to lay back a while."

"Yeah, yeah—there was something in the papers. You and that Bonetti kid. They clip you bad, Mike?"

I shrugged. "One in the side that went right through, and another that fragged my ass. A piece is still in there."

"Yeah, man." He shook his head. "I got one like that in Korea. Worked itself all the way down my leg and came out the back of my friggin' knee. That stuff *travels*. You take care, Mike."

"Sure, man," I said, and got out of the cab.

And there was Pat Chambers, a big rangy guy with gray eyes, an off-the-rack suit, and a mouth twisted in that soft cop grin he gets when the suspect drops it all down on tape and the case is closed on his end. He held out his hand and I took it.

"Welcome home, friend," he said.

"It was a fast year," I told him. "How have you been?"

"Still a captain. I think I'm glued in there."

"Too bad. Inspector Chambers has a nice ring."

"Not holding my breath. Hungry?"

"Starving. I skipped eating on the plane—a TV dinner at thirty thousand feet, I don't need. I hope those Irishers still know how to serve up the corned beef."

"Best in New York. Hell, you ought to know, Mike—you discovered the place."

I nodded, dropping back into the past again. All I did was follow the boys from Dublin who served out their apprenticeships at P.J. Gallagher's and opened up their own spot in real Irish-American tradition. And now their corned beef was a tradition all its own.

The supper crowd was three deep at the bar with all the happy noises that come when the Dow Jones is up and a few drinks are down. I waved at the bartenders, got a wink back, and followed Pat to the booth in the restaurant section.

When we were seated, Pat said, "You drinking anything?"

"Yeah. A Miller will go good."

"You mean with the corned beef special?"

"Natch."

He looked up at the waiter. "I'll have the same." He leaned back then, waited a moment, and asked, "How you feeling, Mike?"

"Fine—another few months and I'll be off the medication. I'm not running any footraces, but I managed to stay in shape."

"I don't mean that way."

His eyes were searching me now, friendly, curious, but still *searching*.

"Why, Pat? You think I might have an attitude problem?"

"Don't you always?"

After a moment, I said, "Not anymore."

"I asked you how you're feeling, Mike."

"And I said fine. Hell, man. I've been shot before."

"Yeah, and you've crawled off to recuperate before. But it never took you this long to show your face again."

"Maybe I'm getting older," I told him. "Why, did you miss me?"

"Yeah. Like an amputated leg that you keep trying to scratch."

The corned beef and beer came then, thick slabs of meat steaming on top of a huge baked potato, the beer foaming down the iced mug. We hoisted our glasses in a silent toast, gulped down half the contents, and got to the main course.

I let Pat take his time getting back to the questions again. They were all the same ones I had asked myself, but this time I had to give an answer.

"Why didn't you ever contact me, Mike?"

"I meant to, pal, I really did, but there was no urgency."

"Come on," he said softly.

When I looked up he was still watching me in that strange way. The expression was exactly the same as the one he had worn the last night he saw me in the hospital. It was my ninth day in the place, I was up and around, but still hurting like hell. Sleep hadn't helped any either . . .

. . . *my head still full of the wild banging of handguns and the crazy booming of shotguns, echoing across the pier, flame belching right past my face and even though I didn't feel the impact of the slugs that took me down I could remember the numbness and the slow drifting away that began to smother me. The face was there, too, blood smeared across the Bonetti kid's mouth, tight in a mad grin as he poked the barrel of his .357 against my forehead and said, "Die, you bastard," as he started to squeeze the trigger but he shouldn't have taken the time to say it because the .45 in my fist went off and his finger couldn't make the squeeze because the brain that should have sent it signals shut off like a switch as Bonetti's head came apart in crimson chunks like a target-range watermelon.*

And now, a year later, I sat in a familiar restaurant with my best buddy and my pulse rate had almost doubled and my breath was caught in my throat.

Damn.

"I got tired, Pat," I said. "I got tired of the whole goddamn mess."

"That kid was a fucking psycho killer. But he did us a favor, losing his cool—or maybe you did us the favor by goading him into that play. Shit. We wiped out damn near half the Bonetti family that night."

"And what good did it do, Pat? Twice the volume of drugs has come into the States since."

"But apparently not the Bonettis doing it," he said with a shrug. "That still leaves five families. Used to be six, till you squeezed the Evello bunch out, ten years ago. Anyway, that's ancient history."

I took another pull at the beer. "Sure. And all the assholes who want to get noodled up on poppy juice make it profitable for 'em. More power to the pricks."

"No. No attitude problem for you."

This time I finished off the beer and put the mug down. I waved for a refill and the waiter took the empty away. "I'm just plain tired of the game, Pat. I haven't got an attitude problem. I haven't *got* an attitude. Period."

The gray eyes turned placid. He smiled just a little. "Good."

I frowned at him. "And before you ask, let me tell you something. I haven't lost my nerve. It's just that it's finally occurred to me that tilting at windmills doesn't matter a damn in this lousy life. Let somebody else do the dirty work—like you cops, for instance."

"I been waiting years to hear this. Don't stop now."

"I *have* stopped. I'm not in it anymore. I haven't got the slightest faintest fucking desire to get wrapped up in that bundle of bullshit again. I've done it, it's past me, I'm retired."

For a full minute Pat went on eating, then nodded sagely. "And maybe it's for the best."

It was his tone of voice that made me ask, "What're you *not* saying?"

His eyes came back to mine. "Right now there's relative peace on the streets. After you wiped out young Bonetti, everybody thought the old man would try to lay a hit on you, and if it didn't take, you'd come roaring back at him with one of those wild-ass shoot-outs that you were so damn famous for. Hell, that's why we kept you under wraps in the hospital . . . until you slipped out on your own."

"Don't lay any blame on the uniforms guarding me—I'm still not that easy to babysit."

"I didn't. I don't."

"So what's Papa Bonetti think about it now?" My second beer came and I sipped the head off it. "Is there still a contract out for this old dog?"

"Not to our knowledge." He shrugged. "We took out so many of his men, and you killed his son—Alberto's a broken man. Sitting out his final years at his Long Island estate, and at that old social club. He's out of the business."

"Balls."

"Okay, so maybe he's not as retired as he says. I mean, somebody's distributing the stuff."

"But not the Bonetti family."

"Far as we know, they aren't major players in narcotics. They may still have some fingers in the racket, but their strong suits are loansharking and gambling. On the other hand, I don't think Alberto Bonetti's losing sleep over evening the score with Mike Hammer."

"You sound sure of that."

"I am. We went through some back channels and put the question to him. As far as he's concerned, the incident is closed. His boy Sal was a hothead who aimed higher than he could reach. The kid's dead, his pop's staying under the radar, maybe retired, maybe not. Either way, any more shooting would be bad all around."

I paraphrased the Capone quote I'd shared with Marty: "Lousy for business."

"And it would make our current administration *very* uneasy, as well."

"I'll bet," I said sourly.

We both went back to our corned beef, the noise around us building up as the bar crowd made its way back to the tables. It was a scratchy sound now, an irritant. I had been away from it too long, much too long, and a scene I once found comforting only annoyed. They sounded like a bunch of damn kids at a ball game, and Pat and I tried to cover it with our own grown-up conversation.

But there comes a time when the small talk fades and all you do is sit there looking at each other, wondering how to work up to the main event.

I said, "What happened to Doolan, Pat?"

His frown had a ragged edge to it, as if he didn't like the way it was going to sound. "I told you. He killed himself."

"Bullshit."

He lifted a palm, like he was swearing in at court. "That's what I thought when I first saw the report. Doolan was never the suicide type."

"Damn well told. There's no way you're going to make me believe *that*."

The gray eyes had a weariness now. "Suicide isn't really the right word, Mike."

"What's that supposed to mean?"

Pat sat back. "Physically healthy men who can't cope, and just plain give up and shoot themselves—*that's* suicide."

"So?"

"So a week ago Doolan had a final report from his doctor. He had a terminal cancer, and was about to go into the final stage. At best, he had about three months to live, and it was going to be a rough downhill ride all the way. He'd wanted to know the truth and the doctor pulled no punches—each day the pain would be worse and there was no way they could stop it."

I knew where Pat was headed.

He went on: "When the doctor confirmed what Doolan suspected, he went home and began putting his affairs in order. Got his will out of a lockbox and laid it out on his desk. His granddaughter gets most everything—the beach house, his insurance, and two fairly expensive paintings he'd bought years ago."

"Doolan buying paintings?"

"Don't laugh, Mike. Their value had gone up many times since their purchase."

"Who else was on his list?"

"The Patrolmen's Benevolent Association and a small bequest to an old buddy in a nursing home in Albany. From his desk, he called a cemetery on the Island and bought a short plot out there, and left a note to that effect attached to the will. It was dated the same day he died."

"Typed?"

"No. It was in his own handwriting and signed. No doubt about it being authentic."

"He did this on the day he died. And he left no other note?"

"No, Mike. But he shot himself, all right."

"Shot himself. And suicide isn't the right word?"

"Let's say it was deliberate self-destruction. Self-administered euthanasia." His shrug conveyed sorrow. "He was cutting out while he still had control."

Knowing old Doolan the way I did, it was hard to accept, yet on the surface that sounded reasonable enough. When a guy hits eighty, a dirty death is something he sure wouldn't want. Still . . . *Doolan?* Damn.

"How'd he do it, Pat?"

"With his own .38 revolver. He shot himself in the heart."

I looked up at him quizzically. "Old cops usually swallow the muzzle, pal."

"There are exceptions. He was one."

"You checked his hands."

"Sure. Doc did a paraffin test on him right there. He fired the gun, all right. Powder and flash burns right on his shirt. No unusual angle to the bullet entry. It would be easy enough to do. We even have a time for the shot. A little old lady heard it. She didn't know what it was at first, but got pretty damn suspicious. Her window opened right onto the air shaft from Doolan's, and she knew he was an old-timer cop."

"She the one who called in?"

"Uh-huh. And she placed the time right on the nose. The M.E. had an easy case on this one."

"How long had Doolan been dead before a car got there?"

"Maybe fifteen minutes." Pat knew what I was going to ask next and beat me to it: "The door was locked. First cops on the scene kicked it open."

"What about the street? Anybody see or hear anything?"

"Nothing. At ten-thirty at night, it's pretty quiet around there. Not like it's crawling with potential witnesses."

"There's a news vendor on the corner."

"I know. And he'd closed down a half hour before."

I shut my eyes and let it run through my mind. Finally I said, "Any doubts, Pat?"

He shook his head. "I wish there were."

"It just doesn't sound like old Doolan," I insisted.

"Mike . . . it is *old* Doolan we're talking about. Not the fireball we knew back in the early days. Not the guy that mentored us both, right after the war. When you get up there in years, hell, you change. *He* changed. You know that."

How could I argue about that? Hadn't I got older, and changed?

But I did argue: "No," I said flatly, "I don't *know* that. I admit the logic is there, Pat. But it still doesn't sit right."

"Hell, man. Cut me a goddamn break. I put *everybody* on it — we blitzed every angle we could before the day was out. Any real enemies Doolan had died a hell of a long time ago. He wasn't involved with any police matters, his circle of friends was small and of long duration. He was well-liked in the neighborhood, occasionally took part in civic affairs . . ."

"Like how?"

"Attended meetings when it concerned neighborhood problems or renovation. Things like that."

"Social life?"

"He would go to departmental retirement parties sometimes — I figure for him that was a big night out."

"What about his granddaughter?"

His wife and daughter were deceased; the one granddaughter was the only relative I knew of.

Pat said, "She still lives upstate with that slob she married. They got in town a couple hours ahead of you."

"Nothing there either?"

"Zilch. The grandson-in-law hasn't missed a day at work all year. Staying sober is probably killing him. If he gets drunk and beats up on Anna one more time, he goes up for a year. The judge really laid on him last time."

"She ought to dump that bum," I said.

"Right now she thinks she loves him. You know, old Doolan beat that kid's ass couple years back — Doolan in his seventies, the guy in his late twenties or early thirties. Funny as hell."

"So there's a suspect already."

He winced at that, and his eyes seemed tired now. "I told you, Mike, I've covered *all* the angles, including that one. There's not a reason in the world to label it anything except suicide."

I nodded, knowing that Pat was certain of his facts, but still reluctant to admit Doolan would renege on his ethical standards and take his own life. Hell, drugs could wipe any pain out right until he died, and Doolan had kissed death often enough not to be afraid of her.

"Take me through it, Pat," I said.

"Mike, imagine how many times I've—"

"One more time."

He sighed. "We got the call, the squad car responded, the officer broke the door down, went back to Doolan's study, flipped on the light, and saw the body—"

"Hold it. The place was dark?"

"Sure. But that's not unusual. You remember how Doolan was. Whenever he had a problem, he'd sit there in the dark listening to that classical music. And he had a problem, all right. That's what he was doing—thinking out a problem . . . a problem he finally solved with a single shot. And before you ask, the music tape was still going when the officer entered. At that point it was about three quarters completed."

"How long was the tape?"

"Ninety minutes." He let me drift over the picture, then added, "Convinced?"

I shrugged. "I keep forgetting the first lesson Doolan ever taught us."

"What's that?"

"Don't get emotionally involved with your cases."

Pat snorted. "Yeah, well, that's a lesson you didn't learn so good, did you?"

I grinned at him, but there was nothing funny in it. "Must've dozed off in class that day, Pat."

His eyes locked with mine. "You're satisfied with what I told you?"

"Absolutely, buddy," I said. "There's no disputing the facts at all. Everything points to a suicide. But are *you* satisfied, Pat?"

"Yes," he said. His eyes were hard, his chin jutted. "I'm satisfied." Then the eyes hooded and the chin lowered, and he let out a deep breath and shook his head. "But *you're* not, are you, Mike? Not *really?*"

"Buddy," I told him, "I'm not doubting you at all. It's just that I feel highly pissed off at Doolan for pulling a stunt like that."

If he pulled a stunt like that.

"He wasn't Doolan," Pat said resignedly. "He was an old man, Mike."

I was older. I was jaded. I had changed. I was tired. I was retired. *But I was still Mike Hammer.*

"Bother you if I look into it myself?" I asked Pat.

"Nope." He let out a sigh that must have started yesterday. "I knew you were going to. No matter what I said. Just tell me why."

"So I can be convinced — like you."

"Fine," he said. "Be my guest." He slapped the tabletop. "*Now* . . . let's go give the old boy a proper send-off."

And that was the real question, wasn't it?

Had somebody already given Doolan a send-off?

Chapter 2

Tomorrow there would be an inspector's send-off for Doolan.

The city would escort the cortege to the county line and the motorcycle squads would pick it up from there. At the gravesite there would be rifles fired over Doolan's casket, bugles blowing, and somebody would present a flag to his granddaughter. Then it would be over and everybody would go home glad that it *was* over so they could get back to normal again, the bureaucrats and the foot soldiers and distant relatives and kids of deceased parents who'd been the old boy's friends having served out their obligation to a dinosaur of a cop who had taken way too long to get around to dying.

But tonight was different.

Tonight would be the gathering of the clan, and like all re-unions, the pack would assemble in little groups according to age, rank, and serial number—the old-timers, long-retired, with their own little clique near the casket, those working buddies of Doolan's getting ready for their own inspector's parades. Gold badges gleaming on freshly pressed uniforms as the brass arrange themselves in ladderlike order of importance, wearing their funeral masks beautifully, but singing no praises to the corpse. In their own way, they'd be working.

We found a parking place down the block and walked till Pat nodded toward the old brick building with the gold lettering on its window.

"Let's go on in," he said. "Just about everybody else'll be there already."

I followed Pat, leaving my bag and my hat in the coat closet. Religious music played just softly enough to be heard but not loud enough to be recognized, and a female employee in her fifties with a white corsage and a trained sad face had us sign in at the book.

A good thirty cops, plainclothes and uniformed alike, were milling, chatting, ranging in age from late fifties to early thirties. Old Doolan had trained a lot of guys—*special* guys. The kind who had gone into some pretty high places—some on the streets, where the pace was fast and deadly, others up the departmental ladder where the air got thin with politics.

For the cops in the trenches, it wasn't a game that you retired out of. The end usually came with a startling suddenness and with little note of it anywhere. A lucky few stayed alive and slowed down enough so that they went into a desk job, where it was the *lack* of pace that killed them.

Pat was one of those organizational types who didn't fit the wildman mold, and had been steered by Doolan into an active but largely administrative role. Doolan was right in that decision, although Pat still could take care of himself on the street.

Me, Doolan had scoped out quickly. As far as he was concerned, I never should have had that early on-the-job army training in the Pacific, a kid who went in lying about his age and came out older than his years. *Lousy goddamn hellhole to go to school in,* he'd said.

"You learn to kill too young, kid," he'd told me, "and something happens. You can get to *like* killing — but on the PD, if you *have* to kill, you make it part of the job and not some emotional damn explosion."

I had a streak that worried him. Doolan had trained me and guided me, but I still lasted less than two years on the department before hanging out my private shingle.

"The rules dictate the action," he told me once.

And, punk kid that I was, I'd just grinned and said, "Yeah? Well, if there *are* no rules, you have to make your own up on the spot, don't you?"

Doolan had lost me my job. I hated him for it — for maybe a month. Years later, he let me read the memo he put through, advising that the NYPD send me to a desk or cut me loose.

"This is a good man," he'd written, "a brave man, and he has brains. But his emotions dictate his behavior, and he is the kind of unpredictable officer who will cause tragedy for himself and others."

I couldn't challenge that assessment.

Still, he had trained me well — all these years later, and here I was, still alive. One of the walking wounded maybe, but alive.

The sweet smell of flowers sickened me. I said to Pat, "Where are all the bad guys? Aren't they required by their dumb-ass code to come by and pay their respects?"

Pat glanced at his watch. "It isn't eight o'clock yet. They like to make an entrance."

"I'd like to help them make an exit. Why, after so many years, do these Cosa Nostra boys bother with all this ritualistic crap?"

"Tradition—gives 'em a sense of structure and pseudomorality. Whether they like it or not, they're still tied to old-country ways. The young guys hate it, but all of that omertà bull is bred into them, and they can't get rid of it."

"You turned into a regular philosopher, Pat."

"Hanging around you will do that." He nodded toward a little civilian crowd near the simple pine-box coffin. "Let's tell his granddaughter hello . . . even though any tears she sheds will be of joy, anticipating what she'll inherit."

"I got no argument with *that* philosophical insight."

I followed Pat, nodding to some of the cops I knew. One, a captain from uptown, said, "I thought you was dead."

"You thought right," I told him.

He frowned, trying to work that out.

Nearer the coffin, the crowd thinned. Pat fell in line by the mass of floral displays from the police and fire departments, a dozen lodges, and a full wall from old friends. I looked at my own watch. Ten minutes to eight.

A red-headed fading beauty, Anna Marina, Doolan's only grandchild, was putting on her own stage play. Her makeup was dutifully smeared, her dark, church-perfect clothes indicated proper bereavement, but there was no real sorrow on display. Her hulking husband stood beside her, not really capable of showing any decent emotion, unless it was a frustrated desire for a drink. His dark suit was rumpled and he could use a shave.

I had known Anna since she was a kid, but no love was ever lost between us. I saw through her manipulative girly ways, so she was never pleased to see me. Maybe in part it was because I busted her wiseass husband in the chops one night for a lousy remark he made about somebody whose color he felt superior to.

22

She looked up at me, her mouth tight.

I said, "Anna. Sure sorry about this. Doolan and I were always great friends."

"I'll never understand that. He got you *fired.*"

"It was the right thing. Doolan put me on my path."

Her upper lip curled. "It would be more respectful if you called him 'Mr. Doolan,' or even 'Bill.'"

"Sure. Bill was a mentor to me, and I'll always love him for it. You and I have never been tight, but if you ever have problems . . ." I glanced at the husband who had sent her to the emergency room more than once. ". . . just let me or Pat know."

Now I swung my head and stared straight at hubby Harry Marina. He was looking at me and gauging the pounds I'd lost, and taking in the looseness of my collar, and he had a wet-lipped expression like a nasty, stupid mutt wondering whether or not to take a bite out of a puppy.

What the hell. I was trying to keep it friendly, out of respect to Doolan. Anyway, I was an old tiger now, and who knew if I could go up against a big slob like this anymore.

So I just grinned at him and his face seemed to freeze and little white lines formed half-moons around his nostrils and almost unconsciously he pulled back a few inches.

Pat was watching me, his eyes narrowing. I nodded to Anna and walked away.

When we were in the crowd, Pat said, "I'd swear that clown wanted a piece of you."

"You think?"

"Man, you shouldn't grin at people that way. You scared the shit out of him."

I was about to tell Pat I wasn't trying for that kind of action, but suddenly he wasn't there, having paused to speak to somebody—a tall, sandy-haired guy with a narrow, well-chiseled face with light blue eyes and a tan even deeper than mine. The guy's dark gray tailored suit with lighter gray silk tie screamed money, but quietly.

"Mike, meet Alex Jaynor."

Jaynor's hand gave up a good, solid grip.

"I feel like I know Mr. Hammer already," Jaynor said good-naturedly. "My admiration goes way back—you've made for a lot of great reading over the years."

"More fun to read about," I said with half a grin, "than to experience."

"Alex is our new congressman from this district," Pat told me.

Jaynor held up a hand as he gave me his own half a grin. "Don't hold that against me," he said.

"I'm not a voting type myself," I told him.

"Why not, Mr. Hammer?"

"The politicians—it only encourages them."

"Ouch," Jaynor said, still friendly. "I'm hoping there are a few of us these days who might change your opinion, maybe even get you into a voting booth."

"You're welcome to try. Where'd you get your tan?"

"Damn," he said with a chuckle, "I was just about to ask you that." One dark hand gestured to another. "What you see here, I'm afraid, comes out of a machine in a little cubicle—one hour a day, every other day. You've caught me already, Mr. Hammer—just another phony."

I smiled at that. "Honest enough to admit it, anyway. And make it 'Mike' . . . me, I'm a beach bum these days—Florida."

He gave me a confused frown. "I thought you were strictly a Manhattanite."

"Call it a leave of absence." I shrugged. "Got to where I'd had about as much of New York as I could stand. You getting a head start on a summer tan?"

Jaynor laughed abruptly. "Hell no. This is show-off stuff. The voters love it. And you know who advised me to do it? Bill Doolan. He said I should follow the JFK model—present myself as young, vital, fresh. Said voters were tired of looking at ward-heeler types."

"So Doolan was *your* mentor, too?"

"Oh, yes. He knew this city, and its inner workings, like nobody else. Now I'll just have to take off the training wheels and learn to ride on my own."

Pat glanced at me and grunted. "Guess old Doolan had angles I never knew about."

"Well, he needed a hobby, Pat—too old to chase women anymore. How'd *you* get to know him, Alex?"

"It was a few years back, when I was a reporter for *McWade's*."

"That's the Canadian magazine, right? Sort of their *Life*?"

"Right. But I covered the New York beat for them, or anyway was one of several journalists who did. There was some juvenile gang activity in Doolan's neighborhood and he pulled out all the stops to help get things calmed down. That guy was damned near unbelievable, the way he could relate to young roughnecks."

"Tell me about it," I said.

"Anyway, I did a big layout on his neighborhood work, and we got to be friends. He's the one who encouraged me to move out of journalism and into politics—to quit writing about problems, and really get my hands dirty solving them." He stopped, nodding toward the door. "Well—here they come . . ."

"Eight o'clock," Pat said with a lift of the eyebrows.

"Rogue's gallery on parade," I muttered.

It took two men in delivery livery to carry each floral wreath, fourteen altogether. When the wreaths were arranged, the donors appeared, somber well-dressed men who made the circuit past the suddenly hushed assembly to the pine coffin, then to Anna and her husband.

Camera flashes started then, not with the wild brilliance of the old bulbs, but the muted winks from the new electronic jobs. I hadn't even noticed the damn reporters and photogs lurking, but they scurried into play like cockroaches when a light switches on.

The press had been waiting for this parade of dapper killers, the other inhabitants of Doolan's world who had come under the inspector's gun, and respected him for it.

Every one of these cops knew every one of them, the young crowd who hated the term "button man," the capos who had the look of progressive business about them, and the elder dons, two under indictment and another just released from a five-year sentence.

And Alberto Bonetti.

The old man wasn't big, but he had the forced rigidity of a soldier on parade. His oval face had a softness to it, but I knew that was forced too, his gray hair combed back immaculately, his eyebrows black as an eightball. He was a man of many masks and this was the one he wore at funerals. Even his hands were under total control and, if you didn't know him, you would think he was merely a dignified old man trying to live out his life.

Only when he was almost past me did he stop, turning his whole body on a swivel to recognize me with a smile. "Ah, Mr. Hammer. *Michael* Hammer."

I barely nodded. "Mr. Bonetti."

His smile widened a bit as I matched the formality he'd given me. "Please know that I am very sorry for the loss of your friend. He was an honest man. A good man. A rare thing in a dishonorable world."

I managed not to tell him to stuff the pretty speeches. Instead I just said, "You knew Doolan pretty well yourself, I understand."

"Oh yes, very well." The old don chuckled. "Don't you recall, Mr. Hammer? A long time ago, he sent me up for seven years."

"A bad rap?"

Again, the mob don let out a little laugh. "Only my being *caught* was bad. I understand, many years ago, he threw you off the force."

"Not exactly threw me off. Recommended I be taken off the street and put on a desk."

"Which, of course, he knew would mean you would resign, and seek other employment. So we have Bill Doolan to blame for Mike Hammer becoming a private vigilante."

"Not vigilante. Not anymore. Just a private detective. And a retired one."

"Really?" He paused to look at me critically, taking in my tan. "You have enjoyed Florida, I see."

I almost smiled. "Well, it makes a nice change from the city."

"Yes. I get to Florida from time to time. My friends there tell me you have quite a reputation as a fisherman. For snook, I believe."

"I'm a rank amateur. But I go out with pros, so yeah . . . I caught a few fish in my time."

That made him smile, just a little. Then: "Maybe someday I will join you in sunny retirement. When a man gets lonely, there are some things better done in another's company."

"Anytime, Mr. Bonetti."

"Good evening, Mr. Hammer."

He turned on a swivel again to join the others, smiling back at the hostility coming at him from the rows of police. The cameras never stopped until the doors closed behind them.

Only then did Alex Jaynor say, "What was *that* all about?"

There was a touch of irony in Pat's voice when he said, "Old Alberto was letting my friend here know that he knew all along where Mike Hammer has been holed up. That he could have had Mike tapped out at any time."

Jaynor frowned. "*Killed?*"

"Certainly."

"But why?"

I said, "Because I blew his kid's head off."

The politician's jaw dropped in sudden remembrance. "Hell, that's right, isn't it? A year ago . . . but you were almost friendly with the man, Mike."

"Old man Bonetti knows his son Sal was a bad seed," I said. "He knows it was self-defense. If he'd decided to have me killed, it would have been to save face, not out of revenge."

Pat was studying me. "You see any of his guys down there in sunny F-L-A?"

"I wasn't looking."

He made a face. "Playing stupid isn't your game, buddy."

"Pat, I just didn't give a damn. And I *wasn't* in the game. Still aren't."

"Now you *know* Bonetti knows your Florida address. Doesn't that bother you?"

"Why should it? If he wanted me dead, it would have gone down a long time ago. And now? Now there's no sense killing me anymore."

Jaynor had the expression of a guy visiting a foreign country who has lost his translation booklet. "Why would you think that, Mike?"

"Because there's no profit in it, Alex—and profit is all those guys live for."

Pat was checking his watch. "Mike—it's time." He reached in his suitcoat pocket and handed me the small canvas pouch with the metallic lump in it.

"Sure you don't want to handle this, Pat?"

"No. Doolan would've wanted you to do it."

So I nodded to each of the men as I walked to the coffin. All of them wore those invisible scars of the field, and they nodded back, each with a subtle look of curiosity because although I was, in a way, one of them, I hadn't played on their team for a long, long time.

I stood there looking at what was left of Bill Doolan. Once he had been young and vital as hell, but what was left was an old gray-headed corpse, barely recognizable. The stupid embalmer had tried to cover up the scar across his left eye and fill out the cheeks that had always been hollow with contained rage. Those bony hands should have been clenched into fists instead of being folded across his chest like all the other dead bodies in the world.

I looked at a mannequin cosmetically prepared to hide all signs of reality. For that I was glad. This wasn't Doolan at all. The real man still lived in memory.

When I'd finished looking at what was left of my mentor, I took a step back and felt the others come up around me. I reached in the canvas pouch, then unwrapped the oily cloth and held out the hammerless Browning automatic for all of them to see.

Carefully, I dropped the clip and let them see me thumb a full load in place, then snap it back and jack one into the chamber. With the rag I cleaned the piece off, then separated Doolan's hands from their frozen position and got the Browning into his right palm as best I could.

The Little Italy bunch weren't the only ones who had rituals.

I said, "Bill Doolan gave this to Pat Chambers a long time ago, and really it should be Pat up here talking now. Pat and the rest of you were really his boys. Yet in my two short years on the force, Doolan twice saved my ass, and if he had notched this gun butt the way they did in the old West, there wouldn't be anything to hold on to now. At least when that pine box he's in collapses under the dirt, he and that gun will fade out of existence at the same time. So long, buddy."

Two of the quiet men stepped forward, closed the lid of the coffin, then hammered it shut with steel-cut nails. In that solemn place the sound of the banging was almost thunderous, and when they were done, what was left was just a box — a rough-cut pine box resting on a pair of sawhorses, as Doolan himself had specified.

Everybody turned their backs when the attendants came in with the table and wheeled the coffin out.

Strange, I thought, *real strange. Like a bunch of kids in their clubhouse, playing at something.*

These cops may have shared a strange little ritual, preparing their friend for the boneyard; but those guys weren't playing. Death was part of every cop's life, whether you bought it on the street or survived into an old age haunted by nightmares or ate the muzzle of your gun as a rookie who couldn't take it or an old soldier who wanted to one-up the Big C.

The guests had started to clear out. The photogs were first, hurrying to get their pictures into the labs, then the police. Pat and I walked Alex Jaynor to the door — he seemed moved by the simple, if odd ceremony. Well, Doolan had been his mentor, too.

Alex got cornered by a reporter, and we left him behind as we headed down the street for a booth in the nearest gin mill.

Pat and I both ordered a Canadian Club and ginger ale, and toasted each other silently.

Over the second drink Pat suddenly said, "What about Velda, Mike?"

The sound of her name hit like a physical blow and I had trouble looking at him. "It's over."

"That simple. 'It's over.' Why is it over?"

"Can't we drop the subject?"

"No. She was too much a part of you. Of *us*. What happened?"

Suddenly the drink tasted lousy. "Hell, I was dying. My life expectancy was maybe a month. I wasn't about to let her watch me go out like a cat that's been half run over, yelling and screaming until they shot the drugs into me again."

"But you pulled through."

"Nobody thought that old army surgeon could bring it off. The odds were ridiculous. I signed the papers and let him go ahead because I thought it would be an easy way to get the whole damn thing finished with in a hurry."

"What are the odds now?"

I shrugged. "If I'm not *too* stupid, I'm going to make it."

He nodded, sipped his drink. "That brings us around to Velda again. When you knew you were coming out of the tunnel, why not let her know?"

I shook my head. "You saw Bonetti in there. His soldiers might have shown up at any time. She'd have been at my side when the bullets started flying."

"She's a big girl. Not your average secretary. She's a P.I. herself, and then there's her military intelligence background. What makes you think she couldn't have handled that?"

"Because she loved me, Pat. You know it, I know it, and we both know I didn't deserve her, but there it is. She would have been so distracted, worrying about me, nursemaiding me, she could easily have taken a hit. And I could stand a lot of things, Pat . . . but after all these years, losing her because she's trying to save me? No. No way. *Now* can we change the subject?"

"Mike, you don't tune somebody out when you love them."

"You said it yourself, Pat. She's a P.I. Probably a better detective than either of us. If she'd really wanted to find me, she could have."

"Really? After your *letter?*"

Barroom noise and chatter filled a pregnant silence.

Finally I said, "You know about that?"

A sad little frown flitted across his face. "Yeah, I know about it."

I tried not to ask. I swear to God, I tried not to ask.

"What's happened to her, Pat?"

He looked past me, gnawing gently at his lip. When he was ready, he said, "Six months ago, she called. She'd gotten your letter. She read it to me, Mike. How could you say those things to her?"

I had to ask him.

"How'd she sound?" I tried to keep the anxiety out of my voice.

He thought about it, then shrugged. "Cold. Remote. Not the way she used to."

"Come on, Pat."

"There was a new man in her life, she said. She said she'd moved on, and called me to say she was leaving town. She did . . . just mention that she . . . wondered if you were still alive, or if you had asked about her."

My chest felt tight and my shoulders bunched up under my coat.

He was saying, "I told her I didn't know where you were, and that we hadn't spoken since you slipped our guard at the hospital. She told me your letter had a Miami postmark, which gave me a starting point, tracking you down. The last I heard, she'd left town."

". . . New man in her life. Well, good. I'm glad for her."

"In a pig's ass you are."

"Let's just say I can handle it, okay? It was a phase of my life."

"A goddamn *long* phase."

"You know me, Pat. Women come and go."

32

"Yeah, you come and they go. But *not* Velda—she was a constant. She was with you for . . . forever."

I'd thought it would be forever.

"Like I said," I said as casually as I could manage, "now it's over."

"I'm supposed to believe you're not hurting?"

"I'm *not* hurting. I won't forget her, but I'm not all whacked out of shape over it."

I leaned back and wondered whether or not I was lying. For sure, I'd never forget her.

Never.

In his typical fashion, Pat turned the whole subject upside-down. He asked very casually, "You have a gun on you?"

He was a winner, all right.

"No. I haven't carried one since that night at the pier."

"You renewed your permit."

"The man's a detective . . . yes, and my driver's license and the one for the agency. The office is closed but the rent is paid up. I sublet my apartment but didn't let it go."

"Why? Why bother?"

Good question. "Some things you just never give up, pal."

"Are you planning on staying?"

"Not long-term. Not sure I could handle that dark cloud you say follows me around."

He waved for the waiter and asked for the check. "You need to crash with me?"

"No thanks. I booked a room at the Commodore." I waited a moment, then added, "I want to go over to Doolan's pad tomorrow."

"I figured as much. No problem. When you're done, we'll turn the place over to Anna, and she and her husband can loot it. Come on, I'll give you a ride to the hotel."

We walked to where he'd parked his old sedan. Pat pulled out and turned left, cruising down one of those sick streets where nobody gave a damn about anything. If you were a stranger, you'd wonder where the slopped-up jokers got the money to buy a pint and who the hell those poor old hookers were going to solicit in *this* neighborhood.

We were in the nowhere zone of a street that had died and hadn't been buried yet. Somehow, nobody had broken the antiquated street lamps yet and a pale yellow blob of light seemed to droop away from the poles.

"What's this, a shortcut?" I asked.

"Just cutting around some road maintenance. Besides, you ought to remember this area."

"When I left it was different."

"Nothing stays the same."

"Just this old car of yours—*damn!*"

"What?"

I gripped his sleeve. "Pat—hold it."

He laid on the brakes.

"Go back," I said tightly. "Between the lights."

He shifted into reverse, gassed the car backward till I told him to stop, then I jumped out and ran to the sidewalk. Behind me, his sedan squealed into a tight turn, then ran up to the curb with the headlights shining like twin theatrical spots on the body sprawled on the concrete.

She was blonde and young but the frozen grimace wiped out any prettiness she might have had. There was terror in her half-open eyes and her chin drooped into a silent death laugh. She hadn't been down more than thirty seconds because blood was still puddling from the gaping wound in her chest.

Pat checked her pulse, nodded at me, then both of us moved at the same time, running away from the body to cover both ends of the street. But there was no movement, no sounds of panicky feet or the odd noises of somebody trying to be quiet when things are closing in. It was one of those damned unlivable streets you find here and there in the city, condemned, partially dismantled, dirty, and only good as a walkway from one avenue to another—that is, if you didn't give a flying fuck for your life.

Back at the car, Pat finished calling in the kill and asked, "Nothing?"

I shook my head. "There are a dozen open basements on either side that anybody could have dropped into. You know these buildings. Those tunnels go right through to the other street."

"There are cars coming in from both sides. We may get lucky."

"No way," I told him. "These street people make a science out of disappearing." I shook a finger at the corpse. "Put the light on her hand."

Pat flashed the beam over and saw what I meant. A thin purse strap was still clutched in her fingers, the cut-off loop of it going around her wrist, the bag itself M.I.A.

The captain of Homicide swore under his breath. "Kid like that, dead—over a lousy goddamn mugging."

"Looks like he came up behind her, and she spun around when he made a grab for the purse, and he stuck her when she started to scream."

Pat thought about it a moment. "Usually this kind of mugging would be a face-to-face job."

"If he were waiting for a patsy around here, he'd have a long damn wait. No—this mugger followed her. And if she's a hooker, she doesn't belong around here, not in that spring frock."

She was maybe twenty-five, slender, and you could tell she'd had a nice shape until death twisted it into a kind of question mark that left her very physicality asking *Why?* The butter-color hair was long and curled and styled, the dress was a pink and white floral with short-sleeve cuffs, worn with nude panty hose and pink pumps.

"Hell, Mike, it's fifty yards to either corner. She would have heard him."

"Not if he were wearing sneakers. These bastards stay in step with the victim, but faster. She only heard her own feet. Dig her shoes—they're heavy leather heels and soles."

Before he could answer, the first squad car turned the corner. Behind it, we could hear the siren of the following one.

But for Pat's taste, they were on the slow side, and he said, "We're going to have to motivate these drivers a little more."

It was less than an hour before they were finished. The area had been covered by a search team that turned up one sodden drunk passed out in an alley, the photos had all been shot, and Pat had given all the details to the only reporter who bothered to show up, a young kid from the *News*. In New York, only muggings with a death involved got any notice at all.

The odd note was the arrival of a new white Japanese sports car that nosed right in between the police cruisers and, with an impatient blast of the horn, signaled two of the uniforms to make room at the curb. Ordinarily anybody who pulled a stunt like that would be snatched out of the car and laid down for a full inspection; but the officers just edged out of the sporty number's way.

Pat was squatting down beside the body, going over final details with Les Graves, a fifty-ish, heavyset, graying detective from Homicide South.

I knelt next to them and asked, "Anything?"

Graves snapped his miniature flashlight off and clipped it on his pocket. "Unless she's got something tattooed on her, she's clean. Any I.D. would've been in her purse."

Pat got back on his feet. "Well, we'll see how we make out with her prints and the laundry marks."

The door to the white car opened, but until the driver got into the glare of the headlights, I couldn't tell who the guy was.

Some "guy."

Some pussycat—a tallish, black-haired doll in a gray pants suit with black trim housing a body with curves even her sports car would find it a challenge to navigate. Self-confidence was there in her face with its hooded yet sharp dark eyes, daring anybody to doubt her—the new breed of professional woman who wasn't afraid to stay feminine while she broke your very balls.

I asked, "Who the hell's that?"

Graves thought I was kidding until Pat said, "He's been away, Les."

"Oh."

"She's an assistant D.A.," Pat told me, "and a real pisser." He turned and waved to the pair on the morgue wagon. "You can take it now."

But the lady assistant D.A. called out, "*Just one moment,*" and clicked over on heels to step in front of them.

I could feel myself starting to grin because this little scene was about to be a real beaut. I had known Pat too many years not to realize what was about to happen, and this pretty little broad—well, not so little—was about to get her ass chewed out by an expert.

But the show she just put on spoke of political clout and I wasn't about to let Pat get hung out on a hook to dry.

So I shoved my hat back and got right in her face where she could get a good look at all my teeth. And I have a few.

"Lady," I said, "I don't know what you think you're pulling, but this is a crime scene. I'd advise you to get your attractive tail back in that un-American bucket and beat it the hell out of here."

One of the uniforms choked back a laugh so hard he farted.

Les snapped his head around and growled at his boys, "Who did that?"

This pulled all the heat out of Pat and, despite his frown, his eyes were grinning like hell. A fart in the night had broken the ice —who'd have thunk it?

Pat pushed me out of the way nice and easy, laying all the apologetic charm he could dredge up. "I'm very sorry, Ms. Marshall, but this, uh, detective didn't recognize you. And this *is* a crime scene."

The cockiness she had rocketed in with had been shot down and she wasn't going to let it get worse. When she thought she had it together, she slowly turned to me to deliver that big stare that withers the weak, but my teeth were still on display and I don't remember the last time I withered.

She took a good look at me and knew not to take me on.

Smart.

Softly, yet loud enough for all to hear, she said, "Captain Chambers, I want this *detective* in my office at nine tomorrow morning," then hip-swayed back to her car, got in, and drove off, in full control again.

The guy with the body bag at the mouth of the morgue wagon looked at Pat. "Now?"

"Sure. Go ahead."

I had my hands on my hips and was looking in the direction where she'd disappeared. "What was *she* all about, Pat?"

"Ms. Marshall came in on the last election."

"Any good?"

Pat shrugged. "Started out a civil-rights attorney. They got good ones and they got bad ones, but this one's a pain in the ass."

"In what way?"

"She has a radio in her car and keeps sticking her pretty butt in where it doesn't belong."

"Well, at least she's interested."

"Interested in spotting the important cases."

"Why, is this one of 'em?"

He shrugged. "Doesn't look like it. But she's always out trolling for headlines. That was a good try you gave, cutting her down a notch."

I said, "Whoever farted wins the medal on that one."

Behind Pat they were lifting the body into the rubber bag. Rigidity had set in and an arm flopped down, something flashing near a cuffed short sleeve, the edge of which the attendant grabbed to lift the limb back in place.

I felt a frown settle across my face. *Back in this concrete purgatory just a few hours, and I find death,* murder, *waiting for me. But this had nothing to do with me. Right? This was just another goddamn mugging gone tragically wrong.*

Right?

Pat said, "Mike — did you hear me?"

I hadn't. "Oh, sorry. What'd you say?"

"Marshall — the assistant D.A.? She doesn't know you, and I don't *want* her knowing you. Tomorrow, when you don't show, she'll call me and I'll put Peterson on her. The inspector's no friend of hers and he won't let any of his guys get hassled, so everything stays clean."

Now I gave him the grin. "Not with that big kitten."

"Mike —"

"What's her first name?"

"Angela."

"Beautiful name for a beautiful woman, Pat . . . only that's no angel."

The morgue wagon pulled away and two cruisers followed it. I walked over to where the body had been and stared down at the sand they had poured out over the spilled blood.

I don't know why these simple kills bother me. There was nothing elaborate about it. Just a lousy mugger punching a hole in a young girl's chest to grab what few bucks she had in a cheap handbag. Bing. One life down the drain. Maybe enough in that bag for a fast snort.

I bent down and picked up a handful of sand and let it sift through my fingers until only a pebble was left. Some great headstone. Fingering it, I stood up and absentmindedly stuck the little stone in my pocket. Now I had a souvenir to commemorate my homecoming.

"Let's get you to your hotel, Mike."

I got in Pat's old sedan and slammed the door shut. He put the key in the ignition, but didn't turn it. "You know, kid," he said, "I can't go anyplace with you. Man, sometimes I think a dark cloud *does* follow you."

"Hey, you're the one invited me back, remember?"

Chapter 3

MY EYES OPENED of their own accord to a morning that was purely New York, a shadowed city whose light strained to get in the hotel room. The digital clock read 6:15 A.M. in Frankenstein green, but twenty stories below, Forty-second Street was already snapping and growling at anybody stupid enough to be down there.

I never should have told Pat my attitude was fine. Hell, I had one great big fat attitude problem right now. Three hours from here the sun was a lively hot thing bouncing off waters so blue it took your breath away, shimmering off white sand soft as flour. From here, even the sand spurs didn't seem so bad.

If I could have woken from the nightmare that was New York into the sunshine reality of Florida, I'd have gladly done so. What was keeping me here? Why not get back on a plane today? This morning?

Doolan had been dead before I arrived, and I didn't even know the name of that dead blonde last night. An old copper with cancer ends it all; a cute dumb kid with a nice shape walks into the wrong neighborhood and becomes a mugging fatality.

What were they to me?

Something. I wasn't sure what exactly. *Not yet. But something. . . .*

A year's habit was too much to break and I rolled out of bed, brushed my teeth, then went into the exercise routine. It wasn't a vanity kick, rather a medically ordered series that got injured muscle tissue back into working order. But I felt like I needed to be doing more, and would do something about that. When I had a good sweat going, I broke it, jumped in the shower, and when I got out, threw on a robe.

The room-service waiter brought the morning edition of the *News* up with my coffee, and I thumbed through it page by page, reading every damn line of every damn item like some suburbanite about to go off to work. But I couldn't fool myself too long, and finally just flipped the pages until I caught the squib almost buried among minor items about the night before.

SLAIN GIRL FOUND ON STREET
Apparent victim of mugging. Unidentified at present. Caucasian, age about 25, five feet four inches tall. Investigation continuing.

Relieved the *News* reporter hadn't recognized me at the scene —I was in no mood to be a sidebar—I tossed the paper and stared out the window, the old juices stirring.

This is a load of crap, I thought, and I had to cut it out. The old days had come to an end a year ago on that pier. There was no profit in getting shot up, and no glory in being made the fall guy.

But at least I got out of it alive. That young girl on the sidewalk was dead. And nobody even knew who she was.

What was it Doolan had said?

"There are some things you just can't walk away from, kid."

I climbed into sweatshirt and slacks, packed a duffel bag of fresh clothes, went down to the street, and grabbed a cab to Bing's Gym.

Nothing had changed. It was still a nondescript old building with dirty windows, and I wondered why health-conscious athletes would want to train there anyway. The interior had that sweaty jock-strap smell of all locker rooms and floating dust mites kept up a perpetual haze in the main gym.

Bing spotted me before I reached the door of his office and came out and wrapped his arms around me.

"Damn, Mike, it sure is good to see you."

He pushed back and grinned up at me, all fat and happy with his hair a monklike white semicircle. It would be hard to guess he'd been a flyweight champ in the thirties.

"Mike, where the hell you been? Look at you, like a nut, brown like a nut. You don't get *that* in New York."

"I'm kind of out of season for the city, kid. This is Florida gold you're looking at."

"Whatever it is, you look great, Mike."

"Quit lying."

He shrugged. "So you lost weight, so you look run-down. What's important is, how do you feel?"

"I feel lousy."

"It's a start. This stems from when you got shot?"

I nodded.

Bing looked at me carefully. "You want to work out?"

"The easy stuff," I told him.

"Like easy for who? I remember what you *used* to handle. . . ."

I let out a short laugh. "Not the big boy weights, pal. Make it a routine for a middle-aged beginner."

"That bad?"

"It's getting better." I glanced around the room. "You got new equipment."

"Sure. Everybody's into bodybuilding now. Don't let it bother you. Tension and weights you can adjust for a kindergartner to a Schwarzenegger. I'll check you out personally on the apparatus."

"Apparatus," I said. "Where did you hear that word?"

"It was in the manual."

"Never too old to learn."

For a full hour I went through the prescribed exercises. My body ached, the sweat poured off me, but there was the satisfying feeling of knowing that I was coming back together again. The one thing I couldn't do was overexert myself. Inside me a lot of healing still needed doing. I put in fifteen minutes of light jogging on the treadmill, then soaked in the shower room a full half hour before I got dressed.

On my way out, Bing asked, "You gonna be a regular again?"

"Long as I'm in town."

"What does that mean? A vacation's one thing, Mike, but you belong in the city."

"Not anymore."

A knowing grin creased his face. "Balls. Guy like you can't escape the city. Hell, you got a blood contract with this place. You're married to the old girl."

I grunted. "I'm about ready to kiss her goodbye."

He just shook his head. "Never happen."

"Think not?"

"Naw, Mike, never. You forgot to sign a prenup."

I laughed, let him have the exit line, went back down to the street, and started walking.

It was a different Forty-second Street at that time of morning, still dirty and noisy, but busy with a freshness that would last until after lunch. I took my time and just before nine reached the official building I wanted. The person I was after had a listing on the directory, and I caught the elevator to the fifth floor.

In an office suite paneled in what we used to call a masculine fashion, the severe young woman behind the desk regarded me with no apparent curiosity whatever. She had dark-rimmed glasses and light brown hair pinned back, but it didn't do any good—she was still attractive.

In a neutral tone that made me long for the day when the girls guarding the gates had flirted with me, she asked, "May I help you?"

I worked on whether to ask for Ms. Marshall or Angela, and settled for the latter.

The familiarity of that shot her eyebrows straight up. "Do you have an appointment with the assistant D.A.?"

"More like a date." I slipped a hip on the edge of her desk and relished the astonished reaction. "I'm surprised, too. It's been a long time since a classy doll like Ms. Marshall wanted to date me this early in the day. But, hell, she was the one who made it."

This was all a little too much for the receptionist, whose eyes behind the lenses were doing a cartoon pop. She punched a button on her intercom and said, "Ms. Marshall, I think you had better come out here right away."

The strained tone of her voice—which implied her next step was to buzz security—got an immediate response.

There Angela Marshall was, in another power suit (charcoal

gray today, skirt not slacks), with a cold, chiseled beauty Rodin might have envied, if he'd worked in synthetics.

At first her expression displayed that open challenge that seemed to be her standard setting, then she recognized me and the dark eyes flared.

"Hi, beautiful," I said. "What's shaking?"

Well, she was. And it wasn't bad to see. She had all gears going, and held the door open so I could step inside her private office.

Maybe she had seen too many movies. The way she strode around the desk, the regal manner she assumed in sitting down, her posture as she leaned on an elbow to study this walking-talking exhibit from the Male Chauvinist Museum — it all seemed too deliberately scripted, a scene carefully broken down into shots and angles, and she was director *and* star.

"What is your name, detective." It wasn't even a question.

"Hammer. Michael."

"Your grade?"

"I made it halfway through the twelfth." Before I enlisted in the army.

"If you made the force, then you must have a G.E.D." She didn't even look up from her notes. "You *are* a detective?"

"Right. And I have a junior college degree, too. Took some night classes."

"Well, good for you. And now as to your rank — what *is* your grade, Detective Hammer?"

This time I gave it a long double beat, and when she finally raised her eyes, I stopped screwing with her and said, "*Private* detective, kid. A plain old-fashioned private eye, licensed in the state of New York with a ticket to carry a gun, and free to buddy around with all sorts of people, including Captain Chambers. I'm even allowed to call a public servant an asshole if he — or she — decides to behave like one."

She may have been a whiz in the courtroom and a political star on the rise, but she'd never make it as a poker player. From her expression, I knew exactly what her next line would be, and beat her to the punch again.

"And don't give me any garbage," I said, pawing the air, "about having my license revoked. That takes cause, not clout, and anyway, I can go a hell of a lot higher up than you can. I've taken more bad guys off the street, one way or another, than any ten plainclothes coppers in this sorry-ass city."

"*Mike* Hammer . . . you're Mike Hammer."

"Right. You start hassling me, little girl, and I'll call in some favors that'll get you squashed right down to handling juvie beefs."

This time *she* took the long beat. "Michael Hammer. Yes, I remember you now."

"What do you remember?"

"What I've read. What I've heard. I feel I know you already."

Everybody was saying that lately.

"So what do you know about me, Ms. Marshall?"

"That you're nasty. Most unpleasant. And very tough."

"That's a pretty good summary. Anything else?"

"Yes. I understand for a long time there was an office pool about which of us on the D.A.'s staff would break one of your fancy self-defense pleas."

"You in on that pool?"

"Oh, no, Mr. Hammer. They stopped doing that. It's before my time."

"Ouch. Now that we've got insulting each other out of the way, how about some breakfast? All I've had is coffee."

From the way the receptionist looked at me on the way out, I knew she had kept the intercom key down all the while. I winked at her, put my hand under her boss's arm, and steered the great lady into the hall.

On the elevator, Ms. Marshall gave me a sharp look and said, "You are such an unregenerate macho bastard."

But she squeezed my hand when she said it.

A taxi took us over to Cohen's Deli, not as famous as the Stage but cheaper, plus they had a Mike Hammer mile-high sandwich on the menu board — pastrami, corned beef, Swiss cheese, American cheese, cole slaw, and Russian dressing. If anybody asked why it was named after Mike Hammer, the waiter would say, "It'll kill you just as fast."

Unaware of my sandwich fame, she went in ahead of me like she owned the joint, but her eyes went back to mine when squat, mustached Herman — in white shirt, black bow tie, and black trousers — said, "Ah, Mr. Mike! You're back in town!"

"Hi, Herm."

"And who is your beautiful young lady?"

"This is Angela Marshall."

"Ah, yes. Our lovely assistant district attorney."

He guided us to a window booth.

Watching him go, she muttered, "Was he putting me down?"

"Never," I told her. "Your beauty simply overwhelms him."

"Bullshit."

"He knew who you are, didn't he?" I said. We were across from each other in the booth.

"Did you hear him say *your* beautiful young lady? And that slight emphasis on *assistant?*"

"Don't worry, kid, you're such a pain in the ass, you're bound to be top dog someday."

"Damn, I hate men," she said.

Looking at the menu, I asked, "Do you?"

She looked at her menu, too. "Not really."

Breakfast with a real doll can be damn exciting. They're awake, showered, and manicured, and all the weapons are pointed right at whatever chump is dumb enough to be sitting across from them. To such dolls, the guy on the other end of the fork is a big, ripe plum ready for the plucking, because that world of economic dominance he dwells in, and whatever male aggression he possesses, are overshadowed by the two most basic hungers.

Just to annoy her, I ordered an enormous breakfast — lox, onion and eggs omelet, hash browns, and pancakes on the side — saying nothing while she daintily dined on a single cream-cheese bagel and coffee. I cleaned my plate with the last of the kind of great buttered hard roll you can only get in New York, burped politely, and sat back waiting like Henry the Eighth to be served my second cup of coffee.

"You're disgusting," she said with her big brown eyes cold and unblinking, her arms folded on the impressive shelf of her breasts.

"And you dig it, don't you?"

She tried not to smile. "Love it."

"Then how come everybody thinks you're such a queen bitch?"

"Because I am." For a brief second I got one of those eye flashes again, that dare that was such a great part of her.

"Balls," I said.

Her smile curled into another challenge. "That's the opening line of a famous poem," she said.

"Oh, I know. One of my favorites."

"Really? Then finish it."

"It's blank verse and loses a little off the page."

"Does it now?"

"It does. *'Balls!' cried the queen. 'If I had to, I could be king.' 'Balls!' cried the prince. 'I have two, but I'm still not king!' And the king only laughed, not because he wanted to . . . but because he had two.*" I took a sip of the coffee. "It's all semantics, baby."

"Actually, it's homophones."

"Naw. I got nothing against the gays."

She chuckled at that, then leaned back, arms still folded. Then she opened her purse, took out a pack of Virginia Slims, and with a quick flip, popped one out at me.

"No thanks," I said.

"Not secure enough to smoke a woman's brand?"

"I don't smoke any brand."

"What happened to Luckies?"

"I stopped about a year ago."

"What happened about a year ago?"

"I shot a bunch of the Bonettis and the Bonettis shot me back. I've been away from the big bad city for a year or so, recuperating."

From all the expression that got out of her, I might have just given her a weather report. "Are you better now?"

"Much better. Kicking the nicotine habit is a nice side benefit of my general recuperation. I don't gasp for breath and I don't burn holes in my pants."

Some motions are exquisitely casual, but this one was so damn deliberate, it didn't belong to a woman at all. Her fingers simply tightened around the pack of butts, squashed them into a little congested mess, and dropped it on her plate.

"Satisfied?" she asked, arching an eyebrow.

"Nice gesture. How long will it last?"

"Remember the old song, Mr. Hammer? Anything you can do . . . ?"

"Good luck," I told her. I reached over and picked up her pretty gold lighter with the engraved A.M. on it and thumbed back the top. A little pressure and I popped the piece askew so it couldn't be used again.

"You don't mind, do you?" I grinned. "I mean, you won't need that anymore. Just trying to help."

There was a deadliness in the way she studied me. Her very manner had a leveling effect—she rather liked the man/woman game play, but only when she could put herself on the same plane as me. In her professional life, she had reached a plateau that few of either sex achieved, and there was no room for anything of the loser in her.

Whoever in the past had challenged this one had only been a neophyte—he'd lost because he was a boy. But surely there had also been real men who'd gotten mired in her charm, only to buckle under the weight of her inherent confidence and educational superiority.

"No," she said, with a glance at the ruined lighter, "I won't be needing that anymore." Very slowly she dropped it in her purse.

Outside the window of the corner deli, the late risers of New York were drifting by. Most of them were the nothing people. Someplace they got money, but they didn't work. The better-dressed were husbands with rich wives, or kids with parents who paid the freight. The shabby ones were sheltered by the city or a church who kept them overnight but didn't let them back in till the evening. They were drifting now, all of them, walking and looking and wondering.

"What makes you such a bastard, Mr. Hammer?"

My mind had to refocus, and when it did, I said, "Maybe it's because I hate this place."

"New York?"

I nodded. "You weren't born here, were you?"

"No. I grew up in Albany."

"You should have stayed there." I was getting an edge in my voice.

"But *you* were born here."

"Unfortunately."

"Did you always hate it?"

"There was a time when it was love/hate, I suppose. But just about everything I loved about it is gone. From the Brooklyn Dodgers to the real Madison Square Garden."

The prosecutor across from me considered that, then asked, "What's her name?"

Velda.

"That's a little personal," I said, "for a first date."

"Is that what this is?" She picked up her coffee cup and smiled at me over the rim of it. "Why do you think I'm sitting here with you now, Mr. Hammer? Why did I accept your invitation?"

"You really want to know?"

She nodded, still watching me.

"I laid it on you last night and I laid it on you today," I said, "and you *still* want to know?"

"Certainly."

It was my turn to sit back and do the looking. I let it all ooze up into me, settle there until I was ready to say it, then I grinned like that day a year ago had never happened.

"To you," I said, "I'm an exercise. A far-out, way-out exercise to test your inherent abilities and your well-honed skills. Until now, everything has gone your way, because you have that glossiness beautiful girls get on their way to being women — that smooth surface that makes guys slide right off them. But someplace, way back, somebody smart warned you to watch out for a guy who had sandpaper on his hands, and who wouldn't slide off at all. You never thought you'd need that kind of guy, but, baby, you do now."

She sipped at her coffee again.

I said, "So why did you accept my invitation? Well, I'd say it has something to do with that crime scene last night—doesn't it, Angela?"

When I used her first name, her eyes tightened.

"You should have let your assistant call security," I said, "when I walked into your office."

Another raised eyebrow accompanied a very pretty smirk. "Would that have done any good?"

"Nope. But now think of the reputation you'll have."

"Maybe I'll just tell people I'm thinking of starting up that office pool again."

"Maybe." My eyes were tightening now and I let her see the edge of my teeth again. "What took you to that crime scene last night, Angela?"

Her face became a pale mask. Lovely, but a mask. "What took *you* there, Mike?"

"Coincidence, I think. I'm the rare cop who does believe in co-incidence. Who thinks fate likes to move things around some-times, like a chess master with a sick sense of humor."

"Not very scientific."

"Not scientific at all. But I do have my inquisitive side. For ex-ample—why would a powerful woman like you rush to the scene of such an insignificant kill?"

She shifted in her seat. "It wasn't so insignificant to Virginia Mathes."

"That was her name, huh?"

She nodded.

"What else do you know about her?"

"Nothing. She was a mugging victim. I was out driving and heard the call on the scanner. Murder is serious where I come from, Mike."

53

"Serious enough to accept a breakfast offer from an obnoxious bastard like me?"

"*Just* that serious," she said. Then she checked her watch and gave me a look that said it was time to go.

I left a three-buck tip, grabbed the check, and we slid out of the booth. I tried to pay but Herman wouldn't take my money.

Outside, I asked, "Want a cab?"

"No, I'll walk back." She reached in her purse and took out the ruined lighter. Looked at it. "Somebody I respect gave this to me."

"Right. You bought it for yourself."

Her smile was automatic, uncontrolled, unaffected. "You're a bastard, all right."

"I don't make a secret of it," I said.

She paused, looked at me very directly for a moment. "Will you tell me one thing?"

"Ask."

"Was *I* an exercise for *you?*"

A truck roared by and a taxi squealed into the curb beside us. A guy with a briefcase got out, paid the driver, and walked away. The driver looked at us and I lifted my finger to claim the ride.

But before I climbed in back, I said, "I already got my exercise today, honey."

Over at the chief medical examiner's office on First Avenue, I managed to get hold of Dr. Adam MacCaffrey, the assistant medical examiner who had been called in when Doolan died.

He was a type I had seen before, a man who had been edged into something he could do well, but didn't like at all. He was about fifty with a perpetual expression of puzzlement, as if he were wondering what he was doing there.

Slender, mustached, and about as pale as his customers, he said from behind his desk, "I really don't see how you can question all the facts, Mr. Hammer."

I shook my head. "I'm not questioning anything, doctor. I'm just looking for a little more information."

"Well," he said, his eyes appraising me over his wire-rimmed glasses, "if I can help, I'll be glad to. Frankly, it's a pleasure to be asked to do anything around here that doesn't involve a scalpel." He found the loose-leaf pad he was looking for, fingered it open, and spread it out in front of him on the desk. "I may not be fast, Mr. Hammer, but I am thorough. Now, what is it you want?"

"Doolan's right arm, principally, the wrist."

He turned a page, then looked up at me again. "Yes?"

"Any abrasions, marks of struggle?"

"None," he said, without referring to the pad. "The victim was quite old, and any sign of a struggle would have been most evident. The skin would have shown even mildly rough treatment." He saw me frown and added, "I know what you're thinking. Could somebody have grabbed his hand and twisted it around on him, then fired the shot."

"Something like that."

"Not this time. The pressure of the trigger guard and the trigger itself would have marked him. Somebody's grasp like that would have left definite imprints. The skin of an eighty-five-year-old man is fairly fragile."

"You're certain, doctor?"

"Absolutely. One reason is that in apparently self-inflicted wounds, there is always that possibility, and I check that out immediately. The victim knew what he was doing. There was no unusual angle about the way he fired the gun. The entry was through the sternum and into the heart. Death was instantaneous." He stopped a moment, his pencil tapping on the desktop. "Tell me, Mr. Hammer, what prompts this inquiry?"

"Suicide wasn't Doolan's game, doctor."

He made a noncommittal gesture with his hands, then said, "That could have been true in his younger years, but this was not a younger man. He was old, desperately ill, and the fact he'd been going over his will, and buying up a burial plot that very afternoon, indicates no doubt as to his intentions."

"You have no reservations at all?" I asked him.

"Not from a medical viewpoint. No."

"From any other angle then?"

"I have no expertise other than medical."

I raised an eyebrow. "Checking his wrist was a little more than medical."

The doctor smiled gently. "That was something I picked up from Dr. Milton Helpern, New York's great forensic medical examiner." The smile broadened a little. "Besides, I'm a bit of a police detective buff. Which is why you're not having any trouble getting information out of me, Mr. Hammer."

"Really?"

"Oh yes. You're a famous character in this city. But you know that."

"Some would say 'infamous.' Did you handle that girl who died in a mugging last night? Virginia Mathes?"

He frowned. "As a matter of fact, yes. Why, does that have something to do with Inspector Doolan's death?"

"Not that I know of. Took place less than two blocks from the funeral home where we were sending him off. But that's a pretty thin connection."

"And it's a pretty routine killing, Mr. Hammer. She was stabbed in the heart—she bled out very quickly, was dead in seconds."

"Her body was twisted when she was stabbed, right?"

"Correct. Her assailant came up from behind, apparently cut her purse straps with his knife, and then she turned and he used the knife again. Tragic, but hardly unusual. Not in this city."

"No," I said, getting up, "not in this city."

I was heading south on Third Avenue, on foot, aware of the graduated flow from one neighborhood into the next. Here, money would swell out like a pouter pigeon's chest, next a block might get skinny with the dust of an excavated building only to erupt into noisy ethnics before getting back into the blender of lower Manhattan, where you were no better than what you could hang on to.

A halter-top/hot-pants girl in a doorway, pretty despite her drug habit, said, "Hey, handsome—you want to party?"

That was New York again, anytime, anyplace. At night in the dirty Forties, or before noon in lower Manhattan, sex was always for sale.

I looked at my watch, pretending to consider it, then shook my head. "Too early, sweetheart."

She let out a little laugh and shrugged. "Your loss."

Actually, my gain. What was funny, after all these years, was how few tourists knew the halter-top honey was only bait. Day or night, upstairs some punk would lay open your head with a sap, grab your loot, and drop you off a block away.

Better off with a pickup in a bar. If you knew the ropes, all you got was a possible VD. Hell, sometimes it was for real too, maybe you found a chickie who really did want some company; but you damn well had better use some finely tuned professional judgment.

I met Pat outside the baroque old building on Centre Street

where TV cameras were filming a documentary on the early years of the city. There was no show-business hype on this one, no stars, no press agents—just a second-unit camera crew doing MOS filming of exteriors, a standard union bunch making a routine buck.

When I spotted Pat on the sidewalk, I walked over and said, "Looking for a part?"

He didn't even turn his head. He had a battered manila envelope under his arm. "Yeah, as the fall guy in your life story."

"Ms. Marshall called, huh?"

Now he looked at me like I'd asked to borrow a C-note. "She was not thrilled with me, passing you off as an NYPD cop last night."

"But you got off with a spanking, right? Worse dames to get a spanking from."

He picked out a stick of chewing gum, unwrapped it, and shoved it in his mouth; he'd stopped smoking, too. "You've been back one day."

"Almost."

"Uh-huh." He chewed on the gum, dragging out the flavor, then asked, "Why'd you have to pick La *Marshall* to move in on, for Christsakes?"

"It was at her invitation, remember?"

"Hey—she invited you through yours truly. You accepting that invite involved *me*. And I have to work in this department, you know."

I shrugged. "I think she enjoyed herself. Women love me, Pat. Remember?"

It was as if no year had passed. It was like those days when we were a little younger and still breathing hard.

He frowned at me, but his eyes weren't angry at all. "Mike—what the hell is going on?"

"Nothing's going on, Pat. I just asked what brought an important gal like her to the scene of some unimportant mugging."

His frown tightened until his eyes were almost shut. "Goddamn you, Mike. Why do you have to be such a fucking catalyst? You come back, and *everything* gets activated."

"Bullshit."

"No. Not bullshit. The guys at Doolan's funeral knew it, seeing you materialize like a goddamn apparition. Those goombahs sure as hell knew it. *Les Graves* knew it, seeing you at that crime scene last night. Now finally *I* know it. Finally it gets through my thick skull that Mike Hammer has decided an open-and-shut suicide is a murder, and so is a mugging fatality so routine it barely made the papers. One lousy goddamn day, and you've turned it all upside down again."

"It's a gift, Pat."

But there was no way to tell him that coming up on the plane, I'd had the same feeling—vague, but there. Not that I was going to do something, but that something was going to be done to me. Done to me good—real good. It wasn't a nice feeling at all.

"So what was Marshall doing at that crime scene?"

His turn to shrug. "Far as I know, just checking out a murder."

"And that's it?"

"She wanted to know whether Homicide was looking into that girl's murder."

"Virginia Mathes, you mean."

His eyes widened. "How the hell do you know her name? It wasn't in the papers."

"Maybe I'm psychic."

"Mike . . . Mike. I'm getting too near retirement to play your kind of games."

A little laugh rumbled out of me. I took a look around, saw

every crack in the masonry, and smelled the garbage in the gutter. Where I came from, the ocean would be warm, the sand squeaky-crunching under bare feet, and the boat ready to nose out into the Gulf Stream.

I said, "Who was she, Pat?"

He made one of those little noncommittal gestures. "You said it yourself—Virginia Mathes."

"Pat . . ."

"She was nobody."

"*Nobody's* nobody."

"*She* was," he told me. "Six years ago, she made a stab at entertaining in a club and got printed as part of our licensing requirement. We ran her through Social Security, got her address and where she worked. She was a waitress at Ollie Joe's Steak House for two years, was well liked, had nothing against her in our files, just walked out of Ollie Joe's last night and got herself killed."

"Just like that."

"You were there, Mike."

"Ollie Joe's sure as hell isn't in that neighborhood. But you've already been to Ollie Joe's, haven't you, Pat? And found out something else, too?"

Ten seconds dragged by; we were just two gawkers on the street watching a film crew. Finally he looked at me.

"Mike, I didn't find out a damned thing."

"*What* didn't you find out?"

I knew he was going to tell me. He ran it around his brain a couple of times, but we had been together too many times on too many things for too goddamn long.

"Before she left," he said with a sigh, "a guy came in and—according to the cashier—seemed to know her. He had a cup of coffee and a piece of pie. She was a little more attentive to this patron than usual, but since there weren't many customers there, the cashier didn't think anything about it. The girl liked to gab, I guess."

"What time was this?"

"Just before she punched out. She signed her paycheck at the desk, picked up her cash, and left."

"How *much* cash?"

"Thirty-five bucks. Her big money was in tips. The cashier said something seemed to be on her mind when she left."

"What about the patron she got friendly with?"

He pitched his gum in the gutter. "He waited maybe two minutes, then he went out too."

"Like maybe she was about to date this customer . . . ?"

"Maybe. And according to the cashier, that was unusual. Ginnie—that's what they called her—never did that."

I gave him the slow grin. "You haven't scratched on Ginnie Mathes's door yet, have you?"

Pat rubbed his hand over his hair, then took a deep breath of polluted air. "I didn't want to spoil your fun, buddy. Here."

He slid the manila envelope out from under his arm.

"What's this?"

"Doolan stuff. All copies, and you can keep 'em—*and* keep 'em confidential."

"Sure."

His gray eyes studied me like I was a fingerprint under a microscope. "You going to his apartment now?"

I nodded. "Right from here."

"Thought maybe you'd hit the Mathes girl's pad first. You're a busy guy for a retired detective—two suspicious deaths to look into, and not back a day."

"You said that before."

"Did I?" He slipped a hand into his suitcoat pocket and brought out a key paper-clipped to one of his cards. "This is for the police padlock on Doolan's door. We have a light cover on the place, so if anybody tries to stop you, give them my card. If I'm not in the office, my guys will confirm things."

I nodded my thanks. "Pat, you're welcome to come along. That'd make it official."

"Since when did you want anything official? Anyway, Mike — what's to see? I told you we picked that place apart. No, this is all yours, my friend. I want you to be totally satisfied with the answers. What I don't want is for you to get a bug up your ass, and go prowling for something that's not there."

I looked at the key like I was imagining things. "You're fine with this?"

"I'm fine with this. For once we have a commissioner who likes your style. Why, I'll never know, but he okayed this bit of action. At least I got my ass covered this time."

"If Doolan's suicide is so open-and-shut, why bother?"

His grin was an odd mingling of amusement, frustration, and maybe affection. "Mike, you're one of those weird Irishers, the kind they say carries little people in his pocket. You've always had a nose for murder, and you've always been able to smell out the bizarre posing as the routine."

"Thanks."

"On the other hand? Sometimes I think when something's going down, and you're riding along, white becomes black, wrong becomes right, and the whole works gets turned upside the hell down."

"My track record isn't *all* bad, kiddo."

"I know, and that's what shakes me up. This Doolan deal is suicide, all right. But I want there to be no doubts. I figure if you're satisfied, *anybody* would be satisfied."

"I hope I am, Pat." I meant it, too. "I'm not looking for trouble."

"Not looking for trouble—do you expect me to believe that? Do you really have *yourself* believing that?"

I said nothing.

He put a hand on my shoulder. "Listen, Mike—on this Mathes thing? I *do* need to come along. I'll be free in a couple of hours. You call me before you go over there."

"If Doolan is a straight-up suicide," I said, "and the Mathes kid is a run-of-the-mill mugging turned fatal . . . why sweat letting me look into it, Pat? What have you got to lose?"

"With you around, Mike? Just my badge. Or maybe my sanity."

I didn't argue the point, just assured Pat I'd call him before I checked the Mathes girl's pad, then grabbed a cab, and gave the driver Doolan's address.

Chapter 4

BACK IN THE LATE nineteen-thirties, this neighborhood had been fashionable enough to attract those who had survived the Depression in style. But that bunch moved outward and upward during the Second World War years, and new generations changed the face of it as the growing pains of the city wrenched neighborhoods apart and then rebuilt them all over.

For twenty years, it had been livable again, a strangely quiet area hoping it wouldn't be noticed. And Doolan had lived there through all the changes, fifty-two years' worth, the last ten as a widower.

I went up the sandstone steps and pushed the street door open. The vestibule was tiny, the four mailboxes on the left, old-fashioned ornamented brass rectangles with no jimmy marks scarring their surfaces. All had yellow lottery announcements in them.

I tried the inner door and that was open, too. When it *snicked* shut behind me, all the street sounds were magically gone and

I could feel the loneliness of the place. No sounds at all drifted down the staircase that led to the upper apartments, no cooking smells, not even the feel of life that should be there.

But there *were* occupants in those flats, all right—the old and unseen, whose very quietness had an awareness to it.

And somehow they were watching me.

Damn, I felt like an idiot letting a thought like that put a tingle at the back of my neck. A couple of years ago, this would have been just another building on another street.

I walked down the corridor to Doolan's apartment door, read the police notice stapled to the panel, then hefted the padlock that held the door shut. Below it, pieces of wood had been ripped out by the force of the kick that smashed the door open.

I keyed the padlock, took it out of the hasp, and pushed the door. It swung open with a small squeak from a twisted hinge, and I stepped into Doolan's life and flipped the light switch on.

There was nothing spectacular about his quarters. I had been there often enough in the old days, and nothing seemed to have changed—the furnishings were nice quality and very functional, everything seeming to belong exactly where it was, as if a decorator had arranged it all and the resident hadn't changed things around to suit himself.

But that's the way Doolan had been, one of those neat freaks. He would have been teed off to see the way the cops had left it, print powder taking the shine off wood finishes, cigarette butts in a pair of Wedgewood ashtrays that were meant for eye appeal only, chairs out of line, cabinet drawers not completely shut.

Suicides don't require extensive shaking down of their premises, but Pat made sure every angle was being covered in this situation. I went through the living room, touching some of the things I remembered, then into the bedroom where Doolan had slept on the same side of the old-fashioned double for so long, one side lower than the other, the place where his wife once slept raised like a pedestal to her memory.

The bathroom was almost clinical, everything in its assigned place. Hell, it was the army again in these quarters, where even inanimate objects seemed to be well-disciplined.

His office/den was different, though. Many years ago it had been his late daughter's bedroom, now it was the place where he had really lived . . .

. . . and died.

His office-style swivel chair wasn't behind the desk, but next to the wall of shelves with his stereo system and its speakers, LPs, cassette tapes, books, magazines, trophies, framed photos, stacks of this and that. The neatness of the rest of the apartment was not reflected here. These shelves held escape and memories and music. He'd been listening to one of his beloved classics when he took the bullet in his heart.

On the floor, outlined in chalk, was the exact position of the chair when he was found, facing the door to the living room, the one flanked with framed photos of old wooden sailing ships and seaports in the distant past. On his left side, against the window, was the antique desk, a handmade oaken relic from the captain's cabin of some forgotten clipper ship.

Twice I walked around that comfortable room, mentally cataloging every item I saw, trying to put it into a perspective that would change a suicide to a kill, without success.

Then I stopped beside the desk, which reverted to Doolan's meticulous form — no unruly work in progress, just an orderly arrangement of pens, pencils, yellow pads, and so on. But a long time ago Doolan had shown me the hidden button that opened the side panel of that museum piece. I pushed it in, gave it a half turn.

Silently, the panel swung open and there, on mounts, were five of the six guns Doolan had so carefully preserved. They were cleaned, oiled, and I didn't have to check them to know they were fully loaded. To Doolan, a gun was only a gun when it was ready to be used and to hell with safety rules. A bag of silica gel lay at the bottom of the enclosure to absorb any moisture, a cleaning kit and a can of Outers 445 gun oil beside it.

A real heavy-duty arsenal, a pair of matched German P38s from World War II, a .357 Magnum, a .44 Colt revolver, and a standard Colt .45 automatic. The missing piece was in the property clerk's office downtown waiting to be claimed.

I took the .45 off the peg and held it in my hand. It felt good. A weapon just like it was sandwiched between piles of clothing in a drawer back at my hotel room. Then a tightness ran across my shoulders, and I put it back. I closed the panel to that secret place and felt my mouth go into a tight grin.

The police shakedown hadn't been that thorough after all.

Strange that Pat had missed that. But then again, there was no reason for him to know that it was there—I imagined precious few of us had been shown that hiding place.

I sat on the edge of the desk. Everything still fit in place—knowing the reality of the world of pain he faced in coming weeks, Doolan would have taken out his old .38 Special, sat there in the dark being saturated by the music he loved, savored the familiar feel of the gun in his hand, then when he was ready, simply shot himself.

I said a muffled "Damn!" and got off the desk like it was a hot burner on a stove. I snapped off the light and went back to the door in the living room.

Doolan had been a typical New Yorker and kept himself barricaded in at night behind four solid locks fastened to the fire-resistant steel shell that backed up the door. Had it been fully latched, no cop could have kicked it in. Only the old original Yale lock had been torn loose, the kind you could open with a credit card, but was okay to keep kids out.

For a while I just stared at the splintered wood around the tongue of the lock, realizing that Doolan didn't have any reason to button himself up completely that night. He had committed himself to a decisive move that didn't concern itself with visitors. That was undoubtedly the thinking that had satisfied Pat.

I stepped into the hall and hooked the padlock back in the hasp.

Everything still fit. Pat was right.

And I still said, Bullshit!

Doolan had been a man of habit. No matter what he had planned, he still would have buttoned up behind locked doors, just as he had done every other night in his life. Nothing cancels out a ritualized, internalized program like that.

At any other time, when he was opening the minimum security of the old Yale lock, he would have had weaponry at hand that he damn well knew how to use. He was well aware that the old lock wasn't able to cope with so modern a chunk of high technology as a piece of plastic.

Pat wanted me to be satisfied that Doolan had committed suicide. I was halfway there — I was convinced Doolan was dead.

But why?

The facts and his doomed situation seemed to say it all, sure. Then why the hell did something bug me the way it did?

Doolan had a motive for suicide, all right, an undeniably perfect motive to call it quits on his own terms in his own special way — papers in order, music playing softly, his own weapon in his hand, and then kiss this life goodbye.

And now I knew what was bugging me.

Memory is a funny thing. You can recall in detail some insignificant afternoon of your childhood, but it takes a while to remember what you had for lunch yesterday. You meet an old pal and regale him with a shared experience that has stuck with you a lifetime, only he's forgotten all about it, then he shares his most vivid memory of the two of you, which stirs nothing at all.

But sometimes something floats to the surface, jarred there — and my visit to Doolan's apartment had summoned a conversation he and I'd had not ten years before.

We were having dinner in the old Blue Ribbon Restaurant when he said, "There is no motive for suicide, Mike me boy. It's a damn coward's way out."

I had thrown him some bait. "Suppose you were trapped in a flaming car and had your gun with you."

"Well, then, I'd burn, kiddo."

"Why?"

"Life's one of those precious things you don't toss away under any conditions."

"You've put a few men down for the long count," I reminded him.

"Only to preserve my own precious life. If somebody ever tries to sell you the bill of goods that I've snuffed myself out? You go look a little harder, Mike. There is *no* justifiable motive for suicide."

Okay, pal, I told his memory. *You made yourself clear. You're dead and you didn't do it, so who the hell did? And what* was *the motive?*

Life takes years to live, but only a few minutes to say goodbye. A eulogy like the one I'd delivered last night doesn't take long to wrap up an entire lifetime, lay it out in a few well-chosen sentences, and send the memory of that intense, complicated structure called a man drifting off to nowhere.

Before long, Bill Doolan would be forgotten.

But not by everyone.

Not by the person who killed him.

And not by me.

The office that Doolan had shared with Peter Cummings looked like something out of *A Tale of Two Cities*. The corner building had opened in 1888, the year of the Great Blizzard, and had watched the city parade pass so long, it had itself become a monument of sorts, the kind two old men found comfortable toward the tail end of their lives.

Ten years younger than Doolan, Cummings had been on the force with Doolan, retired, and become a P.I., specializing in credit-investigations work. Doolan helped his friend out, working only when he'd wanted to, picking and choosing. Two great old guys who didn't know how to quit and, hell, they were still enjoying life, so why should they?

I knocked on the door, heard Cummings's gruff "It's open," and turned the knob.

"I'll be damned," he said. "Mike Hammer."

"Everybody's got to be somebody," I said.

His hair was all gray now, short and bristly. The years had left lines on his face and thinned out his once-powerful frame, but somehow you knew he was still a cop, years away from his era, who still carried a retirement shield in a worn leather case in his pocket. He was in a white shirt with no tie and the sleeves rolled, black slacks, and stocking feet. Argyles.

"I was wondering if you'd show up," he said. He was out from behind his desk, heading to a little fridge conveniently nearby. "Everybody else and his mother's been here. Come on in and sit down. Want a cold one?"

"Sure." I deposited myself in the old walnut client's chair and caught the cold can of Miller. "Like old times."

Back behind his desk, he held his can up. "Cheers."

"Cheers." I popped the top. "You weren't at the funeral."

"No. At my age you have to make a decision—how many funerals are you willing to go to, with friends dying left and right. I decided one more was plenty."

"Your own."

"That's right." He drank. "But don't think I don't feel it. Terrible about Doolan."

"I figure you know the details."

"Oh yeah. Pat laid everything out. He was real shook up over it."

"How're you taking it, Pete?"

"For real?"

"Yeah, for real."

Cummings leaned back, the swivel chair squeaking. "It isn't easy. We were friends for a long time." He took his glasses off, threw them on the desk, and massaged the bridge of his nose. "He wasn't my partner, but he did a lot of work out of here. So I saw him quite a bit. He was the last of the old bunch that I did see. With the others . . ." He shrugged. ". . . you say you'll keep in touch, but you don't. The past goes on a back burner and stays there."

I nodded.

"Now," he said, and sighed, "there's nobody left. Shit, who can blame Doolan for doing the Dutch act? Some days I feel like packing it in myself."

"You're working off a false premise."

"What?" His eyes caught mine and I saw both irritation and confusion there.

"Bill Doolan never killed himself."

71

Time was the heavy tick of the aged pendulum wall clock that seemed to be the only sound not just in the office, but in the world. It went on and on while Cummings slowly edged forward until his arms rested on his desk, his head tilted up to watch me carefully.

Softly, Cummings said, "Okay. How do you know this?"

"Doolan told me," I said. "A long time ago."

The clock kept ticking. It seemed louder now.

"You mind making that clear, Mike?"

I told him about the conversation in the Blue Ribbon.

Finally he nodded, his eyes narrowing. There was no discussion, no argument at all. "What are you going to do?"

"Sure as hell not let it sit the way it is. Somebody's going to get tumbled."

"The old Mike Hammer way?"

"I haven't come up with a new one."

"How can I help?"

"You can start by letting me go through Doolan's files."

He pointed across the room. "Feel free. Everything's over there in the two cabinets on the far end. Other three are mine. Of course, you know, the police have gone over the works. Pat Chambers is no slouch."

"They find anything?"

"Nothing they seemed to think was important. Maybe you can do better. You're no slouch either."

"Thanks a bunch."

Five old four-drawer wooden filing cabinets were pushed against the wall, looking like they came with the building. None of the drawers was locked and, from the way the folders were replaced, I knew everything had indeed been looked at by the police.

I could have told them what was in there—Doolan had always been a clipper. Whatever had looked interesting, he had cut out and saved: newspapers, magazines, anything at all. There was a file of news clippings on every intriguing murder case the past year and a half. Two folders had schematics of the latest alarm systems, including those used in Europe.

When I reached the third drawer, I found a particularly thick folder labeled PERSONALS and pulled it out. I had to crack a grin at that one—old Doolan still had his ego working for him. These were all news photos of him mixing with the public he had served so long. He had been a damn good after-dinner speaker, and there were shots of him in black tie speaking at banquets, a good dozen at political rallies, and just as many at police functions.

The old boy had gotten around more than I thought. Two shots were with presidents of the United States, and eight more were group shots where state senators were listening to whatever he was hanging on them.

What tickled me most was the envelope at the back of the folder filled with 8 x 10s of Doolan posing with dolls. Some of the shots went back twenty years and included movie stars like Marilyn Monroe and Rhonda Fleming up through Raquel Welch and Tuesday Weld; they were all classy ladies, really, even the two who ran elegant call-girl books. The backgrounds were restaurants, theaters, and clubs, the old ones I recognized, the new ones I didn't.

I waved a handful of the photos at Cummings. "What's with these, Pete?"

His grunt was meaningful. "I never asked for details. Doolan would show me new ones as he added them, grinning like a goofy kid. I was too envious to give him the satisfaction."

I chuckled. "Don't tell me the old guy still fooled around."

Once again I got that hard stare. "Mike," he told me, "you're not up in years yet, so you may think it's funny, but even guys our age can still get it up . . . *and* remember what to do with it."

"Sorry about that."

"Maybe it's not as *often,* but . . ."

"Sorry about that too."

"Don't be. Think of the money I save."

The last were three concert-type shots of a woman singing at a stand-up microphone. It partially obscured her face, but it was obvious she was a real beauty. Her platinum hair was straight and long, accentuating her rich brown complexion that went with features that seemed Hispanic and Asian at once. Certainly that red silk dress split up the side to her waist and exposing a long, lush leg had an oriental look, and helped make her look startlingly erotic.

"Who's this one?" I held the photos up.

"Her name's Chrome. Or anyway that's how he referred to her. A performer, pretty famous I guess. Some exotic looker, eh?"

"Not the girl next door," I admitted. "I'm beginning to think our old pal was a dirty old man."

Cummings let out a low laugh. "She was business, Mike. A friend of his in L.A., a reporter, wanted some shots for a show-business rag—this Chrome doll is apparently on the rise."

"So are most of the men in her audiences, I'd guess."

"Yeah, and the rest are gay."

"I didn't think Doolan dealt that much in photography."

"No more than any of us—in the P.I. game, you find your way around a camera. He didn't just work for me, you know. He did jobs for reporters, both local and guys like that one in L.A."

"A lot of that kind of thing?"

"If he was in the mood. If whatever it was appealed to him."

I nodded. "What's in the other cabinet?"

"Bills, mostly. Receipts, bank statements. He never threw anything like that away. Tell you, though, you'll waste your time going through them. He never looked at anything in there—he just *put* things there, every month, every year. You know, real pack-rat stuff. Funny, considering how anal retentive he was about keeping his apartment neat."

I pulled out the bottom drawer. This one was real interesting—one big folder on me went back ten years and wound up with glossy black-and-whites of me on the ground bleeding after that last shoot-out.

I still held the .45 and the lifeless feet of Sal Bonetti were in the background. My side started to throb again and I could feel the fire under my ribs. Something foul seemed to be caught in my throat.

Pete said, "You okay, Mike?"

I could feel his eyes on me. I stuffed the photos back, swallowed, and nodded.

"Maybe you could use another beer?"

I shook my head. "I'm all right. It just happens sometimes."

"What happens?"

"I start hurting in a couple of ways."

The folder had three other pictures in it, front and side views of Alberto Bonetti, in prison casual with his very own number under his name. There was an odd, implied pertinence about those pictures—the total lack of any other information suggested a special degree of importance.

Clashes between Bonetti and Doolan weren't frequent, and those were some years back. Both had come out of the same squalid Lower East Side neighborhood around the same time, hating each other like primeval enemies, one good, one bad.

How much did you hate Doolan, Alberto? Enough to have him killed? Enough to get me back here so you could watch my guts churn, knowing my great mentor was dead like your lousy kid?

Motive? Sure, Bonetti, you have one hell *of a motive.*

From across the room, Pete read my mind. "You speak to Pat about old Alberto?"

"No."

"Well, I can tell you that Pat already checked him out. Bonetti and four of his guys were at Gaspar Rozzi's wedding in the Bronx when Doolan died."

"That doesn't mean much, except maybe Alberto bothered to be seen by a shitload of people."

"Still, how the hell could he have managed it? There are contract killers who can pull off some pretty tricky kills, Mike—but could a stranger have got in Doolan's door and staged *that* suicide?"

This time I stared back at him. "Somebody did."

Cummings came around and knelt at his cooler again and brought out two more beers, tossed me one. "How can I help, Mike?"

I thumbed the can open. I was starting to feel tired again. I didn't remember feeling tired in the old days. "What was Doolan doing this past year, Pete? What was he involved in?"

"Kid, I wish I could tell you something fancy, but Doolan had turned social worker. You got to realize, his action days were long gone, just like me. Hell, working over the telephone was plenty, and when it came to a lot of legwork, forget it. No, his business, if you can call it that, was neighborhood work, a lot of lodge things . . . like giving advice to kids and parents and even political types. He was good at that."

"No action at all?"

"Like what? Every Friday he went to the gun range, and fired off fifty rounds with the boys before lunch. But he's been doing that for years."

"What, a police range?"

"No. It's in Manhattan."

"A gun range in Manhattan?"

"You've heard of it, Mike—the Enfilade. All the society sports go there for a macho kick."

"Yeah. Yeah, I know the place. Pretty stiff fee to belong to *that* club."

"Hell, Doolan had an honorary life membership. Being a big ex-cop has its perks."

I'd check that out. "What about friends? Who was he still close to?"

"He went to too many funerals to have many left. Acquaintances he had plenty of. Everybody liked Doolan."

"Not everybody," I said.

We sipped our beers.

"Pete, you got any ideas? Any leads?"

"Mike, I ran outa ideas a long time ago. Ideas are for young guys like you. And leads are for *real* cops, not old broken-down P.I.s."

"I hope you're not referring to me."

"You? Hell, you're a youngster. No, look at me—I bought the suicide bit all the way. There wasn't one thing wrong with it, not how it went down. I could see myself taking the same route he did under those conditions, and the whole world would've believed it."

"Only it didn't happen that way," I said.

He put his glasses back on and peered at me over the rims. "I hope not. But the facts—"

"You're confusing facts with what we *think* we see." I stood up and put the empty can on his desk. "Okay if I use your phone, Pete?"

"Sure."

I called Pat and said I was ready to check the Mathes girl's place out. He said he'd meet me there in half an hour.

At the door, I said to Cummings, "Anything comes to mind, Pete, I'm over at the Commodore."

"Not at the old stand?"

"My office is closed for now. I'm just looking into a couple of things before I go back to Florida."

"Say, you still with that big, beautiful brunette? My God, she never changes. What a lovely woman. If you had any sense, Mike, you'd have married her ten years ago."

"I'm not with her, Pete. And if I had any sense, we wouldn't have just had this conversation."

His expression said he felt he'd stuck his foot in it, and I got out of there before he could recover.

I knew what Pat was up to. He was the guy who never left the neighborhood, taking the old returnee around the block to show him the changes since he left. It's hard to believe, but unless you've gone away and come back, nothing stands still. Buildings fall, blocks get chewed up, license plates change colors, and faces don't smile right anymore.

Ginnie Mathes had lived in a dilapidated brownstone four blocks from where she'd worked. The super had a basement apartment in the building next door and hadn't known his tenant was dead until Pat flashed his badge and told him so.

There was no hassle about getting in. The guy went ahead, opened the door in the first-floor rear, then left. Pat flipped on the light, we both stood there like dummies, then Pat took the kitchen and I checked out the bedroom.

Ginnie Mathes had nothing much to brag about except maybe cleanliness. Her chief possessions were the clothes in her closet and two drawers of a dresser; to this estate, you could add a little portable TV and a clock radio and not much else. Everything was neatly arranged, the few items of food in the refrigerator fresh, and no garbage in the trash container.

Pat said, "This place has been turned."

"What?"

"Look at the rug."

I hadn't noticed, but it was in a pretty awkward position. Under the sink, the cabinet doors were slightly ajar and he nudged them open with his toe. I saw what he meant. A real tidy girl wouldn't have left them that way.

I shrugged. "Guess I've been away too long, Pat."

"Look at the bathroom."

That one was easy. Somebody had lifted the seat, taken a piss, and didn't flush.

I knew Pat was waiting to see what I'd do next, so I went over and looked at the lock on the door. There were no scratches on the metal, no marks on the woodwork, so I closed the door and leaned against it.

"Okay, Pat—it's a cheap lock and easy pickings, but at the least it was a minor pro job. I don't think they expected to find anything, because she was dead before they got here."

"All right then, Mike—what did she have on her *before* they got here?"

"Thirty-five bucks and tips in cash."

"Somebody was after more than a waitress's weekly pay and tips."

I caught his eyes and got the point. "This wasn't random."

"I'll make a detective out of you yet," he told me.

"Something big enough to kill for?"

"Come on, Mike. In this town *anything* is big enough to kill for."

I nodded. If the mugging had been deliberate, and the killer hadn't gotten what he was after, he still had the girl's address in her purse and figured she wouldn't be I.D.'d until the following day. So he had time to go over her place. . . .

But what was he looking for?

"So whoever shook this place down," I said, "had a whole night to do it in."

Pat was thinking. "We don't buy the possibility that the mugging and a break-in here are two separate events?"

"No way."

"Then there's still something that bothers me."

"Street muggers and B-and-E guys are two different animals."

"Right on," he said. "The only time a mugger breaks and enters is when he's smashing a window in an abandoned building to flop for the night."

I was nodding. "That girl got off a shift after the supper hour on a pay night. It was something she had been doing for a long time. If some creep spotted her routine, saw an easy mark, and followed her just for the cash she had on her, that would be one thing."

"Only she's mugged well away from where she lived and worked," Pat said. "What was she doing there, in that combat zone?"

"That's the question."

"Still could be two people," Pat said. "A mugger is hired to grab her bag, and somebody else is hired to toss her apartment."

"That's *three* people—including whoever hired both of them. Unless it's somebody who did this all himself."

"Or herself."

"You can kid yourself and say Doolan is a suicide, Pat, but *this* is a murder."

"Of course it's murder . . ."

"Not a mugging murder—a murder that needs solving. Are you going to help?"

He raised his hands in surrender. "I'm simply going to make sure you get your fill of this before the system gets it sorted out the old-fashioned way."

I gestured around the sad little apartment. "Really? Then how come the captain of Homicide is messing with a chintzy kill like this?"

"Humoring an old friend. Ready to go over and see Ginnie Mathes's mother?"

I felt my eyebrows go up. "You've been doing your homework, little boy."

"Plain old-fashioned cop stuff, friend. Lots of manpower and the right questions."

Six blocks away, we made a call on Mrs. Lily Mathes, whose dead husband had left her an entire four-story brownstone. Three floors were rentals, so you might think she was well-off; but rent control meant it took Social Security, too, for her to manage a modest living.

Mrs. Mathes was a plump sixty-something in a dark blue dress that may have been as close to black as she had handy. Her white hair was mixed with remnants of the blonde that, along with her attractive face, she'd passed along to her late daughter.

That face wore no makeup at the moment—perhaps it never did or maybe she just was saving herself the trouble of having it run and smear. Her eyes were red, but dry.

She seemed almost glad to see us—maybe it was a relief just to have someone to talk to.

There wasn't much she could add to the picture. Her daughter had been living alone for over two years. During that time, Ginnie had several jobs as a waitress, moving on only when a place closed. No, her daughter had never been in trouble. As far as the mother knew, Ginnie dated once in a while, but lately whenever she had time off, she spent it taking dancing lessons someplace across town.

Pat said, "Did she ever dance professionally?"

"Oh, no," the seated woman told us. "She was too shy for that."

Pat glanced at me, but didn't mention anything about the cabaret license on her daughter. Some things were better left unsaid.

While Pat was getting background, I made a casual circuit of the room. Like most women her age, Lily had her family photos on display. Her late husband was in several with her, a few were of mother, father, and daughter growing up, and one was six snapshots of teenaged Ginnie in a homemade montage — Ginnie and a stocky, blonde-headed guy in two, and with a skinny, shorter guy in the other four.

Lily Mathes smiled when she saw me looking at them. "Those were taken right after Ginnie got out of high school."

"Boyfriends?"

"Oh, you know how girls are."

"Ginnie still see either of these boys?"

She waved a hand dismissively. "That blonde one, he's married and lives in Jersey now. Joseph Fidello, the other one? He's been gone a long time. I think he became a seaman."

When I put the picture back, she said, "I'm afraid you gentlemen are wasting your time. Nobody . . . *nobody* who knew Ginnie . . . would ever . . . *ever* want to . . . to *hurt* her."

A tissue-filled hand covered her eyes and she let her head droop. She went on: "It was just this . . . this terrible city . . . these awful muggings . . . they happen all the time. It's like . . . like living in hell."

I wasn't the best guy to give her an argument.

Pat bent over and took her hand gently. "Just one more thing. Did your daughter always walk home?"

"Yes. On nice nights. If it rained, she took a cab."

"On a nice night—would she go walking farther afield? Or take a cab somewhere, maybe to go to a restaurant or club, or see a boyfriend, and then walk by herself . . . ?"

She shook her head vigorously. "Where they found her, Ginnie wasn't anywhere near her apartment. She wasn't near to her work."

"Yes, we know. . . ."

"She would never, *never* go down a street like where they found her. They tell me it was all torn up and not a safe place at all. I *knew* my daughter. She'd never go down such an unsafe street."

We didn't have to go any further. We said a gentle goodbye and left.

Once outside, Pat said, "So what do you make of it?"

"Three possibilities," I said with a shrug. "Ginnie was going to meet somebody, she was trying to elude somebody, or somebody was chasing her."

"All for thirty-five bucks and tips?"

"For something," I said.

Chapter 5

FOR A WHOLE YEAR I had taken the ordered medication, capsules at regulated times, that were gradually being reduced in frequency and intensity as the physical damage repaired itself. The pain was gone, but so were my dreams. It took two months before I noticed it, and a direct inquiry pinned it down: my unconsciousness was being medicated as well as my body, but since there were no apparent side effects, I let it pass. Missing those surrealistic meanderings was no great loss, unless there were some lovely dolls involved.

But I had forgotten the meds on this night, and for the first time in a year, dreams came through. The first one was a jumble of guns blasting and orange flame chewing the night and exploding skulls and bursts of scarlet and white and gray, and then Velda, and me getting shot, and Velda, crying now, and me, dying now.

This faded into a new dream that wasn't scrambled at all. There was a continuity to it with an aim and a direction, but the light was fuzzy and I couldn't quite make it out. I was back on that war zone of a street looking down at the sand covering the awful puddle of blood on the sidewalk, feeling sand sift through my fingers.

Then it stopped being a dream and I realized I was half awake and thinking.

I kicked the sheet back and hung my legs over the bed. The pain was back again, a big hand feeling for a good grip. I got up, found my pants, and got the vial out of the side pocket. I flipped the cap off, shook one out, and swallowed it, then stuck the vial back.

That was when my fingers found the pebble, the souvenir of a lousy, dirty kill on the sidewalks of New York. It was an irregular oval, the size of a kid's marble, oddly colored with a frosted surface, and there was a distorted picture in my memory of something flashing near the short-sleeve cuff of the dead girl's dress.

Under my fingertip was a flat spot on the stone, and when I turned it over I knew what it was. *What it meant.* Slowly turning it to just the right place, I held my souvenir under the nightstand light and looked into a window that opened onto the pure brilliance hidden in that scruffy little stone.

What I had in my fingers was an uncut diamond with one hell of a carat weight, and somebody had ground a spot on it for absolute proof of what it was.

Ginnie Mathes's death had just taken on a new dimension.

There was a legal probability that I was withholding evidence, but not being an expert in the determination of precious stones, my accountability was limited. Which was nice phrasing, but probably a load of crap. What the hell, I hadn't mentioned to Pat the little arsenal squirreled away in Doolan's desk either.

What was the use of being a private cop if you had to go public with everything? Anyway, Captain Chambers had all sorts of murders on his desk to attend to. I had two. *"Balls!" cried the queen.*

Off Sixth Avenue on Forty-seventh Street is a curbside exchange in the most literal sense, where fortunes in diamonds and cash are traded daily, carried in the pockets of worn coats, wrapped in tissue-paper coverings, and displayed openly to proper customers . . . and the only security is that custom, and the New York police.

It's one of the damndest things you've ever seen, if you are lucky enough to see it at all. A million might change hands when all you thought you saw was two humble Jewish merchants passing the time. It's an ethnic area where all the divisions of the international jewelry trade are busy at it, extending into the buildings on either side. Despite the wealth concentrated in that one block, it is as unpretentious today as it was fifty years ago.

David Gross was an old friend. In 1954 he had retired and left his thriving business to his son. But retirement almost killed him, so he started another business; and in 1965 he retired again and left this one to his grandson. Still he couldn't take retirement, so he went back out on the street, where he had started as a young man, hassling with the diamond traders.

Even among the common black rabbinical garb and the long gray beards, David was easy to spot. His beard had an uncommonly pure black streak on the right side that somehow marked him as the presiding patriarch in the business.

"Well, David Gross," I said. "You never change."

His head craned out and he peered at me through his thick, slightly magnifying glasses. It was hard to make out his smile through the nest of beard. "We have *both* changed, my friend, Michael. But we will pretend otherwise. How nice to see you again! And *alive.*"

We shook hands warmly. "Good to see you too, Mr. Gross. Not bad being alive either."

"Since when to you am I *mister?*"

"David, I'm just a goyim trying to be respectful."

"No—a mensch." He shook his head and the smile became manifest, beard or not. "You have been gone a long time, Michael. Sometimes I would think about you and worry. I remember well what happened in that trouble you had." He paused, the smile gone, looking around uncertainly as if a sniper might be lurking, and said, "This is not an accidental meeting, is it?"

"Not really."

"Nor a social call."

"There's an element of that, but—"

"But there is something we have to talk about?"

"Yes. You got a roof we can sit under, David?"

The old man nodded, his eyes flicking to a building across the street. "My grandson, his office is there. Not that *he* is. Too much money for that boy, it overwhelms him. Oh, he worked for it, but now he wants to spend it all. Always vacations. He's getting fat. That tan—don't tell me *you've* been on vacation? You're not fat."

"No. I've been sick."

"You look good to me. The city, it's good for you. Follow me."

"Sure. Do I have to keep my hat on in there?"

He let out a guttural snort. "That thing you wear with that awful name—what is it?"

"A porkpie. But I'm not asking you to eat a slice, David."

"Better you should eat it than wear it."

"Hey, it's brand-new."

"Then at least do an old friend the courtesy of changing its name."

I laughed. "Okay. Stetson makes it. We'll call it a Stetson."

"Perfect. Michael Hammer, western gunslinger."

"Eastern," I corrected.

Ordinarily, the old man would have wanted to spend an hour

over such kidding pleasantries, but his curiosity got the better of him—me coming to him on a business matter was a rarity. So as soon as we had sat down in wooden chairs on either side of a scarred old table, he poured us each a paper cup of wine.

"Now, Michael, what is it you wish to see me about? A lawyer I'm not. Neither am I a ladies' man. Diamonds I know, but what would you . . ." He paused, looked at my face, and his expression grew curious. "Are you buying for that beautiful secretary of yours? You are finally coming to your senses?"

I shook my head. "We split up while I was away."

"A shame. Is there no hope?"

"I don't believe so. Anyway, David, I'm not here buying."

"Selling?" This time his tone was wary.

"Not exactly."

"So there's a third alternative?"

I held out my hand and let him see the marble-size stone in my palm. He didn't reach for it, just looked at it, then I let it roll over so he could see the ground-in little window into its gleaming soul.

This time he *did* reach for it, felt it, rolled it around in his fingers, then finally brought out a worn loupe, took off his glasses, twisted it into his eye, and examined the pebble carefully. Twice he changed the intensity of the light to be sure of his appraisal.

I let him take his time, not even watching him. Several times his eyes left the stone to peer at me, a strangeness in the silent expression.

I said nothing and waited until he was through. "It's for real?"

"Oh, yes, Michael. It is very much 'for real.'" He paused, then handed the stone back to me. "Do you know how much that is worth?"

I grinned at him. "That's what I'm here to find out."

"Something is funny?"

"How much the stone is worth is *not* the question you wanted to ask me, David."

"Now you are a mind reader?"

"Sure. When a guy like you has no expression just when he's gone into slow motion? Sure."

"So what is it I am supposed to ask?"

I grinned again and waited.

He squirmed because I wasn't playing his game. "Okay, Michael, I will ask—*where did you get it?*"

"I found it, which is the truth, but that's not what you want to know, is it? There's another overriding question, right?"

"How can you *do* this to me?"

"That's not the question."

And then he put me right where I wanted to be in this ball game.

"Where are the rest of them?"

I raised a hand in a gentle "stop" gesture. "Right now, David, I really don't know. But what you have in your head is what I *have* to know."

The excitement in his voice was the gentlest quiver that few would pick up on; he was under control again—almost. "Michael, do you think you can find them?"

I shrugged. "Maybe. I'm guessing this little gem has a history."

"It . . . may have."

"David, don't hedge with me. We're not bargaining yet."

He shrugged. "With one stone, how can I be sure?"

My eyes narrowed and, through a slit of a smile, I asked, "How did you *know* there were more?"

He took a deep breath and sighed loudly. "I am too old to be do- ing this. Such excitement I do not need."

"Bullshit. You thrive on excitement."

"But I could be wrong."

"Come on, David. I'm here because I trust your opinion as much as I trust you."

He rubbed his eyes, then leaned forward, propping his chin on his fist. He tapped on the tabletop. "Put the stone there."

I set it in front of him.

"It looks like an ordinary pebble, yes?"

"Sort of."

"Do you notice on the surface anything peculiar?"

"No. I'm not a jeweler."

"It is like an erosion," he said. "But . . . what has such hardness as to wear down a diamond?"

"Another diamond."

"Very good." He rolled the stone over gently. "Such an erosion as this . . . no scratches, no chipping . . . what does it tell you?" He watched me carefully again.

But when I could only shrug, he said, "I could say it is likely that this precious pebble was carried in a pouch with many other stones for a very long time. Continuous rubbing together, over a period of years, would make the surface like so. They are not like that when they come from the earth."

"David, you're looking at one stone and building a history out of it. Where is this going?"

He was good at long pauses. When he had finished thumbing through his thoughts like a Rolodex in his mind, he said, "Michael, you are my friend. You I can trust. When I look at this gemstone, I get a feeling only a true lover of fine jewels can possibly get. It is almost . . . mystical."

When he spoke, there was a dreamlike quality about the words. Even his tone of voice changed, giving them a hollow ring.

"There is a story of a jewel cutter named Basil, a most mysterious man who came to Germany from Russia when the Communists took over the country. It was Basil himself to whom the tsar went for his jewelry. There have been tales of the fabulous stones Basil produced for the Tsar, rubies, emeralds, diamonds, fantastic baubles few outside the royal family ever got to see. After the revolution, these cut stones all disappeared, probably broken up and sold to make more revolution."

"But Basil himself managed to escape . . ."

"Yes. When the Communists killed the tsar, they searched for Basil, but never found him. Many thought he was dead, but every so often wonderfully cut stones would surface with the remarkable beauty that bore the mark of Basil himself. He became a legend in all of Europe. Whispers had him operating out of Germany, but even there he remained a man of mystery."

"If Basil fled to Germany, how could the quality of his stones remain so high?"

"It is believed he brought a quantity with him from Mother Russia, though it's possible he found some new source. Always of top quality, they were."

"Why didn't he get into the open market?"

For a second, David came out of his reverie. "And show himself?"

I nodded.

"Michael, he was a Jew. Let us say that, on his person, he carried the last of his treasured uncut stones. The Communists would declare them stolen from the state, thieves and mercenaries worldwide would make of him a target. Death could come from any side. Imagine, in a simple leather pouch, Basil carrying a multi-million-dollar value that in this day would be doubled and tripled a dozen times over."

"So he took his time."

"Yes, he was very clever, this Basil. He never showed himself, fashioning his works of art only if he needed the money. But he was a presence, a living legend, Basil and his pouch of huge stones. Just before Hitler came to power, he cut his last known diamond, a ninety-six-carat masterpiece that now graces an oil sheik's collection."

"Do we know if Basil survived the Holocaust?"

"Michael, we do not. We know the Nazis searched for him. Oh, yes, how they searched. But they were dealing with a person who had spent a lifetime in subterfuge, and was an expert at hiding and escaping or whatever was necessary to stay alive . . . and he and his pouch of fabulous uncut stones never surfaced." His eyes burned into mine. "Until *now*, Michael."

"You seem pretty damn sure of what you're saying, David."

He nodded sagely.

"*Why* are you sure?"

His fingers turned the stone until I was looking at the window carved into its surface. David held the loupe out to me. I put it to my eye and drew the stone up to it. I could see, but I couldn't put it together.

I handed the loupe back, shrugged, and he said, "There are facets that are the trademark of Basil."

"Why isn't *it* eroded too?"

David smiled. "That is a . . . shall I say, concave cut? This you understand?"

"The surfaces of the other stones couldn't touch it?"

"That is right."

"Why cut the window at all?"

"Basil never displayed a finished work. It was ordered, paid for, then delivered. Now—what layman knows from an uncut stone?

Not many. To show them what is this pebblelike thing, from which will emerge an art object of untold beauty and value, he would open up a small part of it. And even doing *that* he left his trademark. Yes, the mark of Basil—it was always there."

"You've seen it before?"

"No. Only fine drawings made by a master craftsman who had indeed known Basil. He was no legend, Michael—he was a man. Remarkable men do walk this earth from time to time. I would say, with no intention of embarrassing you, that you are such a man."

"I can cut a throat, David, but not a diamond."

"You are indeed a diamond in the rough, Michael." He shifted in his chair. "Twenty years ago, I was fortunate to be able to study two of Basil's early pieces. Remarkable. There is nothing done like that today."

"You think Basil's dead?"

"Wouldn't he have to be?" the old man asked. "Who lives *that* long? Even men who become legends die. This is something you might keep in mind, Michael, the next time a burst of recklessness comes upon you."

I put the stone back in my pocket. "Thanks, David. This is helpful."

"It is unless I have just been making all of this up. Just an old windbag trying to impress his young friend."

"Not you, buddy."

"Michael . . ."

"What?"

"This is trouble. Big trouble. Trouble as big as man's greed. You do *know* that?"

"David, *that* I really know. That I can give you an expert opinion on."

"Someday . . . you will tell me more?"

"Sure."

"And if you should wish to put this pebble on the market, will you remember your old friend?"

"Of course. Maybe we can get rich and retire to Florida together."

He waved the offer away. "You may have retirement, my friend. I prefer to live."

As I wandered through the many deals being made on that singular street, I could only think how amazed each of these merchants would be if they knew about the rough pebble in my pocket with its window into untold wealth.

It had fallen out of her sleeve cuff.

Things don't fall *into* a place like that, so it had to have been *put* there. And the only people who put things in the cuffs of sleeves are those who wear them.

And now the big question . . . *why?*

David Gross may have put his finger on it when he asked me where the rest of the stones were. Suppose the dead girl *did* have a pouch of them? Why would she extract one, and one with a window in it?

Come on, I told myself, *it isn't* that *hard.*

Virginia Mathes was no heist artist. She wasn't into any part of that game at all. Somebody had used her as a patsy, dropped a fortune in uncut diamonds on her with a story to go with it, and she'd bought the lie.

She was a suddenly recruited carrier, told just to follow instructions, but curiosity had compelled a look at what she was carrying. Not being a lapidary, she couldn't tell one pebble from another, but picked one as a sample, the one with the shiny window — maybe to take to a jeweler herself to find out what this was all about.

Or maybe whoever she was working with only sent her out with one stone — maybe that missing purse hadn't held a pouch of diamonds, and her cuff had been home to a sample to prove to some buyer that the precious things existed and were in her controller's possession.

Still, either way — why walk down a damn dangerous street? She'd have been better off one street over, where it was still hopping and other people were around. Or maybe she thought she could avoid being followed by cutting over onto some out-of-the-way route. A normal person in her position would have been jumpy — checking behind her would have been automatic.

But she hadn't been jumpy, or a guy in sneakers couldn't have sneaked up behind her.

Or *had* she been jumpy?

And a mugger hugging the shadows let her go by, then went at her when she passed. He could have had the knife out as a threatening gesture, but the victim was so on edge that her frightened turn, and readied scream, were so instantaneous the guy just stuck the knife in her, ripped it out, cut her purse straps, and took off with the bag.

But the purse wouldn't have held the rest of the pebbles if she'd brought only a hidden sample with her. And a mugger wouldn't think to go check out her apartment looking for stones he hadn't known existed. He might go there to make a simple heist, only Ginnie's pad had been searched, not stripped.

Somebody else went through her apartment. Looking for the rest of the stones? And found them, maybe?

If a mugger had been the fly in this ointment, he was out of it now — he had his thirty-five bucks plus tips and that was all. Muggers don't hold on to wallets or purses very long. They empty them out, grab the cash, and dump them. Credit cards and checks can be chancy, but everybody takes cash.

Ginnie had been a messenger, a go-between in over her head.

Somebody had sent her to show somebody else one of the stones—that *had* to be it.

It felt like someone had either heisted the stones or stumbled onto them somehow, and was either in the market to sell them to a buyer or back to the owner.

I knew I should turn the pebble over to Pat Chambers and share all of these thoughts with him. I was in no position to do the kind of in-depth investigation it would take to follow all these threads. Pat had an army, and I didn't even have an office.

Or a secretary who happened also to be a P.I. herself, and who could have helped me figure this damn thing out.

So why wasn't I going to Pat?

Because this little kill, which had turned out to be about very big money, had taken place within a few blocks of the mortuary where Bill Doolan had been sent off. What I had blithely written off as coincidence was feeling more and more like something significant, something I didn't understand yet.

But if whoever killed Bill Doolan was also responsible for Ginnie Mathes's murder, only one person was going to settle both scores.

And it wasn't Pat Chambers.

It had gotten dark faster than I expected. There was none of the quiet ease of evening, the way it was at my Florida place, no soft smells and faraway sounds. It was all New York hardness, and the sounds were brazen with impatience, the odors sharp, pungent. Sidewalk traffic had the same hostility the roadway had, everybody in a damned hurry and coming straight at you. Some of the younger wiseass punks even played the chicken game but when they got up close and saw my face, they didn't do any shoulder jousting.

Damn, had it always been like this? What had happened in the one year I had been away?

When I reached the corner of Fifth Avenue and Forty-ninth Street, I stopped and stared around me. I had been walking for a good half hour without realizing it, letting the city get back into my pores again. Now I was hoping the place wasn't going to poison me. If I had been thinking, I couldn't remember what it was about.

The girl said, "Were you looking for someone?"

She was still pretty, like a college postgrad, with a pert smile, brown hair highlighted blonde, and a cute shape in a floral-print minidress. There was even a quizzical expression in her eyes as if she really meant what she said.

But the dress was too short and too tight and her makeup was heavier than back when she was trying to date guys her own age in Bumfuck, Utah, or Arsehole, West Virginia. Before she became a runaway. And a hooker.

A year ago she never would have come near me.

I had paused, so she repeated, "I said, are you looking for someone?"

"Why?"

"You look lost."

I smiled a little. "Maybe I am."

"Then . . ." A smile flashed, and life pretended to come into dark blue eyes. ". . . *I* may be the one you're looking for." She moved, a silken little gesture, and her eyes locked on mine. The headlights of a car turning the corner swept over her face and the little-girl look went hard for a moment.

"You have supper yet?" I asked her.

"What?" She seemed surprised, then: "No."

"Good. Let's get some. And you'll get paid for your time. Is it still a dollar a minute?"

She smirked but it was friendly. "Mister, are *you* out of touch . . ."

"Okay, I'll settle for the going rate."

Her head cocked, like the RCA Victor dog. "You're not *kidding* about supper, are you?"

"No, I'm hungry, and I want to talk."

I picked out the place, since if she'd chosen it, I might still wind up sapped by her boyfriend for my wallet. It was a small Italian restaurant east of Sixth Avenue and she had veal Parmesan and I had sausage and peppers, and for an hour I talked about New York and Velda, and she told me all about three abortions, a bad marriage, and I don't think either of us always knew exactly what the other was saying, the Generation Gap being what it is.

But somehow we both enjoyed the talk.

Going out the door into the evening, she asked, "Are you a tourist?"

"Sort of. I used to live here."

I slipped her two hundred bucks that she didn't want to take until I stuck it in her purse.

On the way out, she said, "I never did *that* before."

"Now that you mention it, neither have I." I glanced at my watch. "Are you done for the night or are you going back to your corner?"

She threw me a quick, impish grin. "I think I'll go home. Why spoil a nice evening. Listen, I could still go somewhere with you—no charge. I *like* you. I can make you happy."

"You could make me ecstatic, kitten."

She laughed. "'Kitten'—that's a funny thing to call a person. How about it?"

I thought about that double bed back at the Commodore, but I said, "Another time."

"Sure." There was something sad in it, which from a realist like this kid was remarkable. "You could walk me back to Fifth. I'll get a cab there."

"Pleasure."

She hooked her arm in mine and we headed east. Halfway up the street, we were crossing over so she could pick up a cab by the stoplight, and we almost made it.

Neither of us saw the car coming. There was no warning blast of a horn or flash of lights, just the roar of an accelerating engine that was right behind us and I heard the dull, sickening sound of the car smashing into a body just as the edge of the fender caught me under my thigh and spun me toward the sidewalk.

For a minute I lay there, dazed, waiting for the sudden flood of pain to come on, trying to figure out what the hell had happened. I moved, sat up, and knew that nothing was broken. The breath was still out of me and inside of me I could feel that everything was still in place.

Up ahead, people were milling about and somebody was screaming hysterically. The crowd seemed to flow in as though drawn by a magnet and blue lights were making psychedelic patterns on the walls of the buildings.

Then the disorientation passed and I remembered the car. Remembered getting the *sense* of a car, its engine roar and the flash of metal and headlights passing as we'd been struck.

But no recall, no sense, of the vehicle's make or color much less a goddamn license plate. Only that it had been big, a Caddy or Lincoln maybe. Or maybe any car that knocks you on your ass seems big in your fragmented memory. . . .

My hat was lying right beside me and so was her purse. Swearing under my breath, I picked them both up and walked unsteadily toward the crowd. They were three thick, but I edged my way through as a lady in front got sick to her stomach, grabbed at her mouth, and forced herself away.

What was there was enough to make anybody sick. The impact had crushed my dining companion's body into odd angles and the force of her head hitting the pavement left nothing recognizable. She didn't look young and she didn't look old.

She just looked dead.

I realized I had her purse in my hand, then edged back out of the crowd. I had seen enough. A uniformed officer was standing beside a prowl car and I eased over to him.

"This was lying in the street back there," I said. I handed him the pocketbook.

He looked at me sharply. "You see the accident?"

I told him the truth. "No, I sure didn't."

Being in the accident didn't mean I had to see it.

"You open this purse?"

"No, but maybe you'd better. Some legalities involved, aren't there?"

That got me a frosty look, then he said, "I'll go get the sergeant."

I didn't wait for him to come back.

Two blocks away I looked down at myself. There was a small tear in my pants leg and street dirt on the sleeve of my coat. With all that jostling, I checked to see if the pebble was still in my pocket.

It was.

My hat needed straightening out, but I wouldn't have been taken for an accident victim, not as long as I was up and walking. Not that that mattered—a guy unconscious on the sidewalk would just be a drunk to anyone running where the action was. If there was no blood, there was no hurt, so who needed to stop, in this town?

My side was hurting again, a dull ache that had all the promise of building into a boiling agony if I didn't get back to my medication fast.

But first I had to make sure of something. I found where the car had made the initial contact and I kept on walking. About two hundred feet down, I found the skid marks that curved out from the curb where the driver burned rubber pulling away. Any squeal noise he made would have been buried in the traffic clatter from Sixth Avenue.

It had to be a big car with a big engine that could pick up momentum fast, but the driver was lousy and never took his foot off the pedal long enough to counteract the centrifugal force of the curve.

He had wanted me, but all he got was her.

And I didn't even know her name.

I got up at six-thirty, showered, brushed my teeth, and shaved. I began to come alive when room service got there with my coffee and the *News*. "I have the *Times* if you'd like, sir . . ."

"*News* is fine," I said.

I signed the bill, fixed my coffee, and opened the paper.

In the photo her body was covered on the stretcher but I wasn't interested in that. The story was brief because she was a nobody who had gotten splattered publicly, a twenty-nine-year-old named Dulcie Thorpe who lived alone in a small East Side apartment. She apparently maintained a nice lifestyle with no visible means of support, no family, and apparently few friends. Her purse had been recovered and had contained a little over six hundred dollars in cash.

So there were still honest cops in New York.

It was strictly a hit-and-run accident and from the damage it did, the car must have been well above the speed limit. No one saw the accident, although several saw a car race by, turn against the light of Fifth, and fly away. One said a headlight was out.

Pat was in when I called, told somebody in his office to close the door, and said, "Well, how are things going, pal?"

"Could be better."

"Yeah?"

"Last night there was a hit-and-run on Forty-seventh right off Fifth."

"Right, a young girl."

"Since when do hit-and-runs hit your desk?"

"It's in the papers this morning. Why?"

"They locate the car, Pat?"

"Beats me."

"Think you can find out?"

"Why?"

"This is where I remind you I'm a taxpayer, and you tell me to go fuck myself and do what I ask anyway."

I heard him breathing hard, then, irritably, he said, "Hang on," and put me on hold.

My coffee was gone and I had finished the paper when he came back on. "Mike . . . ?"

"I'm here."

"It was four blocks away, double-parked outside a bar. The lights and grille were smashed, blood, pieces of flesh, and bits of clothing were in the wreckage. A cabbie parked down the street saw it pull in, a man get out and apparently walk toward the bar. That was all. It was a stolen late-model Caddy and the driver probably wore gloves."

"When was it reported stolen?"

"At eleven P.M. when the police tow-away truck saw what had happened to the front end. They pulled the owner's name from the computer and got him out of bed."

"Who was he?"

"A young doctor who had spent the whole day in surgery at Bellevue."

"And no prints," I said.

"Actually, plenty of 'em, but they all belong to two people—the doctor and his wife." He paused, then added, "It was a real pro job—the entry, hot-wiring, the whole bit. Does this have something to do with you, Mike?"

I let out a little laugh. I could feel Pat stiffen on the other end of the line. My voice sounded strained when I said, "How long have I been back, Pat?"

"Two days."

"Two D.O.A.s."

"Okay, Mike, say it."

"That guy in the car was trying to take me out. He got the girl instead."

"You're not in the report," he said quietly.

"Right, and there's no sense getting me in it either." I took a deep breath, sat in a different position, and told Pat how it had gone down.

When he had mulled it over, he said, "How do you see it?"

"Somebody doesn't appreciate me snooping around. Whether it's Doolan or the Mathes girl that has made me popular, I can't say yet."

"Mike, you were already popular."

"Like with Alberto Bonetti?"

"Hell, man, that makes zero sense. Like old Alberto so cleverly put it to you the other night, he could have had you pickled or fried anytime he wanted to."

"He didn't say it that cleverly, but you have a point. . . . Shit."

"What?"

"Nothing. These damn pills are still working on me. Give me a while and I'll think this thing through."

"And the answer will come out just the same," he told me. "You were inside a hit-and-run, and came out lucky. Try looking at it that way. You're the one always saying coincidences *do* happen."

We said so long and hung up.

Suppose, I thought.

Suppose somebody had picked me up coming out of the hotel, tailed me all day trying to figure a way to nail me, watched when the little hooker and I went to that restaurant for supper, and — knowing we'd be there at least an hour — snagged a car, parked, and waited, hoping he'd get a crack at us.

The possibility was limited, but it *was* a possibility. And if it happened that way, the killer was in a real bind. That "accident" was a murder with the wrong one down, and whoever pulled it would know damn well I'd figure it out.

I felt a grin grow and blossom teeth. Whoever tried to hit me — whether for Doolan or the Mathes kid or both — would have to start all over again.

Only this time I'd be expecting it.

Chapter 6

I WALKED TO BING'S Gym to work out the body ache from the love tap that Caddy gave me the night before. Bing's top trainer, Clarence, knew something had happened when he saw the bruises across my back and on my leg.

"Mixing it up already, Mr. Hammer?" Clarence asked. He was a black guy about thirty-five who'd long since retired from the ring. "You ain't been back in the city that long."

"Maybe somebody mistook me for an out-of-towner."

"Well, they gonna learn a lesson, I bet. You better work an easy routine today, on the apparatus."

Bing had taught everybody that word.

But I still worked up a good sweat, and even with the new aches and pains, I was feeling more myself. Clarence made sure I had a good rubdown and a shower before turning me loose. I was still sore, but clean as a whistle, and feeling better than I could remember. I hoofed it back to the hotel to change from my sweat-shirt and slacks into a suit and tie, and to dump my gym bag.

I had made some changes. You would think I'd have doubled up on the meds last night, after that hit-and-run scrape. You would be wrong. I stopped taking the pills. I didn't flush them—I just put them away. They were mostly for pain and sleep and something that I suspected was an antidepressant meant to cool me out.

Well, a long time ago I had gone to sleep fine in foxholes in the kind of tropical rainstorms that could turn your safe haven into a drowning bath and had artillery for thunder, and if I could deal with those pains and pressures as a kid, I could sure as hell manage without medication as a man.

I'd left the million-dollar marble in an envelope in the hotel safe —nobody knew I had the pebble, so it should be secure. I just didn't want to go around carrying the damn thing. After all, a person could get mugged here in Fun City.

But I *was* carrying something else now—the .45 in its speed rig. With the weight I'd lost, its bulk didn't show under my shoulder at all. Not that it ever had, since all my suits and sport jackets were cut for concealment. This was no simple precaution. Somebody had tried to kill me last night. No time to be keeping the gun packed away in a drawer—time for packing period.

I didn't bother looking around the street for a tail. If he was there, good. Whether a killer with an unknown agenda, or a copper sent by Pat for protection, I'd pick him up sooner or later. The weight under my arm had given a looseness to my shoulders, and I was getting the feeling that I was back in my own ballpark again. I flagged a cab, slipped in back, and gave the driver an East Side address.

The building was turn-of-the-century stylish, a former residence turned into a fashionable men's club. In the basement was the Enfilade, the most exclusive gun club in New York State, snugged away in the midst of Manhattan.

Of course, New York has always had a reputation for being trigger-happy, but these days even buying a gun is a hassle, licensing one is even worse, and finding a place to shoot the goddamn thing is nearly impossible.

So the deep-pocket supersports had come up with their own clubhouse — outfitted with a hundred-foot range and all the technology of a police academy with reloading equipment from cap-and-ball antiques to Israeli Arms .45s.

Membership was pretty damn selective. Social status could always do it, and money generally could too, while occasionally allowances were made for unique personalities, whom the gun fraternity decided could liven up their scheduled events — like the mayor or a Broadway star.

Or a respected retired cop like Bill Doolan.

Ten years ago I had been presented with a membership card so I could mingle during a rare-weapons exhibition, one of the few times select segments of the public had been invited into the shooters' sanctuary. They had a ten-million-dollar display up and I handled the guard duty personally. When the job was over, I was paid handsomely, but they didn't take the card back.

One ancient gent of British extraction said it really was "a bit of a whimsy" to have a member who had actually used a gun to shoot people.

I opened the interior door and the little grayed gnome of a man at the antique mahogany desk looked at me, squinted, then broke into a wide smile.

"Ah," he said. This diminutive guard at the gates wore a dignified black suit and necktie suitable for a high-class undertaker. "Mr. Hammer, is it not?"

"Right on," I told him. "And you're Gerald."

"I am indeed."

You could smell the age when you were inside, the tingling odor of wood polish and real leather, not tainted by the smoke of cigars or covered with cigarette haze. By the door Gerald sat guarding, a brass plate simply read: SMOKING NOT ALLOWED ON THESE PREMISES. A large ornate ashtray stood beside it to make the message clear and provide an exit for any cigar or cigarette that had made it that far. Those with brains would realize that the place was full of barrels of shot and powder, and the ordinance was a safety device.

"Gerry, it's great to see you, and to be seen. But I didn't bring my card."

"No problem, sir—I know all the members. It *has* been some time though, hasn't it?"

"Five years, I guess. Back when Hagley won the International Trophy. Some party that night."

"The exception not the rule, sir. We like to keep our affairs rather dull. Stuffiness has its own benefits, when your hobby is firing off weapons."

"I can dig it," I said with a grin. "Who's lurking in the Enfilade today?"

"At this relatively early hour?" He glanced at the book in front of him. "Only the professionals. A former United States champion in small arms, a gun-manufacturing executive, and our present club president, an ex-Marine marksman, recently retired from Wall Street. Are you going to join them?"

I shrugged. "I don't play with guns anymore."

"I wasn't aware that you ever did, Mr. Hammer."

"What do you mean?"

"Play with them."

"You have a point."

He nodded toward my left arm. "Still, seeing that you've brought your own weapon, perhaps you would like to get in some practice."

"Good eye, Gerry."

"And nose—I can smell gun oil at fifty paces. Would you care to go below and mix with the members in attendance?"

"I would," I said.

Since I'd last been down the stairs into the Enfilade, the place had been renovated. The range itself was walled off from a social area, and from the lack of even muffled pops or cracks, it was either not currently in use or had been soundproofed to a fault.

The lounge area took up perhaps a third of the expansive basement. What had been sheerly functional was now softened with all the accoutrements of a grand billiard room—overstuffed leather chairs, a hand-carved decorative bar, and a table of stainless steel steamer trays for snacks (breakfast items right now). Overhead the soft whisper of heavy-duty exhaust fans sucked out any odor of cordite fumes, but we already seemed isolated from the range. Framed photographs decorated the walls, along with mounted displays of antique pistols, and shelves of trophies gave off a heavy silver glow in the muted light.

The group was having a coffee break, their sound mufflers hanging around their necks like chunky stethoscopes. They were in running togs, though their sport of choice was a standing-still affair.

The former U.S. champion saw me coming, broke into a wide grin, and half-laughed, "I'll be damned, look who's here—my old hero. I always wanted to be *you* when I grew up."

"Good thing you never grew up." I held out my hand for a good solid shake. "How you doing, Chuck?"

Chuck Webb was a compact five eight with sky-blue eyes, a tan rivaling mine, and brown hair cut Marine short. His cream-color polo shirt bore the logo of Smith & Wesson, the company he toured for nationally, giving exhibitions.

He glanced at the others. "This is Mike Hammer," he said to them, "in case you don't recognize him."

The others were quick to say they did recognize me, greeting me with smiles and wide eyes. Maybe the years I'd put on and the weight I'd lost hadn't made too much difference after all.

We had coffee and conversation, then—after the others had gone off to resume their shooting—Chuck asked, "You going to squeeze off a few rounds?"

"Not today, buddy."

"Too bad. I figured on making a few bucks off you."

"At a range, you could. Out where people are shooting back, I might have the edge."

His expression was embarrassed. "No doubt. Man, I was 4-F. Closest I got to combat was that John Wayne movie about Vietnam. Listen, uh, Mike . . . sorry to hear about your friend Doolan. Hell of a nice guy."

Now that the others were shooting, I could make out muffled gunfire. But damn faint for being right next to it.

"You know Doolan well, Chuck?"

He shrugged. "We weren't exactly close, but we were friendly acquaintances at least. He was in the Friday group, and so am I. Plus, I'd run into him at some of the functions upstairs. Caught him at some political meetings too. Such a nice fella, little on the crusty side. Not a bad shooter either, particularly for a guy of his years. Hard to believe he'd . . . turn a gun on himself."

He hadn't.

"Doolan was pretty spry for his age," I said.

He let out a gentle laugh. "Sure as shit was. When you came in, did you stop and look at the pictures on the trophy wall?"

"No."

He jerked his head toward the far side of the room where the stairs emptied out. "Come on—this is worth the trip, Mike."

And there among the many framed photos on display was old Doolan, sometimes when he was not so old. I hadn't realized he'd stayed in active competition at pistol shooting for so long. Only two years ago he had taken second place in an interstate meet.

Of the half-dozen latest photos, I recognized faces in every one—state senators, a Supreme Court judge, a few heavies in military uniforms, and a pair of very lovely dolls.

Chuck saw me eyeing them and said, "I thought it wouldn't take Mike Hammer's eyeballs very long to find their way to that pair. Both those lovely ladies are top marksmen. Or is it markspersons? Anyway, they're reps for an arms manufacturer."

"That's one way to keep a buyer's attention," I said with an appreciative nod. I pointed to Alex Jaynor, who was standing between the dolls, and asked, "Is Alex any good with a gun?"

"Not really. Do you know Alex?"

"We met at Doolan's funeral. They were apparently pretty tight in recent years."

"So I understand. Well, Alex shoots for fun, not for glory. Best I can say is, he enjoys it. Pretty decent guy for a politician. Doolan sponsored his membership."

"They seem an unlikely combo."

The remark brought another shrug. "Not really. Story is, Alex helped Doolan clean up his neighborhood. There was a shooting gallery—and I don't mean the Enfilade kind—and they got rid of that. Ran the druggies and the dealers out."

Cleaning drugs out of a neighborhood could make you unpopular with whoever had been profiting.

Chuck was saying, "Alex and Doolan were both right-wing anticrime, antidrug crusaders, and I guess that bridged any differences in age and background."

"I understand Alex was a reporter and that it was Doolan who encouraged him to quit and go into politics."

"Jibes with what I hear." Chuck tapped the photo under the last guy in the group. "Here's an oddball for you. Know him?"

He indicated a small, narrow-faced, mustached character with dark curly hair and dark eyes too small for his otherwise handsome face.

I had to look long and hard before recognition kicked in. "Shit — is that Tony *Tretriano?*"

"Right. Little Tony. Son of Big Tony."

Big Tony Tretriano had been a minor crime boss who died quietly in his sleep maybe six years ago.

I was shaking my head. "What's a bush-league wiseguy like Little Tony Tret doing in *this* club?"

Chuck was shaking his head, too, but in a way meant to calm me down. "Mike, he's a good kid. You may recall his mother did her best to keep the old man's hands off him."

I did. Tony Tretriano had graduated from an Ivy League school with a law degree and, after his sainted mother died, represented his pop for just a few years. After Big Tony kicked off, Little Tony stopped practicing law. That was the last I knew of the kid.

Chuck was saying, "In recent years, Anthony Tretriano has made it very clear he's severed all ties with organized crime — and in the last year, he's become a very big deal in this town. Jeez, Mike, you *have* been away."

"How has Little Tony become a big deal?"

"You've heard of Club 52?"

The pops in the range were louder. They must have upped their caliber.

"I was in Florida, not dead," I said. "Club 52's the 'in' disco for everybody who is famous, wants to be famous, or just wants to rub up against somebody famous."

Chuck laughed. "Yeah, I wish *I* could get in—any celebrity who comes to the Big Apple hangs there. Anthony owns and manages the club—he prefers Anthony to Tony, by the way. There was an article just a week or two ago in *New York* magazine about how he's expanding to just about every major city in these United States."

"Great. Now every big city will have a club where nobody can get past the velvet rope and the ex-wrestler doorman."

"I'm sure the rich and famous won't have any trouble at any of the locations."

"And 'Anthony' claims there's no mob ties to his club?"

"He seems squeaky clean." Chuck gave me another short laugh. "Funny how kids turn out. Big brother Leo did his bit in the pen for extortion and took over his old man's slice of the rackets when Big Tony died. At least, that's what it said in the *News*. Anthony has nothing at all to do with that part of the family anymore."

"Strange world," I mused.

"Crazy," he agreed. The light blue eyes brightened. "Mike, come on over and try the range. I have a new piece you'd dig—an S & W Model 29."

"What, the .44 mag?"

"You got it. Four-inch barrel. Herrett's Jordan Trooper stock in walnut. Adjustable sights . . ."

"Tempting. But another time, okay?"

"Sure." He shook his head, then laughed. "Yeah, that Doolan, he was still a pisser. Did you know that old fart had a young girlfriend?"

"I knew he still had an eye for beauty. But an honest-to-God girlfriend?"

His shrug was elaborate and his expression amused. "I never saw her, but a couple of the other members did. A big blonde, they said. Hey, *that's* a coincidence."

"What is?"

"You know where one of the guys said they saw Doolan with this young dish?"

"Where?"

"Club 52! How would a coot like Bill Doolan get into *that* trendy a watering hole? Much less land in the lap of some blonde out of *Penthouse*. Of course, just because he was getting up in years, doesn't mean he—"

"Couldn't *get* it up?" I finished. "Good to see you, Chuck. Don't let me keep you from your fun."

"Sure you don't wanna play with that .44 mag?"

"I haven't met the guy I couldn't stop with a .45."

I let him think about that as I waved and headed up the stairs.

Once again, Peter Cummings was in his office when I got there. Crouched behind a pile of papers at his desk, he looked up when I opened the door and motioned for me to come in—he was writing something in longhand. I waited for him to finish, which took maybe two minutes.

Then he let out a weight-of-the-world sigh Atlas might have envied, took the wire-rim glasses off, tossed them, wiped his eyes, and leaned back in his chair. "Well, Mike—are you getting anywhere on your New York vacation?"

I said nothing. I had already plopped down in the same chair as before. Now I put my feet up on his desk.

"Make yourself at home," he said.

"How come you're making me work so hard, Pete?"

"What do you mean?"

"People keep telling me things that you could have. Like how Doolan made a target out of himself by running dopers and pushers out of his neighborhood. Like how the old boy still had a regular girlfriend."

The old ex-cop with the well-grooved face was not intimidated. He just grunted a laugh at the middle-aged child across from him. "You got to learn to walk before you run, kiddo."

"I took a leave of absence, pal. I didn't die."

He studied me a few seconds before he ran a hand through the gray bristles of his hair. "Oh, you died, all right, Mike. You dragged it out right to the last, then you died."

My hands started to form fists and my chest felt tight. "Oh?"

Pete nodded. "Don't fight it, Mike — it's nothing to be ashamed of. When the piss and vinegar run out?" He shrugged. "Just relax and enjoy life."

"Nothing ran out."

"Sure it did," he told me. "The vinegar's all gone, anyway. All that's left is the piss."

"That's enough."

He frowned and sat forward in the old swivel chair. "No, Mike, you're wrong. An old street fighter like you needs the whole schmear, piss *and* vinegar and balls of fucking steel. You go tangling assholes with any of the young turks we have around today, and they'll make a memory out of you in a hurry. In one lousy year, the whole game's changed again . . . and there's no room left for cripples. Physical or emotional."

This time the tension started in my back and I breathed deeply, held it, and exhaled slowly. Pete was goading me. Trying to tell me something that he figured I didn't want to hear.

"Just what is it you call the 'vinegar,' Pete?"

He showed me his teeth; a skull was grinning at me. "The *ag-*

gression, kid, the damn fulminating, wild-assed attack attitude you used to shake everybody up with. *That's* what you haven't got anymore."

"How do *you* know?" I asked softly.

"Ah, I can read you like a book," he told me, waving me away like a wino bugging him for a buck. "It was all over you the other day, like a sick bad smell. And you *know* I'm right."

"You *were* right."

"What do you mean?"

I opened the jacket and I showed him the .45 in the sling. Then I showed him my teeth and let him see my eyes.

"Shit," he said. He swallowed. "Sorry. I, uh, should have given you a closer look, Mike. You *are* back."

"Yeah. Full of piss and vinegar and no fucking medication. Now what's this shit about Doolan having a girlfriend?"

Pete raised his eyebrows quizzically. "And you're not brain-dead either. . . ."

"*Well?*"

"Doolan never told me outright, but I could read the signs."

"What signs?"

Pete rocked in his chair, smiling slightly. "Oh, a certain neatness of dress on odd occasions, a small scent that clung to his clothing that whispered *woman.* A bit of a secretive air, I'd say — like he wanted me to ask him something."

"But you didn't?"

Pete waved me off again. "Of course not."

"You suppose he was fooling around? Maybe with a married woman?"

"I don't know about *married* women, but I always hoped he was out there getting a little in his old age. *Something* was putting life back in his veins and a smile on his puss. Plus, it gives another old goat hope — means there might still be some juice left in *me*, too."

"Look," I said impatiently, "do you know who she was?"

"No, but she'd be about five eight, a person of good taste, fond of dancing, and much too young for him."

The corners of his mouth twitched in a smile. While he waited for me to figure it out, he got up, knelt at his little fridge like the special altar it was, and got us a couple of beers. Tossed me a cold can, popped his own, and sat again.

I popped mine, sipped the icy liquid, and said, "With two-inch heels, she left a makeup smear on him just high enough for dance contact — Doolan was a six footer — and the gift he gave her had class and was selected with a young woman in mind."

"Wise ass," he said. "Just don't put too much stock in this info. Him and younger women, it happened before. Once the daughter of an old friend who was visiting town for a week, another time it was the middle-aged widow of a cop he'd known. You know, some paternal-type romancing here and there."

"You think this last doll was paternal?"

"Maybe. Maybe not."

"Was that why you thought maybe he killed himself? He fell in love with some fine young thing, got dumped, and took the exit ramp?"

He stared thoughtfully at the wall above my head, nodding slowly. "Maybe that did help me buy the suicide bit. The woman seemed to drop out of his life maybe two months ago."

"But now you're not buying it."

"No." He gulped some beer, sat the can down hard on the desk, making a slosh. "Mike, when I think about it, really think about it? Doolan was an old dog. His *fun* times long past. His *looking* times were still with him, and he was smart enough to know the difference. If he made any kind of a run with the babes, it was commensurate with his age and health and all I could say was good luck to him."

"Pat speculate about this?"

"Not outside a vulgar remark or two." He sat forward and leaned on the desk. "Now about Doolan running the druggies out of his neighborhood—he was point man for a citizens' committee, but it was his young pal Jaynor who took the heat. That politician got some bullets thrown at him."

I frowned. "Really?"

"Oh yeah. And if you were trying to make an example out of a local do-gooder like Doolan, why the hell fake a suicide? You'd make him die nice and public, wouldn't you? Right down on the street?"

I wadded up the empty beer can and hit his wastebasket, no rim. "I don't kill to make examples. Any lesson I teach with a gun begins and ends with what comes out of the barrel."

He laughed. "Don't push it, Mike. You trying to talk *me* into thinking you're the same old tough guy, or yourself?"

"Fuck you, Pete," I said good-naturedly. "Where does Tony Tret come in?"

Pete shrugged. "He knew Doolan a little. They were both members of that fancy shooting club—the Enfilade?"

"Doolan and a mob kid like that? I can't picture it."

"Mike, Anthony Tretriano is cleaner than Windex. Every cop in town has gone through the former Little Tony's laundry *and* his garbage, and so has every reporter. That kid couldn't get in the Enfilade unless he was good and goddamn clean, and he damn sure couldn't get by *Doolan's* scrutiny, if *he* thought Anthony was up to something."

"You're calling him Anthony, too, like a guy I talked to over at the Enfilade did. Why?"

"No special reason. Doolan told me young Tretriano didn't like to be called Tony anymore. He associated it with times he'd rather forget."

"Some of us have a better memory than that. Did Pat know about Little Tony being in the same shooting club as Doolan and Jaynor?"

He tossed his beer can and missed the basket. So had several other of his cans. "I don't know. What makes me the expert? Ask Pat."

"I will. What I want from you is your blessing to go over Doolan's files in more detail."

"You think the police missed something?"

"Not necessarily, but I at least want to know what *they* know. And the other day I could only give 'em a cursory look. I got a hunch the answer, or parts of it, is in there."

"The answer to what?"

"Who faked Doolan's suicide. And why. You ever hear of a girl named Virginia Mathes? Ginnie Mathes?"

"Wasn't she a mugging victim the other night? It was in the *News*."

"Yeah. She was a mugging victim. What about another good-looking kid, Dulcie Thorpe? Ring any bells? Were either of those girls among Doolan's little stable of young fillies?"

I had only half of that out before Pete began shaking his head. "No, neither name means a thing to me, beyond that mugging squib. But you make it sound like Doolan was out laying pipe from here to Trenton. Man, I tell you, it was probably more a spectator sport with him. Who's this Thorpe girl, anyway?"

"She was a hooker. She's dead now. Maybe on purpose, or maybe because the guy who ran her down in a stolen Caddy missed me by an inch or two. You wanna see the black-and-blue place on my ass?"

This had turned the old boy a whiter shade of pale, whether from the escalating body count or the prospect of seeing my backside up close, I couldn't tell you.

Pete pushed back in his chair, pulled the top desk drawer open, and reached in back. He found what he was after and flipped it at me.

"Here's a key to the office. I'll be gone for the next two days, on a claim in Philly that requires eyes-on attention. So feel free to do what you want around here. Sleep on the floor for all I care."

"Thanks, pal."

"Any phone calls come in while you're here, take messages and jot 'em down. I don't have an answering machine."

"Thanks, Pete."

"No trouble," he said. "Now get out of here before you get piss and vinegar all over the place."

I got on my feet, exchanged smiles with the ex-copper, and headed for the door.

"And Mike! Try not to kill anybody in here. It's enough of a mess already."

After sixty years or so at the same stand, police HQ had a new address—One Police Plaza on Park Row near City Hall and the Brooklyn Bridge. The new digs were a thirteen-story pyramid of glass and concrete with the personality of a prefab garage. The upcoming move was probably why that documentary crew had been sniffing around the baroque old building on Centre Street the other day. At least nobody was talking about tearing the old girl down.

Pat's glassed-in office off the bull pen was piled with boxes, the file cabinet drawers yawning empty. He was in shirtsleeves and a bow tie, and looked frazzled.

He said, "You took long enough coming in, buddy. I got you off the hook by telling Traffic Detail how banged up you were."

I took the visitor's chair across from where he peered over stacks of paper and file folders. "Pat, what I told you on the phone is all there is."

"Yeah, sure," he said sourly. He pushed a form across the desk at me. "Fill it out."

"You want it typed?"

"There's the machine." He indicated with his chin.

I ran the obstacle course of boxes to the Remington on the little stand, and in five minutes I had the report finished, signed, and handed back.

"What did you find out about the Thorpe girl?" I asked him, returning to the chair.

"Not much more than the papers mentioned. Your little hooker was strictly a loner, not part of a stable. One thing that did surface—six months ago, she dumped her pimp and went out on her own."

"How'd she manage that in this town?"

"Easy," Pat laughed. "She shot him. Aimed right for his balls but got him in the left thigh instead. She told him if he tried coming after her, she'd put the next one in his eye."

"Sounds like she knew how to make a point. Who gave you that? I can't think *that* incident made its way into a police report."

"Not hardly. Her neighbor gave us the story. An older gal. She and Dulcie were friendly enough to talk a lot over coffee."

Speaking of which, he got up and poured two cups from the Silex and handed one to me, pushing across the sugar packs and creamer he knew I required. Not all tough guys drink it black.

"This shot-up pimp puts your theory in a new light, Mike. I don't figure the driver was after you at all. He got who he wanted."

I sipped at the coffee, swirled it around in the cup, and shook my head. "Maybe."

"Maybe hell. She bruised that pimp's ego just a little too much. He came back after all."

"Six months later? Who was he?"

"Fidel Waxman. Waxey for short. A Cuban from the West Side. No known address."

"You looking for him?"

He waved at the air. "Come on, Mike. You know the system. The report's up, and that's about it."

I finished the coffee. "You believe what you're saying, Pat? That I wasn't the target?"

"What have you got says otherwise?"

"You told me yourself—a pro boosted the hit-and-run vehicle."

"Hell, Mike, scumbags like that can double in any kind of low-level crime. Pimping and hot-wiring go hand in hand. So does stripping cars, from hubcaps to chop shops."

"Including murder?"

"Including murder. And one of these days, Waxey baby will surface on something else, and we'll nail his ass for this one. It's the way of the world." He took the coffee cup from me and put them both back on the shelf unwashed. "So, Mike—you've been out sniffing. What have you come up with on Doolan?"

"I hear he had a girlfriend."

This time he gave me a disgusted shake of his head and grunted under his breath as he sat down again. "Come on, Mike. You talking about those photos in his file? I can give you chapter and verse on every one of those—"

"No," I cut in, "this was street talk."

"Okay. I'll bite. What about it?"

"It just doesn't sound like Doolan, that's all. Chasing young tail.

Looking, yes. Cop a feel, maybe. But something serious, with a woman decades younger?"

"Bullshit, Mike, what do *you* know about it? Or for that matter, what do I know about it?"

"What do you mean, Pat?"

"I mean, it's been three years since either one of us even made contact with Doolan, but he was still getting around." He stopped to paw the air. "Man, he didn't even back out of getting involved in some of the hard stuff."

I sat forward. "Hard stuff? What the hell, Pat? What have you been holding back?"

"Eighteen months ago, Doolan dumped information on the narco boys that got an intercept of a hundred-ten kilos of pure heroin. Two months later he gave them a crack lab in Brooklyn and a couple of million bucks' worth of stuff was picked up along with the local chemists putting it together."

This went way beyond helping a budding politico chase some drug-gies out of his neighborhood.

"Jesus, Pat, how did that old coot get into that?"

"Well, you know Doolan. He kept his sources close to the vest, but he always did have his informants. And he was out there doing routine work for his P.I. pal Cummings, and he saw things. He had an eye. A nose. Like you."

"Then even at this late date, Doolan was still making enemies."

"All cops got enemies," he reminded me.

"And enemies like revenge," I reminded him.

"Who the hell would want revenge on an old dog like Doolan?"

"Maybe some other old dog."

"Like Alberto Bonetti?"

I nodded.

"Mike, you are a man obsessed with that goddamn family." He

sat down, folded his hands behind his head, and leaned back in his chair. "Bonetti has enough trouble keeping the ambitious young turks in his outfit from tearing up his own ass. Right now, he still has the bull on them, but keeping it that way is something else." He paused, took a breath, and his expression turned grave. "Mike—you've been goofing off for a year. Do you know what the hell's been happening around here?"

"Not really," I said. "Then again, the Miami area has its own Wild West show going."

"Multiply Miami by a hundred and you have New York. But it's not like the old days—the organizations have tightened up. They have legal covers and the kind of money laundries you could never conceive of. Imagine controlling an entire segment of the *banking* industry—that's what they have now."

I nodded toward the window. "This is *the* stock market town, buddy. If what you're saying is true—"

"It's true. And this city you love to hate, it's also *the* port of entry. Man, I remember when knocking off a dozen kilos of H got us on the front pages. Now you'd better unload tons of the stuff to rate a mention. And damnit, I mean *tons.* Now it's coke that's in the pipeline. Translate that into street value, and you'll see the kind of money power we're up against."

I asked, "So where does Bonetti stand?"

"Maybe not a major player anymore, but still in the game. And he's got a damn good cover, running his own supply line somehow to keep his bunch happy . . . but mainly we figure him for a contact man. He arranges deals. At least we *think* so."

I said, "That's pretty thin."

"Organized Crime Unit does its best. This is more than they have on Don Giraldi."

"Costello's old buddy?"

"Yeah."

"Hell, I thought he was dead."

"That's what people think about you," Pat said. "You know how those old Cosa Nostra guys hibernate—he's still in his place on Long Island, but now his protection comes as much out of lawyers' briefcases as his bodyguards' guns. You remember Pierluigi?"

"Sure." Umberto Pierluigi was a top headhunter for Genovese back in the old days.

"Well," Pat said, "he's got his own cut of the pie now."

"His own *family?*"

"They don't dress it up like that anymore. It's a business organization called Sonata Imports, Inc." Before I could ask, he added, "And it's clean, as far as that goes. They even pay their goddamn taxes."

"So what's the story on Little Tony? Anthony-who-doesn't-like-to-be-called-Tony, I mean."

Pat shrugged. "Kid's out of the loop. He's gone straight. Even *you* have to know about Club 52."

"Yeah, I know about it. It's where the movie stars and recording artists and Broadway cats go to boogie under flashing lights and do cocaine in the backroom."

His face fell. "Knock it off, Mike."

"You're saying that doesn't happen?"

"Of course it happens."

"And you look the other way?"

He didn't say anything.

"Pat? You hear the question?"

"I heard the question. Everybody looks the other way, Mike. A little recreational use by celebrities is something I'm required to tolerate."

"Well, I'm not." I sat forward. "And you're telling me a disco where they got hot and cold running coke doesn't have mob ties? Are you fucking kidding?"

"Beyond what you're talking about, Mike—this social activity that certain parties see to it that we ignore? Anthony Tretriano is a straight shooter."

"Of what? Heroin?"

"Mike . . . he's a businessman. He runs a very successful, famous, well-connected nightclub."

"I'll bet it's well connected. Listen, Pat, Doolan was murdered, and so were those two girls, and I think all three *kills* were 'well connected.'"

"Oh, Mike. Give it a break. What are *you* on?"

"Nothing. Not a damn thing. Not even fucking aspirin. Will you help me?"

"Help you what?"

"You have the men it takes to look into things that I just don't have the time or resources to run down. Things like, did Ginnie Mathes and Dulcie Thorpe know each other? Were they connected in any way?"

His mouth was smiling but his eyes weren't. "Should I take notes, now that I'm your unofficial legman?"

"If you want. For example, have you checked that dance studio where Ginnie was taking lessons? Who else belonged? Was it near where she was mugged?"

"I can tell you that one—it's a little off-Broadway studio. A lot of theater kids train there. And we already checked."

"For a tie between the two dead girls?"

"Well, no . . ."

"Get started, then, if you don't have too much packing to do for your move into that hideous new Holiday Inn they built you guys over by Chinatown."

He scowled. "You got other leads you want me to run down for you, Mike? Anything *else* I can do?"

"Yeah, there's a couple of things. Maybe you should get out your pad and pencil."

"And in the meantime, what will *you* be running down?"

"Hunches, Pat. That's where I excel, remember?"

"As I recall, killing people and banging dames is where you excel, and sometimes there's some blurring between the lines."

I shook my head sadly. "'Dames' is such an old term. You date yourself, kiddo." I looked at my watch. It was later than I thought. "Okay, here's a couple other leads you can run down . . ."

"Gee," Pat said. "Thanks."

But he had his pad and pencil ready.

Chapter 7

NIGHTTIME. *New York. A charcoal sky rumbles and mutes the neon. The taxis have thinned out and those remaining are cruising slower now. More women drivers than I remember. A lot of small, foreign-looking guys behind the wheel. A year ago a lot of hippies hanging out, not so many now. The bar action is slow, almost quiet. Sometimes it gets like that in the city, as if everyone was waiting for a funeral procession to roll by.*

An older, heavy-set uniformed cop on the corner looks at me a few seconds, nods sagely, and winks. I wink back. It has been a year since I've seen him. He's still on the same beat.

Up ahead, Forty-second Street is bathing itself in garish advertising, even the gray overhead can't diminish the commercial glow. The night people are in constant motion. Nobody seems to look at anybody else. If they do, they turn quickly away as if somebody might steal their anonymity.

It starts to rain. Not hard. Just a steady New York rain that doesn't seem to give a damn whether it happens or not. It's no downpour to bother rushing out of, only the kind of insistent drizzle that will make you uncomfortable if you stay in it too long.

You could think, though, on a night like this. You could wander and wonder and reason and begin to get a feel for things, like knowing that the aroma of good cooking will lead to restaurant windows where even on a slow night the tables will be filled with those taking refuge from the rain.

But Doolan's death doesn't provide a nice smell at all. There isn't a logical reason in the world to doubt he knocked himself off. While he was still reasonably functional, he'd kept doing the things he knew best, making productive use of his knowledge and his contacts. He chased a skirt or two. Maybe he even bedded down a couple. Then, before the Big Pain could claw his guts out, he sat down, put his favorite music on, and blew his heart apart. It seemed logical enough, it followed a pattern others had laid down, and I could almost believe it myself.

Almost.

I go back to the Commodore, consider digging out enough medication to address aches and pains the rain has stirred up, and to beat back thoughts that might keep sleep from coming. I decide against it and go to bed, where the thoughts I pursue like uncooperative suspects seem worth the chase, and when sleep finally comes, it's deep but not dreamless, a surreal mix of faces old and new and distinct and vague on streets where the neon is even more vivid, the rain slashing, the odors pungent, and I am at home again in Manhattan, awake or asleep.

Goddamnit.

I am home.

* * *

At five-thirty A.M., I was down on the street in sweats, setting out in an easy jog. I had decided to take a pass on Bing's today, and instead take advantage of the cool, sunny morning.

I didn't have to estimate the distance. Twenty blocks to the mile, and I went forty north, crossed the avenue, and did forty back. There were enough other runners out that I didn't feel alone, and I got back as the early workers were starting to show.

Cooling down slowly was a must, then a hot shower took the ache out of that spot that still bore the bullet track. I don't buy that macho crap about a final cold shower, so I dried off. I shaved and, for better or worse, I could recognize the guy in the mirror again.

"Shit," I told him.

Then I got into shirt and tie and shoulder sling and slacks and sport jacket and put the hat on.

God got melodramatic and let some thunder rip just as I was snugging the porkpie in place. I went to the nearest window. That early-morning sun I'd enjoyed was gone — it was raining again. A little harder than last night. Good thing I'd thought to pack the trench coat.

I had sicced Pat on tracking down various notions I had about the two dead girls — he and his little elves could be useful at times. But Pat didn't buy that Doolan had been murdered, so that angle of the investigation was all mine. And so far I had precious little.

I took a cab to Doolan's address. I still had the key, and there was something up there I wanted to pick up. I did so, but mostly I was here not for his pad, but for his neighborhood, to ask around.

Turned out old Doolan had been a nice guy and he had nice friends who said nice things about him, only "nice" was the kind of well-meaning sweet talk you hear right before and after the funeral, and not the sharp, pointed facts I needed.

And the only facts I was getting were basic — Doolan shopped locally, paid his bills, had a good credit rating, and was a pretty visible guy in the neighborhood, having helped run the druggies out. By the time I had covered all the local businesses, I'd come to a standstill.

It was almost noon and I was damn sick of all the *nice* things I had been hearing. I looked up and down the street, knowing something was missing. Then it came to me: there was no drugstore in sight. Somewhere a guy Doolan's age, with his medical problems, could get his prescriptions filled. And he would likely go to the nearest place at hand.

The Yellow Pages gave up three walking-distance possibilities just outside the neighborhood, and I checked the closest one first, hitting immediate pay dirt.

The store was small, in the middle of the block, had only a handful of customers, one shopping, two at the soda fountain, and none at all at the back prescription counter. Just inside, I shook the rain off my hat and coat, and headed back there.

"I don't talk about my patients," the druggist said, with the strong implication that he recognized the name William Doolan.

He was a small, sour, flat-faced type who didn't seem to want to talk about anything, except maybe what you owed him at the register.

I considered slapping him. His *patients?* He was a fucking pharmacist, not a damn doctor.

But that kind of thing didn't go over so good anymore, and I just got out the card Pat had given me and handed it across to him.

"Why don't you call that number," I said, "and see if I'm square."

Finally his curiosity overcame his suspicions, and he dialed it. He spoke briefly, then handed me the phone. "Captain Chambers wants to hear your voice."

I stuck the phone to my ear. "Pat, could you okay me to this guy?"

"What's it about, Mike?"

"Just checking up on Doolan."

"Come on, man, that's a dead end."

"Maybe, but at least I'm not asking *you* to handle it."

"Good point. Put him back on."

When I handed the phone back, there was another brief exchange and the druggist cradled the receiver on its hook on his counter. "I guess it's permissible to talk."

"Good," I said. "Anyway, I'm not interested in Mr. Doolan's medical history—what I'm trying to pick up are any stray details about his personal life."

"I was just his pharmacist. . . ."

I managed not to say, *Oh, not his doctor?*

Instead I said, "I know, but he had lots of meds to fill, and regularly, and maybe you two talked a little."

"I'm not that talkative."

"Well, anything you can share would be appreciated."

"Like what?"

"Any little thing. You ever pass the time with him?"

He bobbed his head. "Now and then. We'd sit over there and have coffee."

That was a nice surprise. "So what did you fellas talk about?"

"Bill was an old cop. I guess you must know that." The druggist shrugged. "He'd tell me his old war stories—close scrapes and busting bad guys and that. What *else* has an old cop got to talk about?"

"Nothing about what he was up to lately?"

"Well—he went uptown a lot. He sat in Central Park, he said, and people watched. Sometimes he would dress funny."

"Funny how?"

"One time I told him he looked like a Bowery bum and he said I was making a good guess."

Christ—so he'd been staking somebody out. Who at this point in his life would Doolan be watching, undercover?

"Funny thing, though."

"Yeah?"

"A couple of times he looked pretty damned sharp."

"Sharp."

"Yeah. Nice suit. Like he really had dough. Mostly he was dressed like, well, any old bird his age. I asked where he was going all duded up, and you will not believe what he said."

"Try me."

"I say, 'Where are you going tonight, Bill? Club 52?' And you know what he says?"

"What?"

"'You must be psychic, Fred. That's exactly where I'm headin'.' Right. An old coot like that, going to Club 52. I gave him the horse laugh, but then a week later, he came in all duded up again, and I say, 'Expectin' another wild night at Club 52, are ya, Bill?' He says sure, and says if I don't believe him, have a gander at this . . . and he shows me a plastic card, signed by that guy Anthony Tret-something, who owns the joint."

"Yeah?"

"It's a plastic card with Club 52 on it and it says ALL ACCESS. You *believe* that?"

"Did you ever ask Doolan why a guy his age would be going to Club 52?"

"Sure I did. Get this—he says to me, 'Don't be a stick in the mud, Fred—don't you *dig* disco?' Dig *disco?* Was he kidding?"

This was the Doolan who died listening to recordings of the great symphonies, a lover of all the fine classics—and in his final days, he dug disco?

"When did you see him last?"

"Couple days before he killed himself."

"So did he seem really sick? Was he depressed, or in pain . . . ?"

"Not really, but then he was taking strong painkillers before he died, and wouldn't be feeling it much if at all. Who knows—maybe there at the end, he was having one last fling. Hell, twice, he bought some rubbers from me."

"Maybe he didn't want to be a daddy at his age."

"Nuts. Didn't want to catch a dose, I'd say."

Either way, it was an interesting purchase for an octogenarian.

There wasn't much else Fred the druggist could tell me, so I said thanks and left. He'd warmed up—I was glad I hadn't slapped him. For a nontalkative guy, he and Doolan had gabbed plenty.

But all I had was one more screwy bit about my old friend that didn't make any sense at all—he had not only been to Club 52, he'd been a regular, or enough of one to rate a signed entry card from Little Tony himself.

I was going back in time now.

Down at the end of the street would be an old barroom with scarred furniture and artifacts dating to Prohibition days. Some of the customers would look like they had been there that long themselves, and the old sportswriters would be gathered at one end arguing about something that never happened anyway.

I would meet Velda at the back booth where the phone was right on the wall and she would have a cold beer and a meatball sandwich already ordered for me and we would compare notes of what had happened in the world of sports that day, with Ernie and Vern constantly butting in.

The taste in my mouth was sour and I spit it out. This time there would be no Velda and I shut her out of my mind. Vern had died the way a sportswriter should, of a heart attack after filing a story about a no-hitter at Yankee Stadium last year.

Two old-timers looked at me, surprised, then grinned. Somebody said hello from a booth and I waved in that direction while I moved through the modest crowd.

There in back was Ernie—a dark little balding mustached guy with a stubby pencil behind one ear, rolled up sleeves, a loose necktie, and baggy trousers, looking like he was trying out for a revival of *The Front Page*. Vern had been sports, but Ernie was police beat.

Right now he had the phone stuck to his ear, his waving hand describing something that couldn't be seen on the other end of the line. Not unless the rewrite man was psychic.

When I sat down in the booth nearby, he gaped at me, then hung the phone up without saying goodbye.

"How you doing, Ernie?"

"Man . . ." He shook his head, whether in disgust or amazement, I couldn't quite tell. "You *are* the fuck alive. I hardly believe it. Somebody *said* you were at Doolan's funeral, but I said they were either lying or hallucinating."

"I was there, all right. One of the youngest."

"That's not much to brag about," he said with a snort of a laugh. He slid in the side where his half-drunk beer was already waiting. "Where the hell have you been, Mike?"

"Away."

"Oh, so it's twenty questions? You think I don't ask enough questions in a given day, that you have to play cute?"

"I was living in Florida." *That was the first time I'd used the past tense for that.*

"No shit? I thought you died. Everybody thought you were dead.

When the Bonetti kid popped you, and you just disappeared, everybody figured you'd bought it. Either crawled off to bleed out someplace on your own, or got followed there and put out of your misery." He shrugged. "Mike Hammer's dead, there goes New York, I said."

"Sure you did, Ernie."

"But here you are back again, right?"

"Right."

"And you don't even look like some old shot-up piece of shit."

"Thanks a bunch."

"You look fit in fact. Packing heat?"

"I'm warm enough."

"That old glow in your eyes is there and everything. Somebody gonna die?"

"Somebody might."

He shifted in the booth. "So something big's going down, right?"

"Right."

"And if I ask what it is, you're going to tell me to shove it up my ass, right?"

"Right."

"Shit." He threw the rest of the beer down, then waved until the waitress saw him, and he held up two fingers. "So where's Velda?"

"I don't know, Ernie."

"Was she in Florida with you?"

"No."

Everything seemed to stop in midair, then he frowned.

I said, "It's over."

That got another snort of a laugh out of him. "In a pig's ass it's over," he said. "You don't just drop a broad like that. George Washington don't drop Martha. Tarzan don't dump Jane."

"Maybe Jane dumped Tarzan. Anyway, I hear she's got somebody else. And she's not in the city anymore." I managed a shrug. "These things happen."

"Jesus, Mike—this is like when the Yankees dropped Babe Ruth."

"Yet somehow the Yankees survived. Now forget it."

A young waitress came up and set down two foaming steins of beer in front of us..

"Want some pretzels, fellas?" she asked.

We both nodded.

"I'll bring 'em," she told us.

Ernie was smiling at me.

"What?" I said.

"That kid doesn't even know you. Maybe you gone out of fashion."

I was in no mood. "I need some information, Ernie." A frown started and I added, "Not asking you to share anything off the record, if you're not so inclined."

He wiped foam off his mustache. "Hey, if it's news, Mike, everything's on microfilm and you can look it up."

"You're quicker, pal." I took a pull of the beer. It was icy cold and tasted good. "This disco, Club 52—what goes on there?"

"It's popular and expensive and harder than hell to get into. It's where that dance, the hustle, got famous. You see everybody from movie stars to the big politicians inside."

"Even though they do coke in back?"

He frowned. "I've never been in there, Mike. I don't know *where* they do the coke."

"But they do it."

"Probably. Sure. Everybody in the upper register seems to."

"And nobody cares?"

"Hell, no."

"Because the 52's mobbed up? Little Tony Tret's running it, right?"

Ernie's head shake said no, but his mouth said, "Yes." Then he amended it: "Only, Mike, it's not a mob thing. Tony divorced himself from his family a long, long time ago. He was just a young entrepreneur who had the right idea at the right time. This cocaine kick, it's no big deal. It's just social. They keep it discreet, and nobody complains. It's not like there's piles of stuff on tables and everybody's bending over and snorting it."

"The clientele is the young and the beautiful, right?"

"Sure, and the old and the rich. Now and then tourists get in, if they know somebody or throw a hell of a tip at the doorman. But it's a hard ticket, man."

"Yeah? I know a guy who had an all-access pass."

"Like for backstage at rock concerts? Well, it makes sense. It's called a disco, but they do live music, too."

"That right?"

"Big sensation now is that Chrome broad from Spain or Mexico or somewhere—she was on Johnny Carson, you know, and got signed to a major record label. Gonna tour at these franchise clubs Tony Tret is opening all around the country." He chugged his beer, thumped the stein down, and cocked his head at me. "Who the hell would a middle-aged type like you know that would rate *that* kind of backstage pass?"

"You knew him, too—Bill Doolan."

"Aw, balls."

Said the queen.

"Oh, he had that kind of pass," I insisted.

He was shaking his head, not buying it. "Come on, Mike, you knew Doolan better than *that.*"

"I thought I did. Story is, he was taking pictures for some newspaper guy out in L.A. Which is funny, since I don't remember Doolan being any kind of photographer."

Ernie made a farting sound with his lips. "Doolan was a photographer like all you dicks are photographers—point it at a naked broad through a motel window, and shoot. Hey, if he was doing pro-level photographic work, I'd have known."

"Didn't he feed you tips in recent years?"

"Sure he did—old Doolan came onto stuff, usually when he was working for his pal Cummings, who's a real P.I. Unlike you, Mike, who just pretend to be one so you can find excuses to shoot people, and not with a camera."

"If it's not likely Doolan was shooting photos for an L.A.-based reporter, then what *was* he doing?"

He leaned forward. "You can bet that old son of a bitch wasn't just chasing young tail. He was working."

"Like how?"

"Beats the shit outa me. He was always into somethin'. He was an old pro and just liked to keep his hand in. Some guys never learn how to quit. Right, Mike?" Ernie paused, chewed on his lip a moment, then said, "Hard to believe he killed himself."

I just looked at him without saying anything at all, then all his gears started to mesh and I saw him tighten up across the shoulders.

He darted a look around, then said very softly, "So *that's* why you're back. You don't think Doolan snuffed himself either, do you, Mike?"

"No," I said.

He sat there thinking for maybe thirty seconds. Then he said, "Somebody you should talk to."

"Okay."

He slid out and came back two minutes later with a young guy about five ten with the long hair and mustache of his generation and a canary shirt with a pointed collar over a sport jacket that looked like couch upholstery.

"This is Lonnie Dean," he said, making room as the younger man slid in next to him.

"Christ, you *are* Mike Hammer," the kid said in a thin baritone. "I heard you were back in the city."

I just nodded.

Ernie said, "Mike, Lonnie wrote that story a while back about the new breed of organized crime family. Won a bunch of journalistic awards."

"Didn't see it," I admitted.

A grin blossomed under the younger reporter's thick mustache. "You wouldn't have, Mr. Hammer. The mob shake-up I wrote about followed that shoot-out on the pier you walked away from."

"Crawled is more like it," I said. "So I was an instrument of change, huh? Like the kids say, groovy."

His eyes were bright. He seemed enthusiastic and nervous, like he was meeting a movie star. "Mr. Hammer—"

"Make it 'Mike,' Lonnie."

"Mike. I could hardly believe it when Ernie came over and told me you were over here . . ."

Christ. Not a damn autograph hound.

". . . I mean, we've never met, I've only been on the O.C. beat for a year. But you are *news*."

"Yeah, well. Some people would be flattered but—"

"No, I mean news right now. Didn't make the media, but that hooker who got run down? You got clipped, too, didn't you? And walked away from it?"

I frowned. "Where did you hear that, son?"

"I have sources."

"In the department?"

"Sure, Mr. Hammer . . . Mike . . . but those aren't the sources I'm talking about." He used a forefinger to bend his nose in the time-honored fashion to indicate he meant wiseguys. "Do you know who's claiming credit for almost running you down?"

"Surprise me."

"Alberto Bonetti."

I squinted at him. "Why? It wasn't his people."

Ernie got in a question: "How can you know that, Mike?"

I shrugged. "Alberto would've used a pro. A pro wouldn't have got the girl, if I was the target."

Lonnie said, "You mean, you'd be dead now."

"Maybe. I've been out of the game. But hit-and-run isn't the mob's style either. Too many potential witnesses, too imprecise. And that driver was strictly amateur night." I sipped beer, thought about it. "The word on the street is Bonetti hired it done?"

"Yeah." If the kid's eyes had been any brighter, I would have needed sunglasses. "And there's more, Mike. Your pal Doolan may not have been a suicide."

I managed not to smile. "Do tell."

"Bonetti's taking credit for *that* kill, too. Well, that may be over-simplifying it . . . *You* have something to do with that, too."

"Me?"

The shaggy-haired crime reporter nodded. He looked like a fucking Muppet, but he seemed to know his shit. "Nobody was figuring old Bill Doolan for murder until you came back to town. Word got out you were starting to nose around, which people took to mean Doolan musta been whacked, and the credit started going to Bonetti. Whether the rumors began with the old don, or just grew . . . that's where it stands."

I was nodding slowly. "So the street says . . . or anyway *thinks* . . . that Bonetti took Doolan out to get back at me, and lure me out of hiding . . . ?"

Lonnie nodded. "That's right, so he could have you taken out."

Ernie said, "Like in a hit-and-run."

The other reporter nodded.

"But it's bullshit," I said.

Lonnie shrugged. "Possibly, but it comes at a good time for Bonetti. He can use what it does for his rep among the other crime families right now. That shake-up is still under way, Mike — somebody new, somebody not so overt, is moving in on drug distribution. But the old-timers, like Don Giraldi and Pierluigi, if they solidify behind Alberto, the Bonetti family could be a power again."

It made sense.

Lonnie was chuckling. "You coming back to town, you really did old Alberto a favor. You ought to send him a bill for the good PR in his circles."

"I may," I said.

That stopped Lonnie's chuckling. "What are you going to do, Mr. Hammer?"

"Well, right now I'm going to ask you for a favor. You do me that favor, Lonnie, I'll give you the inside track on what'll be a big story."

"All right."

"Check your sources. I want to know two things."

"Okay."

"First — is there any activity involving rare gems going on in mob circles? Rip-offs involving gems, or valuable stones being used for money laundering — anything of that nature."

"You got it."

"Second — has Tony Tret really gone straight? His family was once associated with the Bonettis, loosely, but associated. Could Club 52 be a front for drugs?"

"Okay, but I doubt this Club 52 angle. As you must know, Mike, the authorities look the other way on the recreational stuff that goes down at that place. The club is in itself a goldmine, and I can't imagine Anthony Tretriano—who seems to despise his rough background—risking it."

I smiled. "How long have you been working the organized crime beat?"

"Just about a year."

"Have you seen any evidence that those people will stop at anything where making money is concerned?"

Lonnie laughed. "You got me there, Mr. Hammer. Mike."

I reached a hand across and we shook. "Nice knowing you. I'm at the Commodore."

"Not your office?"

"Naw, it's closed up."

"For good?"

"Don't know, son. Don't know. Ernie, thanks for introducing us."

"No problem, Mike. You always look out for your friends, don't you? Glad to do the same for you."

And it was time to wander out into the rain and hail a cab.

Alex Jaynor was listed in the Manhattan directory, an address on East Fifty-third Street. I took a chance on his being home and dialed from a pay phone around the corner. On the third ring, the phone was picked up and a smooth voice said, "Hello, Alex Jaynor here."

I had to grin at the way he merchandised his greeting.

"Hi, kid," I said. "Mike Hammer here."

"Hey, Mike—where are you?"

"Damn near on your doorstep. You have time to talk to me or are you busy?"

"Not at all. Come on up—or would you rather meet some-place?"

"I'll come up," I said, and cradled the phone.

The building was an old one, but nicely refurbished, the kind of place up-and-coming people used until they got to the top of the ladder where penthouses became their style. Meanwhile, they lived in quiet opulence with a gray-haired doorman who had a genuine Irish accent. I gave him Alex's name, he let me in, then pointed to the elevator in the lobby. "Apartment 4-C, sir."

I thanked him, went upstairs, found 4-C, and pushed the buzzer. The tall, sandy-haired politician came to the door grinning, holding his hand out, and practically pulled me inside. He was in a dark blue shirt without a tie and navy slacks, casual but crisp.

"Good to see you again, Mike. This is a nice surprise."

"Really?"

"Not often I have a living legend stepping over the threshold."

I had to laugh at that one. "Never mind about legend—I'm just glad to be living." I followed him in. "Anyway, Doolan was the leg-endary one, not me. I always felt I walked in his shadow."

"Well, having known the man, I can understand that. Make you a drink?"

"A CC and ginger will do it."

"Coming right up."

While he built the drinks at a wet bar, I took a look around. The apartment was a small world of rust-stained wood, modern and high-ceilinged, with open stairs going up to a loft-style bedroom. The kitchen was tucked under the loft and was small, metallic, and utilitarian—nobody in Manhattan seemed to think much about eating in, at least in this part of town.

There were doors off to a spare bedroom and a little study, but—with its comfortable leather chairs and sofa, and functional glass-and-metal tables—mostly the apartment had the feel of one big room, a masculine refuge from the world.

Alex handed me my drink and said, "Like the digs?"

"You got it made, kiddo. Good address, too."

"Doolan found it for me about a month after we met. *How* he found it, I'll never know. It's still a little expensive, but I'm making the nut now."

I said, "Cheers," and sipped the highball.

"So, to what do I owe this visit?" He pointed to a dark brown leather chair and matching sofa and he took the former while I settled onto the latter. I tossed my hat on the glass-and-metal coffee table separating us.

"You know, Alex, I wish I could lay a question out that made sense, but what I want to know is—what was going on with Doolan in the last, say, six months of his life?"

"Not sure I follow."

"I've been off the scene for a year, I hadn't seen him for at least a year before that, and now that he's gone, I'm trying to find out how he was dealing with what he had left of his life—facing that medical death sentence."

Eyebrows lifted and came back down in the chiseled face. "But you were closer than *I* ever was with Doolan . . ."

"I was then. You were now. Look, you two were tight during the time I was away. What was he like?"

"Compared to what?"

"Describe him," I said.

He swirled the drink around in his glass, the ice chinking the side. "Doolan was a damn good friend. It's an overused word lately, but he was a real mentor."

145

"You said you met him when you were a reporter for *McWade's* magazine."

He grimaced, then chuckled. "You make it sound like more than it was, Mike. I was a *roving* reporter. It wasn't the cushiest of jobs—low pay and minimum expenses."

"It's a Canadian publication—but you're not Canadian?"

"No. I'm originally from Boston. It was just a job I was able to land out of college. Headquarters are in Toronto, but the general circulation is bigger in the New England states than it is in Canada. Most of the news is collected from the Northeast U.S. anyway."

"*McWade's* send you to New York?"

"On special assignment. All the major cities are troubled by teenaged crime, and Toronto wanted to see how New York handled it. They really wanted drama more than information. Sensationalism posing as journalism is, I'm afraid, what sells magazines. Even in Canada."

"And what you were covering fitted in, huh?"

Alex nodded and tasted his drink. "I guess you know there's been some pretty heavy stuff going down with youth gangs, and some of that activity leaked over into Doolan's neighborhood."

"So I heard."

"They had the residents in a state of terror until Doolan got involved. With his connections, that place was swept clean in a week. There were arrests, convictions, and by damn, nine of those punks are pulling time now."

I grinned. "Doolan appreciate the publicity you could provide?"

"Hell no—he wouldn't even let me go back to *McWade's*. Refused to let me turn the story in!"

"How did he manage that?"

"He promised to connect me with some New York–based publications, and thanks to him, I got into freelancing articles on a regular basis, and did some things that caught attention and won some awards. Even did some TV work. Somewhere along the line, Doolan steered me into politics."

"He must have seen something in you he liked."

"We were close. I lost my father when I was very young, and he did fill a void. And I think having somebody my age, who could handle himself, to wade in with him into the rough parts of that neighborhood, well . . . it's probably the kind of thing he'd have leaned on you to do, if you'd still been around."

"I'd like to think I would have helped out. Did it get rough?"

"Enough. That was the first time I had shots thrown at me."

"But not the last?"

"No. Hell, Mike, I'm no hero. No tough guy. I was in the army during Vietnam, but never saw much action. I know my way around firearms, but that's mostly because of gun clubs as a kid, and, of course, the Enfilade now."

"Tell me about getting shot at."

"Nothing you can pin down. I was in my car, the first time. On the street, the next. And when I was campaigning for office, on an anticrime platform, it happened again. That was when Doolan talked me into wearing a bulletproof vest whenever I go out."

"That can get a little bulky."

"Well, I'm a wiry type. It doesn't show. But sometimes I don't know why I bother—vests don't stop head hits."

"Do you know who was throwing those shots? I don't mean the specific shooters, but whatever group sent them?"

His grin was wide and turned up at either end, Cheshire Cat–like. "Well, you saw them the other night, Mike—at the funeral home? Doolan was convinced it was the Bonettis behind not only the drugs in his neighborhood, but the attempts on my life."

Maybe the word on the street giving credit to old Alberto for taking Doolan out wasn't misplaced after all.

"What if I told you, Alex, that I think Doolan may have been murdered."

He said nothing for a moment, his light blue eyes unblinking. Then: "It may sound terrible, but I'd prefer that to suicide."

"I hear that."

"So goddamn out of character."

"If I'm right, Alex, you may be the next target."

"Yeah? Any advice?"

"Keep wearing that vest."

"Oh yeah."

I shifted on the couch. "Did you know Doolan hung out at discos?"

"What?"

"Well, at one disco—a famous one. Club 52."

He tried his drink again, frowning. "No, I didn't know, but in a way I'm not surprised."

"Really?"

"For a man his age, he did a lot of offbeat things, and went a lot of places, that conventional people would find strange."

"What about women?"

This time he put his drink down on the glass coffee table and another smile creased his face. "Hell, Doolan was an ass patter, Mike. You know the type—you can get in trouble for it these days."

"Sure can."

He laughed. "But when you get to be his age, you can get away with murder with the ladies." Then he realized what he'd said, and added, "Poor choice of words."

"He ever talk about particular women?"

"Not really, but I had the feeling he had some sort of friendship with a woman or two. Doolan and I were close, sure, but it was father-and-son close, which meant some doors were closed to me."

I leaned back and stared up at the ceiling. Long shadows from the table lamps made an eerie pattern on the slats of wood.

I asked, "What was his lifestyle like in the last month?"

Alex considered that a moment, then spread his hands apart reflectively. "Normal, as far as I know. I saw him a couple of times every week. Hell, he never missed going to the Enfilade. No, wait a minute, that's wrong . . . the last two times I saw him he *did* seem kind of, well . . . down. The old buoyancy just wasn't there."

"Enough to be suicidal?"

"Who knows?"

"Was he sick? Was it really kicking in?"

"I admit I didn't think about it—I mean, everybody has moods, off days. But it certainly could have been that. If he was really getting to be in bad shape, I'm surprised he never mentioned it to anyone."

"Doolan wouldn't," I said. "You're right—he was a great friend, but certain doors stayed closed." I finished my drink, reached for my hat, rose. "Thank you for the hospitality, Alex."

"Oh, my pleasure. Anytime."

"Take care. I may need to give you a call again. I'm trying to put some pieces together. You might have the glue."

"I hope I do," he said.

Down on the street, the rain had let up. But a low rumble of thunder echoed across the city. There was an occasional dull glaze of cloud-hidden lightning in the south, and when the wind gusted past, I could smell more rain coming—the kind that was held above the buildings until it was soaked with debris and dust, and when it came down, it wouldn't be a cleansing rain at all.

Chapter 8

AT NINE P.M., West Fifty-fourth between Broadway and Eighth Avenue was an artery clogged enough to give Manhattan a heart attack. The taxis slightly outnumbered the brave, foolish souls with their own wheels, and it was so hopeless, even the horn-honk symphony seemed halfhearted.

The fuss was over a fairly nondescript entryway for so famous a nightspot—a bunch of doors, a velvet rope, and a modest overhang that said CLUB 52 in light blue art deco lettering on a black background.

The sidewalk was as jammed as the street, although a passageway from the curb cut through the crowd, maintained by security types in black 52-monogrammed blazers, so that the limos that somehow managed to crawl through traffic could disgorge celebrities and other beautiful people. These were gods and goddesses—these were that rarefied breed.

They who were on the list.

On either side of this red carpet were photographers whose flashes popped at each passing fur or gown or Armani suit while gawkers yelped and yelpers gawked as the blazer boys held them back. These were the unfortunate rabble who didn't even bother crowding up to the velvet rope for possible selection.

I encouraged the cabbie to squeeze in behind the nearest limo and by nine-thirty, I was stepping out of a Yellow cab onto the red carpet. The rain had let up but I still had on the trench coat and porkpie hat as I walked in no great hurry up to where the shrimpy kid in the cream-colored sport jacket and no tie would be checking his clipboard, should he not recognize me.

The photographers knew me, at least some of them, and just as many flashbulbs died in my wake as had for Andy Warhol, a skinny broad on his arm, the last ones out before I made my entrance. Warhol was that fifteen minutes of fame clown—weren't his up yet?

Over at my right, standing on a little platform ringed by security guys, was Little Tony Tret—Anthony Tretriano himself. He was skinny and short and dark with a well-trimmed mustache, little dark eyes, and Roman emperor curls; he was in a black tuxedo but his bow tie was a big floppy red thing, vaguely obscene.

When I got to the row of painted-out black doors, the guy with the clipboard asked me for my name and I told him and he clearly didn't know it and also couldn't find it. He glanced at the nearest blazer bully, but a voice called out from above.

Not God. Better.

The boss.

"Steven, don't you know a native New Yorker when you see one?" Anthony said, in a nasal Brooklyn tenor. "That's Mike Hammer. Let him in. . . . Love the fedora, Mike."

I didn't correct him. That would have been ungracious of me, and we all know how gracious by nature I am. So I gave him a little grin, nodded, tugged the brim of the porkpie in a tip-of-the-hat manner, and got a big smile out of Anthony, who immediately returned to picking lucky numbers from his human lottery.

If human was the word—I paused at the door and glanced at this group, who were dressed up in various ways, from high fashion to low self-esteem. A number were in oddball outfits, gladiators, barbarians, even one doll in a Marie Antoinette getup. A few were playing it cool, and these were the ones most often selected, as those yelling "Anthony!" and "Choose me" and so on were not making it with the exalted arbiter of the worthy.

I went on in. Admission was slow, as Nero took his time with his thumbs-up (and mostly -down) routine, so I was alone in a vast entryway, with the half-dozen black doors behind me. Darkness encompassed me. So did thunderous disco music, only slightly muted here. The only light in this space came from a glittering chandelier and an indirect purple glow splashed on the arched ceiling. Up ahead was a lot of light, flashing and colorful but indistinct, like a city making itself known on the horizon.

Somewhere in the darkness, off to my right, a female voice called over the music: "Want to check that Bogart wrap, big man?"

I found my way over there. Behind the counter, two girls in their early twenties wore Roman togas with necklines that allowed the brunette's big ones to spill out and the blonde's perky ones to point accusingly at me, twice. They wore way too much makeup for my taste, but I forgave them even while wishing I'd invested in the blue eye-shadow industry.

The brunette took my trench coat and I was about to pass the porkpie to the blonde when Little Tony was suddenly at my side, a hand on my sleeve.

"Hang on to the fedora, Mike," he said lifting an advisory finger. His speech was slurry and his eyes were half-lidded. Drunk? Quaaludes? "People here dress to identify themselves."

"As who they are?"

"Or who they want to be."

His hand was still on my arm. I wanted to flick it off, like a bug, but he was my host.

As we moved toward the flashing lights and pumping music, I said, "To what do I owe this honor? I mean, escorted by Little Anthony himself. So where are the Imperials?"

He only smiled at that. "We'll find time to rap later. You'll soon understand, Mike, that there's no need for the old hostilities."

"Water under the bridge?"

"My feeling exactly." He was guiding me toward the flicker and flash and the storm of sound. "You need to get a feel for my party. It's a party I throw every night, and you may find it addictive."

Some straight lines are just too easy.

So I ignored it and said, "I'm hoping we can sit down and talk, Tony."

"Please call me 'Anthony,' Mike. You're comfortable being called 'Mike'?"

"Have been for some time. Can we talk now?"

He shook his head. "I'll be on the door for another half hour at least. You run a tab and I'll take care of it. In an hour I'll meet you at my office. Just tell any one of my security guys that you have an appointment."

Then he waved and disappeared back into the darkness, illuminated briefly when he opened a door onto the street to resume his duties — he had people to crush and others to elevate. The way those Italian heels elevated him.

When I made it to the flashing lights, and was no longer solitary but one of a crush of people, I still felt encased in darkness. Light was a pulse, timed with the booming bass beat of the deafening disco music — yellow, blue, momentary baths of color in a cavern carved by occasional green laser lights. Cigarette smoke swirled, but the ventilation wasn't bad, and busboys in athletic shorts and running shoes and nothing else were keeping the bottles and glasses picked up and off the packed dance floor.

The bare-chested busboys were part of a bisexual motif — for every nude male statue there was a female one; for every bartender in a hot-pants toga, there was a waitress in a miniskirt toga with a neckline to the navel. I'd heard the term sensory overload kicked around, but never understood it before. I just stood there like Dorothy getting a load of Oz for the first time.

Around me were bizarre towering hairstyles, tuxes, bikini tops, spandex, gold lamé, masks, body paint, glitter, hard hats, athletic T-shirts, pointed collars, berets, sunglasses. Above it all loomed a giant silver man in the moon with a gold coke spoon with glittering lights in its bowl near the moon man's Bob Hope proboscis. Below was a sea of partying souls on a central raised plexiglass dance floor, hands waving as if to heaven as they writhed like the damned, washed in that throbbing red and blue illumination against a painted backdrop of Pompeiian pillars.

The crazy joint did not seem to have tables, other than in a V.I.P. section behind a gossamer-type screen, home to comfortable booths and nonstop champagne. Among the pampered elite were Truman Capote, the mayor of New York, and various models whose faces I'd glimpsed on fashion magazines when I was picking up *True* and *Guns & Ammo* at my favorite newsstand. Mirrored bars were at left and right, and the bartenders were muscular young males in vests and no shirts, doing dance moves as they served a frantic nonstop customer onslaught. The only quiet in the storm was the stage — it seemed to have been abandoned for the records the d.j., high in his omniscient booth, was spinning.

I did find tables and booths upstairs, in the balcony, but they were filled with necking threesomes, fornicating twosomes, and the general funky smell of sex. The great ventilation didn't seem to be able to take the edge off that. I was able to find a place at the front rail of the balcony to have a look down at the self-absorbed dancers — many had no partner — whose fluttering hands suggested a revival meeting run amok as they immersed themselves in the repetitive, senses-numbing music.

From my vantage point, I caught some interesting items. For one thing, the bartenders seemed to be dispensing pills and coke vials as much as drink tumblers and champagne glasses. This perch made that obvious, but they didn't seem to be hiding it particularly. I could also see the cash registers at the nearest of the two bars. Starting at about ten-thirty, at staggered intervals, the cash drawers were emptied into garbage bags, and the register tapes were changed.

Clearly a skimming operation Vegas might have envied.

Anthony Tretriano and his curly Nero hair and his black tux and floppy red bow tie had taken his d.j. booth box seat at this coliseum of decadence and was now interrupting the thudding, mechanical songs with celebrity announcements. Most of those he introduced were the kind who were recognized by a single name and he had a kidding put-down for each of them.

Funny thing is, there was never applause. Just smiles of recognition. Maybe Club 52 was too cool for clapping. But probably not the clap.

I had been here before, in this space, even in this very balcony, long before it was the trendiest club in town. This had been a theater, or anyway a radio and television studio, its traditional seat-ing long since ripped out. CBS Studio 52—that's why a club on Fifty-fourth was called 52—had been home to Jack Benny, Captain Kangaroo, and countless game shows, *What's My Line? To Tell the Truth, The $64,000 Question*.

The $64,000 question I was mulling was whether that stage was still used for anything. Like a black hole, the proscenium where so many mainstream entertainers had performed was a void in the midst of flashing lights.

Then the recorded music was cut off and dead silence filled the room.

Little Tony's voice burst forth: *"She's Manhattan's favorite Latin, my children—everybody's favorite pink taco . . ."*

Lots of laughter at that.

". . . Chrome!"

This time the room did erupt in applause.

On the wall behind the stage, a rainbow of neon tubes finally illuminated the stage as the star performer strode from the wings with a wireless mike in hand and all the confidence that could fit into one tall, curvy, leggy frame. A backup band was revealed as well, but just a drummer on a riser and one guitar player and a guy at a synthesizer. The sound coming from speakers all around conveyed more instruments than were up there, and whether they were miming their performance or not, I couldn't say.

But Chrome was singing all right.

She had a strong alto that cut with authority through all that disco noise and made her delivery of this updated "Boy from Ipanema" appealing. Against the now-alternating neon slashes of yellow, pink, blue, green, her bronze flesh made the white of her teeth startling, her almond-shaped eyes big and brown and lavishly lashed, her nose pert, her mouth moist and ripe and scarlet red. Exuding a charisma that seemed to shimmer around her, she stalked the stage in pink platform heels carrying long, almost masculinely muscular legs that climbed all the way to the fringe of her shocking pink dress.

If you could *call* it a dress — it was skintight with a cutout that exposed her supple midsection, navel and all, and a V-neck that did its best to contain those firm D-cup globes. I hated the *thud thud thud* of that disco beat, but her strong voice and her confident manner, and the rhythmic bounce of her bosom, won me over.

Of course, in that place a star performer was just so much window dressing. Nobody in the balcony stopped necking or fucking to watch Chrome, and the dance floor remained filled with Holy Roller hand wavers lost in their own narcissism. Come to the cabaret, my friends, and why not? Liza had.

Chrome and I did have a moment, or maybe I just imagined it. As I stood in the balcony, twelve kinds of sex behind me in a living Hieronymous Bosch tapestry, I thought I saw her look right at me, and hold my gaze, and smile, before she moved on down the stage on those magnificent, endless legs.

She did only half a dozen songs, and was gone. No encore but Tony praised her over the sound system and the applause rang, just like in a real nightclub.

When I left the city a year ago, this had been an empty theater, out-of-date studio space the TV network had been trying to dump unsuccessfully for many months. Now it was the most famous nightclub in town, maybe in the world. And it had all been the doing of that punk Little Tony.

The office was one flight up from the balcony. Tony had said to meet him in an hour, but it was more like two — I didn't bother asking one of his flunkies for my audience until I saw the party's host move out of the d.j.'s perch. The blazer boy who led me up was as polite as he was muscular. On the stairs, he glanced back at me.

"Ain't I seen you at Bing's?"

"Could be."

"I do some boxing. Why's an old guy like you working out for? No offense."

"It's a Zen thing."

That stopped the conversation.

The honcho's office was nothing fancy—drywall painted light blue, some framed Broadway show posters, a bulletin board with news articles about the club, a metal desk cluttered with Rolodex, business-card caddy, ashtrays, pill bottles, a few drink glasses, and a pile of register tapes. On the floor next to the desk was a garbage bag, twist-tied shut, but I knew it was full of cash.

Skinny little Tony had tossed his tux jacket on a couch under the Broadway posters and undone the red tie, the fabric flaccid around his collar. Under the fluorescent lighting, his curly Roman emperor locks appeared shiny and wet. He had the casually drowsy demeanor of a guy who'd been doing an untold combo of drugs, and seemed like anybody but the mastermind behind Manhattan's biggest success story.

He was probably thirty-one and looked like a kid on prom night who'd overdone it.

"Excuse the mess, Mike," he said, not rising, but gesturing genially toward a hard wooden chair opposite his comfy-looking black leather swivel job, the only class appointment in what could have been the office of the manager of a Dunkin' Donuts in Queens. If that manager was into Broadway shows, anyway.

He was beaming at me, the small dark eyes red-tinged and half-hooded. Were those caps under that perfectly trimmed mustache?

"Well, Mike? What do you think? What do you think of my party?"

"People are having fun." The never-ending pounding bass was a reminder of that—no music could be heard in the office, but that relentless thudding went on.

He threw his hands up and the grin got even bigger. "Exactly! That's the point. That's what I was after. Famous people need a place to let their hair down, and not be bothered. Not-so-famous people, if they're good-looking and know how to party, this is their place, too." The dark little eyes flared. "Say, what did you think of Chrome, Mike? Isn't she something?"

"Oh yeah. Crazy. I can see why you're having her open your new clubs."

"She'll hit the top of the charts, wait and see. She'll win a fuckin' Grammy. Love of my life, that woman."

Was that for real, or just show biz talk? In the old days, Little Tony made a point of going out with big, bosomy babes on his arm. But the word was he swung the other way. And with all those bare-chested bartenders downstairs, I had to wonder.

"Tell me, Anthony—that curbside circus out there. Why do you run the door yourself? Can't you trust anybody else to do the picking and choosing?"

He shook his head firmly. "Mike, this place is . . . it's my living room. You don't just let anybody into your living room. When you invite guests in your home, you make sure it's a good mix, right?"

"I don't do that much entertaining."

He chuckled. Shook his head. "You're perfect for 52. You're a legend. Larger than life. You are welcome here anytime."

"Do I rate an all-access pass?"

His smile turned pixie-ish. He raised a cautionary palm. "Let's not get ahead of ourselves. It's your first night."

"Bill Doolan rated one."

Without hesitation, Tony nodded and kept nodding. "Great guy. Perfect fit. Best addition to the family since the Disco Grandma."

"How the hell is an old-time copper like Doolan your 'perfect fit'?"

Tony lighted up a cigarette, swallowed smoke through a smile. "Mike, he was famous in this city—not as famous as you, but the papers were full of him. He cleaned up his neighborhood, the capper of a career full of putting thieves and robbers and hoods away."

"Some of whom you're related to."

He waved that off. "That's history. That's the past. That's not who I am anymore. But Doolan, he was a real character. He could put away the booze like Sinatra. He liked the ladies, too, the young ones. I think he had a thing for Chrome, y'know. Whether it went anywhere or not, I couldn't tell you. Probably just a flirtation."

"How often was he here?"

Tony shrugged. "Maybe once a week—for a couple of months. Not a regular, but a familiar and always welcome face."

"He took photos here."

"Did he?"

"Is that allowed?"

He gave up a sluggish shrug. "We let media types in, if they behave. If we got somebody here, Princess Grace or Baryshnikov, and they don't wanna get photographed, they don't get photographed. That must be understood."

"Is that who Doolan was to you? A media type?"

"No! He was just another wonderful eccentric. I never saw him shoot photos. If he did, it was probably just snapshots for his scrapbook. To paste pics of Chrome in next to his grandkids or whatever. Or to do whatever dirty old men do with photos of sexy young women in the privacy of their own homes."

"A dirty old man? Doolan?"

"Why, won't you be one someday, Mike? And me, if I live long enough?"

I shrugged. "If you live long enough."

Not much threat had been put into that, but it sobered Tony. Anthony.

The little emperor leaned forward. "Listen, Mike, this place is legit. I got no mob ties whatsoever. My brother Leo and me, we haven't spoken for two years. You saw the mayor downstairs. We got councilmen and congressmen as regulars."

"Like your friend from the Enfilade, Alex Jaynor?"

"No, Alex has never been to 52. And we shoot on different days at the Enfilade. We've spoken a few times at events. Why?"

"He was tight with Doolan. All three of you belong to that gun club. Just wondering what the connection was."

Tony shrugged again. "Just what meets the eye. I think Jaynor and Doolan were in the same regular shooting group, but I wasn't. We got along. Were polite. My hunch is Jaynor may harbor suspicions about me. About my background. He's a do-gooder, and I frankly don't trust do-gooders."

"Yeah. They *can* spoil a party. No mob ties at all, Tony?"

"Please, Mike — it's Anthony. No. None."

I gestured to the garbage bag. "But that's a mob-style skim you're running."

The smile under the mustache froze. Then it melted and he said, "We don't need the mob for that. It's a cash-and-carry business, Mike."

"How much are you carrying that the I.R.S. doesn't know about?"

161

"Why, are you a fan of the I.R.S.?"

"Not particularly. They did a nice job on Capone. What have you made in a year, Anthony?"

Another shrug. "Seven million."

"Before or after the skim?"

He shrugged. "After. Skim's around two mil. See, Mike? We got no secrets, you and me."

"And you're not worried? If I could spot that action from the balcony, so could an I.R.S. agent."

That smile again. "He'd have to get past the velvet rope. Look, Mike, we're hot right now. Everybody loves a winner and we're winning."

"So the drugs your bartenders peddle, and the coke I saw those orgy girls and boys using in the balcony—local law enforcement looks the other way?"

"These are hedonistic times, Mike. It's not criminal activity, it's a lifestyle! My God, an individual like you surely can't object. You've laid more pipe than all the plumbers in the Bronx! You killed more people than Audie fuckin' Murphy."

"Not as many at one time."

Little Tony shook his head; the Roman curls stayed put. "You are a pisser. You always have been a pisser." He got up from behind his desk, clearly ready to walk me out.

So I got up. At the door, he stuck his hand out and I shook it. He was my host. But, my God, his palm felt greasy.

"You are always welcome at 52, Mike. You are on the list."

He was on mine.

I said, "Like Doolan?"

"You said it earlier—he had all access. He could go anywhere in my world."

"Like, where *can't* I go in the club, without that pass?"

This seemed to amuse him. He opened the door and the young boxer in the 52 blazer perked up like a puppy who heard the rustle of a candy wrapper.

"Louis," Tony said, "show Mr. Hammer to the V.I.P. room."

"You mean the lounge, Mr. Tretriano?"

"No—the *room*."

The kid from Bing's led me down the stairs into the balcony and below to the main floor, then to a door near the stage that was guarded by a pair of blazers. We went down creaky wooden steps into the basement. A path cut between chained-linked supply areas, decorative crap on one side, boxes of liquor and beer on the other. Then I followed my escort down a drywall corridor to a guarded metal-grillwork door through which could be seen another, smaller party.

Like the upstairs, the lighting was dim though no flashing lights or laser lances were cutting through the darkness. The illumination came from the yellow and orange of an old Wurlitzer jukebox, an Elton John pinball machine, some funky vintage neon signs, lava lamps, and glowing fiber optics sprays. The limited lighting provided mood, sure, but it also concealed a multitude of sins. And not just those that might be committed by the guests.

As that grating door yawned open for me, and I stepped inside, I realized Little Tony Tret really was a hell of an entrepreneur. After all, he had transformed a dank, nothing basement into a celebrity lounge that the likes of Mick Jagger, Cary Grant, and Liz Taylor were dying to get into.

I'm not saying Mick, Cary, and Liz were present in this rec room for degenerates, but you would recognize just about every face. The furnishings were strictly thrift shop, mostly '50s atomic-age junk but also comfy easy chairs and couches and even plastic lawn furniture. A wet bar had a single bare-chested bartender, but there was a corner for pot smokers, too. A few of the famous faces were just standing around, chatting cocktail party–style. There was a bathroom marked HIS & HERS off to one side with an OCCUPIED card hanging on the knob.

But the main attraction was a massive glass-top coffee table with a mirror the size of an LP cover that was heaped with cocaine — a staggering pile of the stuff, like an ungainly pyramid of powdered sugar. Celebrities of every stripe were on the edge of couches and sofas, worshiping at this white altar, leaning in to cut lines with razor blades and sniff through rolled-up C-notes, lolling back laughing with white stuff on their noses, like kids who'd stuck their faces in the snow. And hadn't they?

I moved around the room nodding at people. I'd met some of them before. A lot of them recognized me — I did have the porkpie on — and sometimes laughed and pointed and occasionally patted me on the back as I passed. To them I was a cartoon character come to life out walking among them.

I spotted a big platinum blonde at the bar getting herself a glass of champagne. She had on a pink minidress with shoulder straps, lots of well-tanned flesh on display, and an ass that could make a man sit up and beg. I asked for a beer and was given a bottle of Michelob. The big blonde turned to me and it was Chrome.

Not a tan, then — she was natural bronze, if not natural blonde. That shade of platinum on a brown-eyed doll took help. And I liked the Asian look of her eyes.

"You were in the balcony," she said, with a musical accent, faint but there. Brazilian?

"I thought I imagined it."

A dark, well-shaped eyebrow arched. "Imagined what?"

"That we made eye contact."

We left the little bar for the next customer, finding a two-seater sofa we could plop down in. She crossed her legs and unleashed her very white smile on me.

"Your hat, I like it."

"So do I."

"You are some kind of cowboy?"

"Close. Private eye."

She nodded and laughed. "You are that Mike Hammer person. You are not so well known in my country, but here at 52? They whisper about you being here tonight. Much excitement."

"I make friends everywhere I go." I patted her hand. "You sing good. I hate disco, but I like you."

She shrugged. "I did not start with the disco music. I like the jazz. Jobim? I was one of the first to record his songs, you know."

"I didn't know."

She bobbed her head; the feathered platinum locks bounced off her shoulders — I'd thought that might be a wig, but it was real.

"The records," she was saying, "they were never released in your country. I have six gold records in Latin America. But I have the American contract now. My boys and I, we will do a big tour."

"Of the new Club 52s that Little Tony's opening?"

She smiled. "Little Tony, you say. He hate to be called that."

"Yeah, I know. He prefers Anthony. But I knew him when."

"When?"

"When he was a little punk in his old man's crime crew. They pulled heists and pushed dope."

She smiled a little, but no teeth — it was a pursed kiss of a smile. "The drugs, do they offend you?"

I was looking toward that coffee table with its jet-set worshipers. "It's poison."

"I myself do not use them. I *do* drink. And that is a drug, too, they say."

"Maybe."

"You are a funny one."

"Yeah, I'm the life of the party."

"I would guess you *could* be . . . if you were in the mood."

I grinned at her and it shook her.

"Ooooh . . . that is a nasty smile you have there, Mike. And your eyes—they are very strange."

"Watch this."

I got up and went over to the central coffee table where the rich and famous were tooting it up. I said excuse me a couple of times, and then I edged in close.

An actress I used to know looked up at me and said, "Not *you*, Mike! Indulging? Oh how the mighty have fallen. . . ."

"Think so?"

I leaned over and picked up the mirror with its pile of coke, and with surprised yelps of protest at my back, I carried it like a busboy with a tray of empty glasses over to the HIS & HERS. Ignoring the OCCUPIED notice, I yanked the door open and found a guy in the middle of a perfectly good blow job, and from a female, too.

"Hate to interrupt, but would you excuse me?"

The guy, who acted on a cop show, hopped up off the lid of the toilet with his pants around his ankles and almost stabbed the girl in the eye. A redhead with her top down, she quickly got to her feet and plastered herself to the wall in the close quarters.

I lifted the toilet lid, seat and all, and dumped all of the white stuff into the crapper.

People were yelling, even screaming behind me, crowding around, but nobody touched me.

It didn't all go down in a single flush, which meant I had to wait a little while for the toilet water to fill back up again.

Just making conversation, I said to the actor, "Give me a call if you ever have research questions," and he just smiled over his shoulder at me nervously, while the little actress, who was on a top ten sitcom and had lots of Orphan Annie curls, gave me a wide-eyed look and was shaking. Like I was a maniac or something.

After the second flush had done its work, I said to the actor and actress, "As you were," and shut them back in there. I had a hunch they may have lost their momentum. Pity.

I went back to the coffee table and flipped the mirror onto the glass. It skidded a little through the remaining white lines.

An Academy Award–winning tough guy got in my face. Either he thought he had plenty of backup or the coke had made him foolish and brave.

"What the fuck's the idea, you goddamn Neanderthal?"

I pushed him away, gently, then said to the startled, outraged bunch, who were all on their feet now, "I hate to be the turd in the punch bowl, kids. But that stuff is illegal, and I don't want to risk going down for it."

This elicited lots of comment, running mostly to "Oh, *Jesus!*" and "Do you *believe* this asshole?"

I said, "I mean, not on a night when there are rumors of a police raid."

The place emptied out faster than that theater when King Kong broke loose.

And then it was just me and Chrome in the wet cellar that posed as a V.I.P. room.

She was laughing and applauding, saying, "Mike! I think maybe you *are* a cowboy."

Chrome came over and took my hand and led me to a big comfy leather chair near the ruined fun of the coffee table. I sat down and she nestled onto my lap, slipped her arms around my neck, like I was Santa and she had a wish. She was a big woman, and not light, but I didn't mind. Her lips found mine and they were moist and hot. I glanced over at the guard on the other side of the grating door. His back was to us.

"Listen," I said. "I want to talk to you. . . ."

She was nuzzling my ear. "I want to talk to you, too, Mike. We will talk later. . . ."

"Did you know Bill Doolan?"

Her head reared back and the big brown almond eyes locked on to me. "Yes. I did. Not well. So sad that he die. He was very nice."

"How nice?"

"What do you mean, Mike?"

"Nice, like . . . this?"

And I put my hands on her breasts and just squeezed gently, like I was checking the freshness of fruit at a market. They were ripe and firm, all right.

"No," she said. She kissed me again, warm, sticky with lipstick, full of promise. Then her tongue was flicking and licking at my ear, darting like a snake's, as she whispered, "He was just a nice old man. He come stand and watch. Never dance. Just watch."

"Some people *like* to watch. . . ."

"Some do not."

She slipped off my lap and onto the floor where a shag carpet was waiting for her knees and her hand found my zipper and tugged it down. She had me out and in her grasp and her mouth was about to descend when I held her back, the heel of a hand at a shoulder.

"I don't like sex in public places," I said.

"There is no one here but us."

I nodded toward the guard beyond the grating.

She shrugged. "Like I said . . . there is no one here, Mike."

"I thought you were Little Tony's girl."

"I'm nobody's girl."

Her head bobbed down, but I pulled her up.

"No," I said. "Not now. Not like this."

Her full lips teased me with a smile. "And here I think they say that you are the wild man."

"Wild, yes. Not kinky."

She rose, sat on the arm of the easy chair, slipped an arm around my shoulder; her other hand still grasped me and gently, gently stroked. "We could go to your place."

"I don't have a place."

"We could go to mine."

"We could. But not tonight. Not now. This place . . . your precious 52 . . . Chrome, doll, this is not my scene."

The aftermath was expectedly awkward. My fly got zipped, her makeup got unsmeared, and so on. But she gave me her address written in mascara on a Club 52 cocktail napkin.

"*Where* do you live?" I asked her.

"Rio de Janeiro. Why?"

"This is a Park Avenue address. You staying with somebody?"

"No. I have a Manhattan apartment now. I will be spending much time here. Much time in America. You see, Mike . . . you have not escaped me. You will *never* escape me."

"Is that a promise? In the meantime, where's the nearest exit? I got a feeling after Little Tony hears about this, he may take me off the list."

Chapter 9

BY TEN THE NEXT morning—after an early swim in the
Commodore pool, another Bing's workout, and a deli
breakfast—I settled in for a day of the kind of detective work that
doesn't make it onto the TV shows.

I had to delve into those ancient filing cabinets in that ancient
corner building where two old men had shared an office but kept
their secrets to themselves. Pete Cummings, on his job in Philly,
had left me a tidy desktop and a comfortable swivel chair and an
icebox full of Miller. He was my idea of a good host.

But I was glad I'd got limbered up with a swim and a workout, because you have to have good knees to go through every
drawer of two five-drawer files. And with an information pack rat
like Doolan, those drawers contained plenty of chaff to go through
trying to find a few kernels of wheat.

I paid special attention to any clippings that dated within the last year. Doolan put together a fat file of the press he and Alex had got for cleaning up the neighborhood, but I couldn't find anything that wasn't laudatory fluff—RETIRED POLICE OFFICER LEADS NEIGHBORHOOD REFORM. Nothing with specifics about the criminal element he'd helped run out. No other names at all except some of the merchants I'd met when I canvassed the neighborhood.

So I went back and started at the beginning of the newspaper stuff—right around Doolan's retirement twenty years ago. It was a lot of loose, yellowed clippings—two full file drawers—and started with puff pieces about the brave officer stepping down, and included clips on any hood, thief, or rapist that Doolan had put away who'd got out and made the papers again.

At first I thought I'd struck pay dirt, but virtually every series of clippings wound up with the bad guy returned to the slammer. Had Doolan's fine hand worked behind the scenes on any of these arrests? Did that mean a family member of some sorry incarcerated son of a bitch might have settled a grudge with the old warhorse?

But that didn't cut it. Doolan hadn't been chopped down on the street in a drive-by shooting—it was a staged suicide in his own damn apartment. That required a kind of sophistication and access unlikely to be found in the loved ones of some recently rejugged recidivist.

I made a list of the names anyway, on a yellow pad. It was the kind of thing I could hand over to Pat if everything else was a dead end.

One file drawer seemed to be nothing but crimes from all over the world that had, for whatever reason, piqued Doolan's interest. These went back many years, well before his retirement, some brittle with age, a number from true detective magazines. At times he would underline in pen some nice piece of detective work, sometimes deductive, other times forensic.

I would walk a stack of file folders to Cummings's desk and sit and flip through the contents, and occasionally I'd get distracted by the interesting stories he'd clipped, everything from Jack the Ripper and Lizzie Borden to Kid Twist taking that flying leap out a six-story window at a Coney Island hotel (there'd only been six cops to keep track of him). So it sucker punched me when I found myself holding a crumbling clipping from an old *Saga* mag headed THE MARK OF BASIL.

There, in details echoing what diamond merchant David Gross had told me, was the tale of the tsar's favorite stonecutter, with blurry photos and hand-drawn re-creations, winding up with the questions, "Whatever happened to the great Basil? And what became of his precious stones? Has a glittering trail of death continued on through the years?"

My hands were trembling. It might have been a coincidence. After all, it wasn't like Doolan worked the Lizzie Borden case. These clippings seemed random, just material that got his juices going enough to honor them with a place in an already fat file folder of nothing special.

But for the first time I had a connection between Bill Doolan and the pebble I'd absentmindedly plucked from a pile of bloody sawdust used to soak up the life that had spilled too soon from young Ginnie Mathes.

It was almost one P.M., so I had a beer and unwrapped the ham and cheese on rye my host had bequeathed me. The "Mark of Basil" clipping stared at me from the desk as I ate and drank, and dared me to make something out of it.

Beyond its existence, I couldn't. It remained nothing but a glimmer of a place where three murders connected — Doolan's staged suicide, the fatal mugging of Ginnie Mathes, and the hit-and-run of Dulcie Thorpe—and it provided nothing more than the hope that maybe my efforts were worth the trouble.

Nothing else presented itself in the folders of clippings, though I lost an hour plowing through a full drawer of mob material, with plenty on the Bonettis and a full file on the Tretriano family, right up to recent stories on Anthony and Club 52. Nothing underlined in these.

I moved on to the drawers of photos. I skipped the folder on myself and went right to the folder stuffed with shots of beautiful women, sometimes with Doolan posing with them, often indifferently composed, indicating he'd elicited help from some bystander to snap these visual keepsakes. The final dozen or so were from Club 52, including the sexy onstage shots of Chrome that I'd seen before.

This time I noticed another blonde, up by the stage, but her back was to the camera—tall, shapely, her sleek ash blonde hair curling under just before it hit her shoulders. Wearing tight jeans and a white blouse, she was in all of the performance shots. Never more than a sliver of her face was revealed, yet something about the way she stood jogged my mind. . . .

Laying the photos out like panels of a comic book, I got the overall picture—the blonde was running point for Doolan! Obviously she would carve herself a place out near the stage, and when Doolan was ready to snap his camera, she would move to one side, taking the patron or two next to her along for the ride, giving him a path for a clear shot.

In addition, there were three photos of Doolan posing with Chrome, the singer's arm around him in one, another where she was kissing him on the cheek, and a final one where they were hugging, the old boy looking happy as hell. Couldn't blame him.

But the other blonde, the ash blonde, her presence was felt in those three pics as well. They were the work of somebody who knew her way around a camera—better than just a recruited bystander, superior to Doolan's own amateur-night photography.

Who was she? Was this the younger woman who had smudged her makeup dancing with Doolan that Cummings had told me about? Who Doolan had bought a gift for? Trying to make Chrome into Doolan's girlfriend was a stretch. Maybe the ash blonde was the real woman in his life. *Who was she?*

One of the photos was still in my hand when the office door opened, as if in answer to that question. And it was an attractive woman, all right, but not a very good candidate for Doolan's late-in-life lover—since this was his granddaughter.

"Mike," Anna Marina said, and forced a smile. "I'm glad you're here. Pat said you might be."

She was probably thirty-five and had a nice shape on her, well served by an orange paisley silk blouse and a short rust-color skirt with matching pumps. Good colors for a redhead like her, with her pug nose lightly dusted by freckles and her big dark blue wide-set eyes; even her lipstick was an orange-tinged red on thin but nicely formed lips. Her hair was in a shag that had been out of style for a while, but I didn't mind. I'd been out of style longer than that.

"Hi, kid," I said. "Come in and stay a while."

She shut the door carefully, as if afraid she might break the glass, and crossed the creaky floor to the client's chair. This was Cummings's office but I was feeling like a private detective again. And something about her manner told me this was business.

"Pat said you're looking into my grandfather's death." Anna had a nice voice, breathy, high-pitched but not squeaky. She sat on the edge of the chair, knees together. No purse.

"Yeah," I said. "I have my suspicions."

"Frankly . . . so have I."

"Really?"

"Not about his suicide. I think he took his life. I mean, who wouldn't, facing that kind of death sentence?"

I frowned at her. "I can share my thoughts, Anna, if you want to know why I—"

"You've been in and out of his apartment, right? Looking into things, I mean."

I shifted in Pete's chair. What was this about?

"Yeah, Anna, I have. Why?"

"Did you notice something missing?"

"No."

"From the walls, I mean."

"No. Everything looked like it was where it belonged. Always did in your grandfather's apartment."

She nodded, then shrugged. "It's true that other things had been hung in their place."

"What things? In whose place?"

She sat forward, wide-eyed, and an urgency that had been bubbling under her surface made itself known. "The two paintings. By George Wilson? The famous abstract painter?"

"Never heard of the guy. Are these the two paintings Pat told me about? The valuable paintings that were left to you in your grandfather's will?"

She nodded. "Mike, they're worth a lot of money. Twenty-five thousand as a pair. They are just a bunch of colors and shapes, but the artist died recently and the value has skyrocketed."

I nodded. "And these paintings should have been in Doolan's apartment?"

"Yes. But they're gone. And I'd like you to find them—no questions asked."

"I could look for them, I guess. But there was no sign of a break-in."

She winced. "Mike . . . are you going to make this hard? We are willing to give you a . . . a twenty percent finder's fee. No questions asked."

"What's this 'no questions asked' stuff?"

She rose. She smoothed her skirt out. Tugged at her blouse as she thrust out her breasts, which were nice full high handfuls that went well with her narrow waist. Her face was pretty enough but with an odd blankness that hid calculation, or anyway tried to.

Then she was sitting on the edge of my desk, bracing herself with the heels of her hands pushed against the edge, which gave her a breasts-forward posture. Her crossed legs were bare, her knees white. Nice calves on her. She was a natural redhead, and I always get a kick out of that, when it comes time to compare the drapes and the carpet.

Anna Doolan, now Marina, had always been able to work guys into a lather without trying, which was how she'd won her high-school-football-hero husband. Who had gone on to further glory as an hourly worker at an upstate dog food factory.

"You never liked me," she said, chin up a little. "But you always liked to look at me."

"I never disliked you. I just saw through you."

"We could have a weekend together, Mike. Just you and me. Harry goes to Vegas with some friends of his in June. We could go someplace else. Any place you like."

She started to unbutton her blouse. I was going to stop her, but what the hell—no charge for looking. The blouse hung open and then she helped it a little, letting her twins out for some air.

She didn't have a bra on. She didn't need one. Her breasts were creamy white and dusted with freckles, just like her face. Her areolae were barely darker than the smooth flesh around them and the nipples just a little darker than that, pert eraser tips that could rub a man's face until he'd forgotten any mistakes he ever made, or might ever make. . . .

"Twenty-five percent," she said, and I got it.

"Get the hell off my desk, Anna," I growled, "and button up. I didn't steal your damn paintings."

She frowned, and slid down off the desk with her shoes hitting the floor like two little gunshots. The blouse hung open and the view was fine, but all I could think was *How could this little tramp be related to Doolan?*

"I'll go to a lawyer," she said. "I'll get a *real* private eye. We'll prove—"

"I didn't take the paintings, kiddo. Maybe whoever killed your grandfather did. If your grandfather was murdered, aren't you interested in finding out who—"

The door opened and a big guy stormed in.

Whether it was on cue or not, I don't know. I found it a little hard to believe that Harry Marina was smart enough to cook up such a scheme, although Anna was. Anyway, he'd either been waiting just outside the door through all this for the right moment, or had been parked down on the street and came up to see what was taking so long.

Anna stepped away from the desk, bumped against the little refrigerator. Finally she got around to starting to button up.

"Hammer made a play, Harry," she said nervously. "Do you believe this guy? He said he'd give me the paintings back if I—" She shivered at the thought of my hands on her pale flesh. Not too convincingly.

Harry was six two in a black T-shirt and blue jeans and work boots, two hundred plus pounds, little of which was brains. The shirt may have been part of Anna's plan, as it showed off his muscles. But Harry had some gut going, too, so I wasn't that impressed.

I could have taken the .45 out from under my arm and really got his attention, but that would have been overkill.

He came over like a halfback finding his way through the line and kicked the client chair out of the way.

"You goddamn sleazeball, Hammer," he said. "I oughta break your fucking neck."

"I don't have the paintings," I said.

He reached across the desk and yanked me over it and clippings and photos went everywhere, and he tossed me. I landed hard on the old wooden floor, right where the bullet had gone in. He stomped over and leaned down over me — he had booze on his breath but was not drunk — and his teeth were bared and his eyes were stupid as he grabbed me by the lapels.

"You come across with those paintings," he said, "or I'll—"

I threw a forearm into his chest with enough power to send him backward. He didn't lose his balance, but he did have to work to maintain it, which gave me enough time to get to my feet, and as he was straightening, I threw a hard right hand into his breadbasket and he bowed to me, polite bastard that he was, and I brought locked hands down on the back of his neck and sent him to the floor with a *whump*. I was about to kick him in the head when I felt her hands on my arm, gentle not gripping, and her big blue eyes were pleading up at me.

"No, Mike. Don't. Don't hurt him. Can't you just please give us the paintings?"

This distraction allowed Harry to tackle me, and I went back past a yelping Anna, who jumped out of the way, and I hit the floor again, not hard but he'd let go of me and got to his feet and was diving at me now, and there wasn't room between the desk and the fridge for me to get clear, so I stopped him with a foot that caught him in the balls and his eyes popped and his face turned white as he dropped, his dead weight coming right at me.

I did manage to scramble out of the way just before he *whammed* and get back behind the desk against the window. Anna had retreated over by the couch opposite the file cabinets, a clawed hand to her mouth. Her hubby was curled in a fetal ball, hands buried between his legs, his pain so great he couldn't express it other than to show me a bright red face with a vein-popping forehead and bulbous eyes.

I grabbed him by an arm and dragged him to his feet. He walked like a monkey as I guided him to the door. I opened it, shoved him out on the landing, hoping he wouldn't fall down the two flights of stairs. Half hoping, anyway.

When I turned, Anna was right there, looking ashamed, with that wide-eyed expression I'd seen from her when she was a kid and Doolan caught her stealing money from her grandma's purse.

"Thirty percent?" she asked.

I took her by the arm and flung her out, too, slammed the door on them, and locked them out using the key already in there. The sound of them picking themselves and each other up, and their footsteps going down the stairs, was a pleasure to hear.

I picked up the place.

I had another beer.

Maybe she was adopted.

Irritated that the thought of those freckled breasts persisted in my mind's eye, I ignored the pain in my side from hitting the floor and got back to work. Soon I was digging into the most boring but potentially illuminating of the file drawers—the paid bills, bank statements, and so on. Again I worked backward, starting with the most recent.

And a little over two months before Doolan's death, there it was: the receipt from the Soho Abstract Art Gallery for payment of fifteen thousand dollars for two paintings by George Wilson.

"If you are thinking, sir," the prissy male voice at the gallery told me over the phone, "that we underpaid your friend, I can assure you that we gave a reasonable price."

"I understand you have to make a buck. I was told they were worth around $25,000 for the pair."

"That's the approximate retail value, yes, but Mr. Doolan was in a hurry. He said he needed to raise the money quickly and was willing to accept a strictly wholesale offer if cash was available."

"Cash?"

"Yes. That was, of course, a red flag to me, but he did have the provenance. Do you know he bought those paintings thirty years ago for a pittance? Several hundred dollars each! I would say he made out quite well on the deal."

"Not that well."

"Oh?"

"He was murdered."

I thanked the guy for his help and pressed on sorting through receipts, wondering what the hell Doolan had needed the money for. Fifteen grand was a lot of dough for an old coot to spend in the last months of his life, even if he was hanging out at Club 52.

A possible answer came quickly—here was another receipt, from a travel agency, for $956.75. One round-trip ticket to Bogotá, Colombia, with the return date open, for a Georgina Wilson. Cute alias considering how the money was raised. The receipt was in the Wilson name as well, so she must have made the booking herself.

I called the travel agency, and the woman on the phone, who was the manager and very efficient, remembered the ticketing.

"Yes, Ms. Wilson is an attractive blonde in her mid- to late thirties, I would say. I remember her well because she wore her sunglasses throughout the interview, and her hair was quite lovely."

"Platinum?"

"I would say more . . . ash blonde. She had her passport with her, which really isn't necessary for ticketing, but she had me look it over to make sure everything was in order."

Probably to see if it passed muster, since it was the passport for the nonexistent Georgina Wilson.

So for some reason, two months before he was murdered, Doolan had sent his blonde friend—girlfriend—to Bogotá. If the fifteen grand had been raised for this occasion, the plane fare only put a small dent in it, a top-notch phony passport maybe another grand. So he was funding what might be a long stay, judging by the open-ended return ticket. A vacation for her? *Without* him? That made no sense.

But what did make sense? Colombia was among the biggest exporters of cocaine in the world. Was that it? Was this Doolan's last case?

And on the desk, the *Saga* clipping with the headline THE MARK OF BASIL taunted me.

By late afternoon, I was punchy from research—at least the visit from the Marinas had provided a little exercise—and I was about to give my blurry eyes a rest and close up the office when the phone rang.

It was Pat.

"Remember Joseph Fidello?" he said.

"I never met the guy. But isn't he Ginnie Mathes's former boyfriend?"

"He's a former everything now. I'm heading over to take a look at his body."

"Fidello's dead?"

"Well, his throat was cut ear to ear."

"That'll do it."

* * *

The shabby brownstone rooming house on West Forty-sixth was one of many in the neighborhood, and Joseph Fidello's one-room flop was typical of its kind—peeling wallpaper, a battered dresser with a two-burner hot plate, a standing lamp, some odds and ends of furniture, and a daybed that folded out with a wafer-thin mattress.

The latter had Joseph Fidello on it, and the mattress had soaked up a lot of his blood. He was on his back, a slender but muscular guy about thirty, maybe five nine, with an anchor tattoo on his left biceps. He was in an athletic T-shirt and boxers, his arms and face tanned and the rest of him pale as a blister. Not much body hair. He looked like a kid.

His eyes were open in frozen terror and his mouth was peeled back in a silent scream. His gaping throat made a second screaming orifice, the blood congealed and almost black. He'd been dead a while. Rigor had set in. His bowels had given way, so it smelled rank in the little room.

We had beat the lab boys here—nobody around but the uniforms who'd caught the squeal, and they were out in the hall. What seemed to be the murder weapon had been tossed on the mattress near the corpse's right hand.

"Gee look, Pat—it's another suicide. He cut his own throat."

"Very funny. Check out the knife without touching it."

"And here I was going to play mumblety-peg." I leaned in. It was a stiletto with a black enamel handle with J.F. inlaid in pearl. "Pretty fancy blade for a guy in a fleabag like this."

Pat was looking at a billfold taken from a pair of pants on a chair nearby. "He's a seaman—Seafarers International Union card. But I knew that already."

"You checked up on him like I suggested?"

Pat gave me an irritated glance. "I'd have thought of it without your help. Fidello didn't keep a regular residence—probably just rented between jobs. Worked passenger ships in the engineering department."

"You're going to want to get a list of what ships he's been on and where he's been."

"What would I do without you?"

"*You* called *me.*" I glanced around. "This room's been searched."

The closet door was open, and clothes had spilled from hangers onto the floor—nicer clothes than somebody in this kind of room might normally own. On the other side of the room, the dresser drawers were askew, and a scarred-up nightstand's drawer was halfway out.

"Searched like his late ex-girlfriend's apartment was," Pat said thoughtfully. "For what?"

A pouch of diamonds?

"Sailors bring in all kinds of valuable contraband," I said with a shrug. "Narcotics, maybe."

"Maybe," Pat said. He scratched his chin, his hat way back on his head. "*Something* small, anyway. Something Ginnie could have been carrying in her purse the night she died. A fat roll of bills? Stolen gems, possibly?"

I just shrugged.

We were at the foot of the bed in the cramped little room. He pointed at the corpse, who seemed to be studying the ceiling. "Suppose Fidello got in over his head smuggling gems into the country and got his ex-girl involved. Innocently involved perhaps. As a go-between, a delivery girl—and got her, and then himself, killed. What do you think?"

"Reasonable theory," I said with another shrug. Pat was a smart guy. Damn near made me feel guilty, not telling him about the pebble.

From out in the hall came a female voice: "I'm Assistant D.A. Marshall. Is Captain Chambers in there?"

The uniforms made way for her, and she came in and found somewhere to stand. I'll give her credit — she didn't register the stench. Not even a nostril twitch. She was in a black pinstriped pants suit with a gray silk blouse and all that dark hair was up. She looked like a schoolteacher you were really afraid of and also wanted to jump.

"Captain Chambers," she said with a nod. "Can you fill me in?"

"Ms. Marshall," he said. "It's early days. Forensics hasn't even shown yet. Meet Joseph Fidello. He was Ginnie Mathes's boyfriend, or ex-boyfriend. The Mathes girl was the victim at—"

"The crime scene three nights ago," she cut in. "I know. I heard the name Fidello on the scanner and made the connection. I'm keeping up with your reports, Captain."

She hadn't acknowledged me yet, which took balls of a sort, because I was standing there grinning at her, fists on my hips like Superman. I stayed that way, listening as Pat filled her in on what little we knew about this crime scene — the knife handle looked to be free of prints, probably wiped — and when the lab boys showed, we moved into the corridor.

Pat was at the doorway filling Forensics in while I took Angela by the elbow and walked her a few paces down for some privacy. Somebody was cooking pork and beans.

"We have to stop meeting like this," I said.

"Hello, Mike."

"Another itty-bitty kill, and great big beautiful you shows up at it. What gives, Angela?"

She cocked her head and her smile had a devilish cast. "What are you doing for dinner tonight, Mike?"

"Are you asking me for a date again?"

"We can make it separate checks."

Even so, I had the feeling that with this doll I'd pay, all right.

"P.J. Moriarty's at eight," I said. "I'll book the reservations."

"See you there, Mike."

She returned to the latest crime scene and I got out of there before Pat Chambers guessed anything else right.

Lonnie Dean and I sat in the same old-time bar in a different booth. Ernie, who'd introduced us, wasn't around. The young reporter on the organized crime beat may have had the mustache and long hair of a hippie, and the ridiculous pointed collar of a circus clown, but he was a pro, all right.

The kid lighted up a cigarette and sucked some smoke down, held it like it was grass, then let it go, adding to the fog in the crowded gin mill. It was just after six and the bar was three deep, and the voices and laughter of reporters topping each other made a harsh music punctuated by the clinks of glass.

The young waitress smiled at me—she knew me now, especially since I'd left her a five-spot last time—and delivered an icy draft Miller without my asking. She might get another fiver.

"There's no talk of gems being used for money-laundering purposes," Lonnie said with an apologetic shrug. "I have good contacts on that front—the freelance fences, the pawnshops who work the angles, nobody indicates anything along those lines."

"New York's a big town. You can't have contacts with everybody."

"No, but these are the major players, Mike. If we are talking mob, and we are talking the kind of valuable stones it would take, then I would say nothing's shaking."

"Be a good laundering operation."

"Sure it would. Something as small as stones, and uncut ones would be virtually untraceable, no photos in insurance company files to cause trouble. . . . Cash for stones, then stones for cash. Put a jewelry store or two in the mix, and the green's clean again."

I sipped the cold brew. "Also be a good way to make a big payoff. A million in cash makes a big bundle to move around. You could set a lot in motion with a simple handoff."

Lonnie nodded. He was having a beer, too. A bottle. Heineken. Kids. "Look, Mike, it's not all bad news, or I wouldn't have called you for a meet."

"Okay."

He sucked a little more smoke. His eyes were bright. I was his hero and he was about to please me. "I did a little digging on the Club 52 front. I called the guy I replaced at the *News*—you remember Tommy Bellinger?"

"Sure. I know Tommy well. He's out in Arizona, right?"

"Yeah. It's good for the lungs." This he emphasized with another pull on the cigarette. A good thing young people live forever. "But he's got a phone, and I called him. Turns out this Chrome used to be the main squeeze of somebody you know. Or, somebody you knew."

"Such as?"

"The late and conspicuously not great Sal Bonetti."

. . . *blood smeared across the Bonetti kid's mouth, tight in a mad grin . . . Bonetti's head came apart in crimson chunks . . .*

"I didn't know Sal ever had a main squeeze," I said. "Word was he would diddle anything with two legs, including little boys and billy goats."

"That's four legs, Mike. Yeah, they say he was a twisted mother, but Tommy says Sal discovered Chrome on a South American trip—she's a star down there, you know—and booked her into a showroom at a Vegas casino that old Alberto still has a piece of. Apparently Howard Hughes doesn't own every damn craps table in Nevada. Anyway, Sal panted after her like a horny puppy dog and she liked the attention. That was the word on the Strip, anyway."

"So Little Tony probably saw her perform there. Maybe stole her away from Sal."

He shook his shaggy head. "No. He didn't get interested till *after* you rid the world of Sal. Who, one would think, would find plenty of billy goats and little boys to diddle in whatever circle of hell you dropped him in."

"Let's hope the little boys and billy goats are doing the diddling, Lonnie. So what's the deal with this Chrome broad and these bent lasagne boys? Is she their beard or what?"

He waved that off with the hand holding the cigarette. "Naw, she's just another show biz type who cozies up to whoever has the money to make her famous. She's gone as far as she can in Latin America—like anybody in her game, Chrome knows she's not a *real* star till she makes it in the *real* America."

"You think Tony really digs her?"

"Who knows? I heard those young bartenders of his march in and out of his penthouse like a parade of little tin soldiers. My guess, and it's just a guess, is Chrome and Anthony are strictly business partners. But, hell, maybe he *does* love her, considering the money he's spending on the broad."

"What do you mean?"

"Man, he's laying out hundreds of thousands launching this tour of his new locations, nationwide. They have their own Lear jet, and are taking her full band and all of their gear."

"Their own damn *plane?*"

"Yeah, like Hefner or Sinatra. Lavish layout, lounge with a bar, plus she can fly home and see her folks and do gigs down south of the border that she already had booked. Maybe Tony *is* crazy about her. She is one big, beautiful animal."

"So I hear," I said.

"Anyway, this wild-ass seventies lifestyle — guys like Sal and Anthony, they swing in ways that even an old prowler like you could never imagine. No offense meant. You been at Club 52, right?"

"Yeah."

"Well you saw the scene. Men and women, women and women, men and men, two men and one woman, it's a Rubik's Cube of fleshly delights. To guys like Anthony, gender labels are just labels. Lot of that going around these days, Mike." The reporter flashed me a mocking smile. "Hey, man, aren't you into androgyny?"

"I don't dig science fiction," I said.

I let him wonder about that and slipped out of the booth, leaving a sawbuck behind to cover the damage and the tip. I needed to get to the hotel to clean up a little.

After all, like the old song said, I had a date with an angel. Even if she was an assistant district attorney.

Chapter 10

WE SAT AT THE bar at P.J. Moriarty's at Sixth and Fifty-second, waiting to be seated. It was a straight-ahead steak and chop house that the restaurant critics looked down on and hungry patrons packed. John, the Irish bartender, brought me an icy Miller without asking and took Angela's drink order. She said she'd have the same, so I slid mine over to her.

"You look great," I said.

And she did, in a cream-in-the-coffee silk blouse and a simple short black skirt, her long, full black hair touching her shoulders. The strength of her face and the intelligence and beauty in those big dark eyes recalled Velda, even if this one lacked my ex-secretary's distinctive fashion-flouting pageboy. This woman's forehead was high with a strong widow's peak, as if the brain in that lovely noggin demanded air, like electronic equipment that might otherwise overheat.

"You clean up pretty well yourself," she said. Her beer arrived and I took it — it had taken almost thirty seconds. John was slipping.

"Thank the Commodore Hotel," I said, gesturing to the dark gray suit. "If they didn't have in-house dry cleaning, I'd be screwed, with as little wardrobe as I brought up from Florida."

Her eyes tightened, just a little, and she sipped her beer and didn't look at me when she asked, "When this is . . . over . . . are you going back there?"

"Don't know."

Half a smile blossomed. "Well, that shows the city's back in your blood. Before, you were just vacationing here."

"I know. Maybe I love smog and panhandlers."

Her half smile was both sweet and teasing. "How do you make a living, anyway? Everything I hear about you says you've spent decades doing favors and cleaning things up for friends and, well, mostly dispensing a sort of rough justice, when you deem it necessary."

"The big-paying cases don't make the papers." I shrugged. "All that publicity attracts business. I do all right."

"Will you open your office back up?"

"Maybe. Is that why you asked me out to dinner? To get my life story? I mean, this *is* our second date, and it's your idea again."

She laughed just a little. "No. We have things to talk about. I saw the questions in your eyes in that hallway outside Joseph Fidello's apartment."

"That place was an apartment like a matchbox is a fireplace. But I do have questions, yeah."

She cocked her head and the dark hair fell nicely. "I'll try to give you some answers. But first — can we eat? I'm starving."

Her timing was impeccable, because the head waiter, Samuel, motioned me from his stand that our booth was ready. I'd asked for one back by the kitchen, normally a lousy seat but I liked that the clatter and in-and-out of waiters would cover our conversation.

But Angela hadn't lied—she was hungry, all right, and she was no vegetarian feminist, despite the light breakfast I'd witnessed a couple of days ago. She got the lamb chops special and she put it away like a stevedore who missed his last meal.

"Watching you make those chops disappear," I said, working on my medium rare New York strip, "makes me wonder if I'm the next lamb set for slaughter."

"I skipped lunch," she said as delicately as possible with a mouthful. "This always happens. I try to skip a meal, to be good, then dinner comes around and I'm very bad. Good thing I burn a lot of calories. But it's tough, watching my figure."

"Not from where I sit," I said.

We shared cheesecake off a communal plate. The dessert was almost as good as the sense of shared intimacy. She was a strong woman, smart and big with the kind of curves the fashion magazines abhor. Like Velda. I frowned at my mind's damn insistence on bringing up past history. . . .

"Something wrong, Mike?"

"No. I want to ask you something—were you working with Bill Doolan on a case?"

She shook her head. Her tongue licked whipped cream off her upper lip. "I never even had the honor of meeting him. He was a legend."

"No, he wasn't. He was a man. Flesh and blood. He had his weaknesses—like an eye for pulchritude."

She laughed.

"What?"

"I don't think," she said giggling, "I ever heard that word spoken out loud before."

"My vocabulary might surprise you."

"You're a surprise in general, Mike. Why do you ask if I knew Doolan?"

I gestured to her. "Because here you are — sniffing around the edges of my investigation into his murder."

"Don't you mean suicide?"

"No. It's a murder. It might not be ready for presentation to your office, Angela, but I'm completely convinced Doolan was murdered. Somebody close to him did it — a woman, maybe. That was his weakness."

"Pulchritude," she said, not clowning it. "My interest is strictly Club 52. I can't imagine your late friend was a habitué of that Weimar Republic flashback."

"Actually, he was. He was viewed as a lovable eccentric by Little Tony."

She nodded sagely. "Anthony Tretriano." Then she frowned. "*Doolan* was a regular at 52?"

"For a while, anyway."

"Why in the world would *he* be? And if you say 'pulchritude' —"

"He was taking pictures, Angela. Mostly of that disco doll . . . Chrome?"

Her expression changed so radically it was damn near comic. Her eyes tightened and popped at the same time, and her face turned so pale the bright red of her lipstick was like blood on white linen.

"We shouldn't talk in public about this," she said quietly.

"We're all right. With all this kitchen noise —"

"Not here."

"Well, if we're at the 'your place or mine' stage, I don't have a place, other than my room at the Commodore."

"That should do fine. But we shouldn't go up at the same time. We're both well known, and I don't want anybody getting the wrong idea."

I grinned at her. "Including me?"

Her smile had a nice naughtiness to it that was brand-new. "I've already learned, Mike, not to try to control *your* thoughts. . . ."

The Commodore near Grand Central Terminal was probably due for an overhaul, and at twenty-six stories wasn't much in skyscraper terms, but it remained my favorite hotel in the city. I always used it for out-of-town clients and maybe now and then for a conference with a good-looking female, sometimes work-related, sometimes not. My stay here so far had been just fine. And it looked to improve. . . .

Angela Marshall was lounging on the dark blue spread of my brass double bed, facing me as I sat in the comfy chair in a corner by the window. I had ordered room service for four more cold Millers, in bottles, and those had arrived. My guest, in her silk blouse and short skirt, had her shoes off, leaning on one hand, sitting on one hip, with lots of stretched-out bare leg showing as she spoke animatedly, like a girl at a slumber party. With the lucky guy who'd crashed.

The only light on was the nightstand lamp on the other side of the bed, and the limited lighting and the shadows thrown made for a nice mood, enhancing the already beautiful features and shapely form of the assistant district attorney.

My hat and coat were tucked away in the closet, and my tie was loose. We had a nicely cozy thing going.

She was on her second beer (fourth, counting those at Moriarty's) and that may have accounted for her lively manner.

"Mike, I've been investigating Club 52 as discreetly as I can—I went there a couple of times myself, but that really told me nothing. But I'm convinced the club has been a major conduit for cocaine and other controlled substances in this city since the day it opened. And now Anthony Tretriano is opening up Club 52s in half a dozen major cities, all around the country. With more to come."

I nodded. "You figure he's not just franchising his club, but setting up a nationwide distribution system."

"Yes! And there's a kind of twisted genius about it. The blessing given by local law enforcement to the recreational use of drugs by his celebrity guests, the hands-off, benign neglect bit . . . it plays right into Tretriano's ability to move narcotics in and out of there."

I was frowning. "Why do you have to investigate discreetly? Since when does the New York County District Attorney's Office give drug running a free pass?"

"Have you been to Club 52?"

"Just the other night."

"See anybody interesting there? In terms of officeholders?"

I grinned. "Only the mayor and two local legislators and one national one. I see your drift."

"I have no way of knowing who in the current local administration, or on the national scene, are just naive, starstruck nincompoops buying the Club 52 glitz, and who's been bought off all the way. Mike, these are dangerous waters to swim in. God, you don't know how relieved I am to be able to finally talk to somebody about it."

"What about this new federal group, the D.E.A.? Have you contacted them?"

"That's the plan, when I feel I really have something more than hunches and suspicions."

She was ambitious. If those hunches and suspicions were right, she might become the city's first female D.A. And then mayor, and . . . ?

I sipped the Miller. I was still on my first (or third, but who was counting). "Baby, these *are* dangerous waters. The kind a girl can drown in."

"I'm a big girl, Mike. But I admit . . . I admit liking to have a guy like you on my team."

"If I'm on your team, I have a right to ask a few questions."

"Yes you do."

I sat forward. "What brought you to that crime scene the other night? Ginnie Mathes is a small kill for such a 'big girl.' And then there's earlier today, this afternoon, over at that flophouse—why does the late Joseph Fidello get on your radar? And don't say because he was the Mathes kid's ex-boyfriend. I want the whole story."

She reached for the beer, chugged some. A little Irish courage for the girl.

Then she said, "Mike, Ginnie was in a dancing class, off Broadway, using the same private tutor as Club 52's star attraction."

"Chrome?"

She nodded. "I talked to the tutor, and I think I did so in a way that raised no suspicions. I'm not as skilled an investigator as you, but I didn't dare use any of our investigative team, and—"

"Skip it. What's the connection?"

"Chrome had been grooming Ginnie to be a backup dancer in her act."

"She doesn't use any backup dancers in her act."

"Well, not her current act, maybe. But Chrome's preparing for this big national tour, and she'd been dangling that opportunity over Ginnie's head, as recently as the day the young woman was killed. Chrome had really been courting her—otherwise Ginnie wouldn't have been on my radar at all. They often had lunch together, after dance class, and Ginnie seemed enthralled to be in the star's company."

I sipped more beer. "If you did your research, which I'm sure you did, then you know Ginnie took out a cabaret entertainer's license a while back. Making it as a performer was apparently a long-held dream."

"Right," Angela said, nodding. "And when I heard the description of the dead girl who was a mugging fatality, it sounded awfully close to Ginnie—not just physically, but down to the clothes I'd seen her wearing earlier . . . so I checked it out."

"And we had our first star-crossed meeting."

She smiled. "Boy, did I hate *your* guts."

"I wanted to ram that Japanese sports car of yours up your rear highway."

"Really?"

"Yeah. Or ram something somewhere."

She almost blushed at that. Damn, she was cute.

"But, Mike—now Ginnie's boyfriend has been murdered, and there can be no question about that. Nobody could write Fidello's death off as a mugging. And it's sure not a robbery, considering where he lived."

"No," I confirmed. "That was as cold-blooded as kills get. So how do the pieces fit? You're looking at Tony Tret as a drug kingpin. What does that have to do with Chrome making friends with Ginnie Mathes?"

"Simple." She shrugged. "Chrome works for Anthony. She may even be his main squeeze, if rumor can be believed."

"I say Tony's gay, but go on."

"Whatever the case, this may just be a matter of Chrome enlisting Ginnie for some purpose. An errand of some kind, which might explain what Ginnie was doing on that rough patch of real estate where she died."

Delivering Basil's diamond to somebody. But who? And why?

"Mike, what's on your mind?"

"Just thinking, doll. Just thinking."

"Can you figure why Fidello was murdered?"

My eyebrows hiked. "Possibly he was getting back with Ginnie, and overheard something, and maybe became the kind of loose end that needs cutting off."

"Somebody is killing awfully casually."

"Little Tony comes from that kind of stock."

She put the beer bottle back.

"I have to tinkle," she said.

"As long as you put it so sweetly, you don't even have to leave a quarter on the porcelain."

Angela laughed at that, tipsy enough for my quip to seem funny. She snatched her purse off the nearby nightstand and scampered off. Always a kick to see a big, beautiful woman scamper.

I sat there thinking about a young woman who dreamed of a show biz break and had done a star a favor, maybe delivering a valuable pebble. Her reward had been a quick, nasty death. If Angela was right, Ginnie was doing Tony Tret's bidding, in a roundabout way.

What was Tretriano doing with Basil's diamond in the rough? And assuming Tony was using it as a small-size big payoff, whose palm was he greasing in such a magnanimous fashion?

The toilet had long since flushed and she wasn't back yet.

Then the door opened and she stepped out in the shaft of light, and all she had on was the silk blouse, buttoned up discreetly, but with the tail not quite hiding the dark tip of her pubic triangle. Her legs were long and with a little flesh around the thighs, which was fine with me because I hated these skinny kids. She was tiptoeing, like she was sneaking up on me, though I was right there staring.

She stood before me like a good soldier waiting for inspection. But I was standing at attention, too, even if I was still sitting down.

"Am I too forward?" she asked.

"Not forward enough," I said. "That blouse is ruining the view."

She made me crazy, working those buttons one at a time, taking several seconds each that made sweat bead on my forehead despite the cool spring breeze coming in the crack of the window under the closed blinds, which made a metallic rustling.

When she'd shrugged out of the silk blouse, she put her shoulders back and the full breasts jutted proudly, displaying large, round, puffy nipples whose erect tips pointed slightly right and left, as if a practical joke to turn me cockeyed. Her waist was narrow and her stomach firm and well defined without losing its womanliness, and the dark, dark tangle of pubic hair promised a jungle well worth exploring.

"Should we have some fun?" she asked.

"I'm gonna say yes," I said.

"Check my purse. See if anything interests you."

I stood up and she giggled at the tent I'd made, and grabbed it, pulled it down, and let go. "Boiiiing," she said, and laughed.

Maybe not just a little drunk.

I went over and got in her purse and found what she was talking about—handcuffs. Well, she was an officer of the court.

I stood by the bedside and dangled the shiny pair, which caught what little light was in the room. "I don't wear bracelets, honey—I'm a man."

"I can see you're a man. But I'm a woman."

She threw the sheets and blankets back, and crawled up on the bed, pointing a well-rounded, dimpled behind at me with a little teasing tuft sticking out from in between, where heaven met the earth, and she snapped her right wrist to the bedpost at left. Then she lay on her back, spread-eagled, pink peeking through the curly black, and looked over to where I stood getting out of my own clothes, and she said, "You'll never make me talk, officer."

I didn't make her talk, but I did make her holler, and laugh, and even cry a little. She was moist and tight and wild, a prisoner gyrating for freedom that she didn't really crave, and as I was buried in her dark hair with her moaning in sweet pain, I thought, *So like Velda . . . so like Velda. . . .*

"Velda," I whispered.

Out loud. Not meaning to.

"What did you say?" She stiffened under me. "What did you call me?"

"Old Celtic term of endearment, baby."

"What does it mean?"

"Love of my life."

"You're sweet . . ." Her hips began to grind under me again. "You're so *sweet. . . .*"

Wasn't I?

She fell asleep almost immediately, despite her cuffed wrist. She was on her side, her back to me with the covers over her, snoring softly, when I slipped out of bed. I left my clothes on the floor, but got into my shorts. I went to her purse to find the handcuff key, though when I started to rustle in there, she stirred and made a protesting sound that made me shrug. If the cuff didn't bother her, it didn't bother me.

We'd turned all the lights off, but I'd been in this room for enough days to easily make my way to the john without any help. I didn't even turn the bathroom light on until I'd sealed myself in.

What a wonderful, smart woman this was. I'd thought Velda was one of a kind, but another had found me, and took me on my own terms, rough edges and all. It seemed a kind of miracle. I wouldn't say I loved her, not yet, but the sex had been great, hot and loving and crazy. The kind of memory you save up for your deathbed, when you can really use it.

I did a few things in the john that don't really move this story forward. What may be relevant is that the lovemaking had been spirited enough to make my side ache like hell, particularly that hot spot under my ribs. The pill bottles were lined up behind the sink like members of the jury.

The pill bottle for pain, which I knew to be a goddamn narcotic, I grabbed and held and sat staring at, like a kid in school with poor reading skills trying to make sense out of Dick, Jane, and Spot. My hand was shaking a little and my side was burning, like some sicko bastard with a red-hot poker was having a horse laugh at my expense, and I heard the door snick open out there.

I got onto my feet without a sound. I put the plastic vial carefully on the counter without a single rattle of pills.

Somebody was out there.

I did not believe it was Angela, up and dressed and slipping out on me. No, she'd been too drunk to accomplish that quietly, and anyway she couldn't reach her purse for the precious little key, not in that handcuff. Not without my help.

Somebody was out there.

I had no weapon. The .45 in the speed rig was on the shelf in the closet. Just across the way, but it might as well have been in New Jersey. I was in my shorts and the closest thing to a weapon in here was a toothbrush.

That room out there was dark. Pitch black. If I was someone's intended target, an intruder could easily take the slumbering Angela for me. The blinds were shut, I knew, no city light to speak of seeping in. Just enough to make out the vaguest shape, like that of a sleeper, primed to be an unwitting victim.

The only weapon I had going for me was surprise.

Leaving the bathroom light on, I opened the door, stepped into the shaft of brightness, and yelled, *"Hey!"*

He was big, stupid big for the role he'd taken on, wearing the white shirt and black bow tie and black trousers of a room-service waiter. The sudden light had him squinting, and his whole face seemed to be clenched, his hair dark and curly with muttonchops, his nose a blobby thing, his chipmunk cheeks acned and pock-marked.

And he was at the foot of the bed with his fist raised high, a long, wide, gleaming Bowie-knife blade reflecting the bathroom light back at me.

This registered in a fraction of a second, and in the next fraction I was on him. He had two inches on me, but I was able to grip his wrist with both hands and stop its downward swing. We did an awkward, grunting dance for a few seconds, and Angela had woken up at some point, because she said "Mike!" softly and then, rattling the handcuff against the brass bedpost, trying vainly to escape, shrieked, *"Miiike!"*

He was strong. Cords in his neck were standing out and veins made a nasty bas-relief on his forehead as he forced his knife-in-hand down, taking my gripped hands with him, edging that wide, pointed blade toward my throat even as his arm sent one forearm after another into me, making that hot spot under my ribs issue lightning bolts of pain all through my torso.

I let the knife inch its way toward me, then pulled back, and with all my strength, brought the blade down, all right, in his hands and mine, but swung it around into his midsection. Deep—the sound like a boot stepping in thick wet mud. His eyes bulged in fear and agony as we did the final steps of our dance, face-to-face, almost nose-to-nose, his mouth moving silently, maybe in a prayer, and I grinned as his hand fell away and my two hands gripped the handle of the knife whose blade was already all the way in and jerked it upward on a terrible path and then made a circular sideways motion, taking the blade on a grim ride.

Then I stepped away.

And grinned at him some more as he looked at me, astonished, then down at the red spreading across his white shirt and the knife pitching to the floor as a flap of flesh opened and he caught the tumble of bloody slimy intestines in his fingers, though some of the scarlet-smeared snakes slithered from his grasp, and I would swear he fainted before he fell to the carpet to die.

That was when I realized Angela was screaming.

I crawled up on the bed where she was still jerking that cuff and said, "It's all right, baby. He can't hurt you. He's dead."

Only her horrified eyes weren't on the corpse, but on me.

I had Angela uncuffed, and she had padded into the bathroom, taking her clothes with her, when the phone rang. It was the front desk, complaining about noise, which was quick, because the guy had only been dead a couple of minutes. I told the desk man to tell any on-duty manager that there had been an assault on a guest, me, and that the hotel doctor should come up, and the police should be called immediately.

I hung up, got the switchboard, and gave the girl Pat Chambers's home number.

"I need you to get over here," I told him.

"Over where?" he said sleepily. "Jesus, Mike. I'm at home. I have a life, you know."

"Is there a woman in bed with you?"

"No."

"Then I'd argue the point about you having a life. There's a dead body on my hotel room floor. I've already had the desk call for the cops. But I figure you'll want to be in on this."

"Mike . . . Mike. Did you make him dead?"

"I didn't shoot him."

"You didn't?"

"He had a knife."

A long pause.

Then he said "Mike" again, almost sorrowfully, and hung up.

I went to the bathroom door and knocked. "Are you all right, honey?"

". . . Yes."

"I've called the police. A doctor'll be up soon to check on our friend."

"He's dead! He *has* to be dead!"

"Yeah, he's dead, all right, but there are procedures. Hell, I'm telling *you*? Listen, if uh . . . if you want to slip out before anybody gets here. . . ."

"No. No, I'll stay."

"Fine. Do you want the doc to check you over?"

"No. No."

The doctor came up, a sixty-ish gent, looked the dead intruder over, and got to his feet, a ghastly white. "This is a first at the Commodore," he said.

"Come on, doc, people die in hotels all the time."

"Not like this."

"Oh. Yeah, well I can see that."

The doc was long gone when the uniforms got there. The older of the pair wanted my story and I told him I was Mike Hammer and that Captain Chambers of Homicide was on the way. That satisfied him, and Pat made it in less than half an hour. He looked a little rumpled and he'd forgot his hat, but he made it.

Pat stood looking down at the dead guy, shaking his head, hands on hips. "This tears it. This really fucking tears it."

"You want to hear what happened?"

He grunted something that wasn't quite a laugh. "Why not?"

I told him, referring only to Angela as "a lady friend." I left the handcuffs out, too, basically starting with me getting up to go to the john.

He glared at me. "You call this self-defense?"

"Hell yes! The prick comes into my hotel room, with a goddamn Bowie knife, intending to cut me up while I slept."

"But you disemboweled him."

"Yeah. And?"

"*And?* How the hell do you disembowel somebody in self-defense?"

I shrugged. "He got on my bad side."

Pat closed his eyes. I thought maybe he was praying. Then he opened them, but he didn't look at me. "Well, where is she, your lady friend? I hope she makes a good witness."

The toilet flushed again. I figured the first time was her puking; the second was anybody's guess.

She came out, looking fairly spiffy in the silk blouse and short dark skirt. Not a lovely hair out of place, but her eyes were off. I don't know whether Pat noticed that, because he was just gaping at her in general.

"Angela Marshall," he said, to me, not her. "The assistant district *attorney* is your witness?"

"She should make a good one," I said.

Pat sighed heavily, then went to the phone and called for the lab boys. Then he gently walked Angela out to the hall, away from the body, and asked her to wait. After that, he returned to take a brief statement from me, just inside the door.

When he'd slipped his notebook away, Pat said, "I don't mean to encourage you, but I do have a couple of pieces of information you might appreciate hearing."

"Go ahead. Liven up my evening."

"Remember Ollie Joe's Steak House, where Ginnie Mathes worked? Where she talked to a patron at some length before she left and went out and got killed?"

"Uh huh."

"Well, the register girl at Ollie Joe's identified Joseph Fidello's picture as the chatty patron."

"Really. What do you make of that?"

"Nothing yet. But there can be no question we're looking at murder, not some random mugging. Not with both of them dead. On the other hand, I believe we've confirmed that the little hooker, the Thorpe girl, was not the intended hit-and-run victim. It was all you, Mike."

"Why do you say that?"

Pat arched an eyebrow. "Washington kicked back some interesting info on Dulcie Thorpe's former pimp, the one she shot?"

"What's the deal?"

"The deal is he's dead. And has been dead for three months. The feds had him on tap because he was involved in some interstate heisting of stolen stereo equipment. Got killed in one of those falling-outs among thieves you hear about. Appears he gave up pimping, after Dulcie popped him."

"Tough to keep discipline with the rest of the stable," I said, "once one of the girls shoots your ass."

He glanced toward the dead body. "So . . . I'm sure you've noticed something significant about your caller tonight."

"You recognize him, too?"

Pat's laugh rumbled out of his gut. "Oh yeah. That's Frankie Cerone. One of the top Bonetti guns. Seems old Alberto may still have a grudge against you after all, Mike. For taking out his boy Sal."

"I don't think Alberto gives a shit about Sal."

"What?"

I shook my head. "Word is, old Alberto's been getting credit for staging Doolan's suicide, though I don't think he did. And for trying to have me run down, too, which I also don't think he did." I nodded toward the gutted killer. "I think he decided he might as well really get in the game."

"What, to build up his rep?"

I nodded. "My guess is the old man is trying to stage a comeback. Maybe I'll have a talk with Alberto."

"Mike, you stay the hell away from him. I will throw your ass in jail so fast—"

"How can you make that speech and keep a straight face? Listen, I'm going to call the desk to arrange for a new room. This one's a mess."

I went over and stepped carefully across the corpse and called down to the desk. When the arrangements were made, I returned to Pat and said, "Take it easy on Ms. Marshall, Pat. She's had a bad shock."

"I will. For political reasons if not humanitarian ones."

"Give me a second with her."

I went out in the hall. She was smoking a cigarette.

"Thought you quit," I said gently.

"So did I," she mumbled. "Bummed one off an officer."

The two uniforms were milling. We were down a ways and had enough privacy to talk.

"You need to give your statement to Captain Chambers," I said.

She nodded. Drew in smoke, closed her eyes, exhaled a blue-gray stream.

"Listen," I said, "I arranged for another room. You'll love this, doll—a thousand rooms in this dump, and they only had one available. It's the Honeymoon Suite."

She looked at me like I was a ghost that had materialized before her. Not a good kind of ghost either.

"You have *got* to be *kidding* me. . . ."

I held up a palm. "Just to crash. Just to decompress from all this crap that went down."

"Really?" She shook her head, sort of shivering, then she took another drag, let it linger, finally exhaled, and said, "Mike, I know you saved my life. I *know* you did."

"You don't have to thank me, baby."

"I'm not thanking you. I mean, I am grateful, but . . . I *saw* what you did."

"That was self-defense."

"In its way, it was . . . and I will back you up. I owe you that much. But you went over the line, Mike. You didn't have to do . . . what you did. You enjoyed it. How can you *enjoy* killing? What is wrong with you?"

"I don't enjoy killing just anybody," I said defensively.

She laughed at that. There was hysteria in it, but she seemed otherwise calm as she stroked my face, and the gesture held genuine affection.

"I was falling in love with you tonight, Mike. I was drunk, a little drunk, yes, but falling . . . only now? I can't be with you, Mike."

She went over to one of the uniforms and said she was ready to give Captain Chambers her statement.

I could only sigh.

And here I thought this doll was like Velda. . . .

Chapter 11

ALBERTO BONETTI HAD a distinct advantage over most of his associates—he was an Ellis Island baby. Nine months earlier, he had been conceived in a squalid area of Poldosti, Sicily, fathered by a young anarchist with a passionate hatred of authority and nurtured in the belly of a plain and plump wife who was madly in love with her impetuous husband. Alberto's mama never even considered the fact that the child's father had no feeling at all for her, except that their marriage contract and her dowry bought them tickets out of that oppressive country to the new land of America.

By the time all the arrangements had been made, their baby was approaching term, and upon disembarking at Ellis Island, New York, Maria Bonetti promptly gave birth to Alberto, a brand-new United States citizen . . .

. . . and already a headache to officials, who didn't quite know how to deal with a sudden birth right on their literal doorstep.

But citizen or not, Alberto remained a Sicilian at heart. And not in a good way. One day New York's Five Families woke up to find they had a new neighbor who had grown up while they were warring, whose wealth and power had made him into a quiet, deadly force that could not be ignored and, rather than invite him into their conclave, they simply moved over and made room for him.

The early dons seemed to relish holding on to their early beginnings. The decrepit old buildings where they started their empires were like the hills of their old, beloved Sicily, the caves they had to return to every so often to make them remember who they really were.

A half block off Second Avenue, in the shadow of the Manhattan Bridge, the Y and S Men's Club took up all three floors of an old brick building whose considerable renovations were not visible from without.

On the street level, behind frosted windows and a wooden door marked MEMBERS ONLY, was a recreation room with pool tables, pinball machines, and booths along one side for sipping cold cans of beer from upright pop machines that needed no coins and held no pop and were lined up against the opposite wall like the victims in the St. Valentine's Day Massacre. This lineup included a 1950s-era jukebox that played old rock 'n' roll and new heavy metal, no fuckin' disco, and similarly required no coins. Toward the back was the latest thing, a massive rear-projection television that ran continuously with beat-up easy chairs and a threadbare couch arranged for worship at its cathode altar.

This ground floor was the province of the young turks, the bodyguards, muscle boys, and pistoleros who had graduated from street gangs and relaxed here between duties, criminal and otherwise. An open staircase climbed the rear right wall and on the opposite side was a small elevator. There were presumably other avenues of entry and escape known only to the occupants.

No snotty kids or teenaged punks ever touched the muscle cars parked out front, or the luxury rides with vinyl tops and whitewalls in the rear lot. Reprisals for that kind of action were swift and severe. No ongoing police surveillance was maintained either, unless a member was out on bail and being watched. The Y and S Club was well protected and well defended.

The second floor could have been a Madison Avenue millionaire's hideaway. A curved, thirty-foot-long bar with chair-back stools dominated a chamber whose richly dark wood-paneled walls were decorated with gilt-framed paintings in oil, watercolor, and pastel by famous artists, the kind whose work had been copied onto the nose cones of planes during World War II. The subject matter was female nudity, of course—this *was* a men's club—but nothing outright vulgar.

In addition to a civilian bartender, a staff of four was on hand to take coats and hats, serve drinks, and do whatever their benefactors required. These minions were a special breed—their training suited them for the finest private club in any major city, but they were also armed bodyguards. They wore dignified black suits with black bow ties, and the cut of the jackets did not betray the holstered guns on their hips. Among their duties was never remembering what went on in this sanctuary of smoking, drinking, and privacy.

The members were an odd mix. Men in their sixties and seventies, in sweaters and threadbare pants, would sit at a pearl-enameled table and play cribbage, whist, and other old-fart card games. A table of sharply dressed younger members—in their forties—had a poker game going that took up a corner with a felt table and a hanging Tiffany-type shade. This game had been continuous, as far as anybody knew, for decades. Always money on the table. Always players coming in and out. Whether six A.M. or six at night, no matter.

In the middle of the room was a little reading area, easy chairs and a couch around a coffee table littered with upper-tier girlie magazines, plus *Sports Illustrated, Ring, Variety,* and various boating periodicals. No TV had been installed in the second floor clubroom—anybody wanting to watch sports could join the kiddies downstairs. No radio either—if you wanted to keep track of the horses, go to a fuckin' bookie joint already. There was, however, continuous music, soft but easily discerned, Italian crooners singing hits of the forties and fifties.

No disco allowed on the second floor either.

On the third floor were the suites. Each one had a living room with TV and wet bar, a well-appointed bedroom, and a luxurious bath with a large hot tub. There were three such suites, used by important out-of-town guests and by various members who wanted a little overnight getaway from the wife and kids. A larger fourth suite, however, belonged to the master of the brick castle.

This was Alberto Bonetti's home away from home.

As a kid, he and his gang holed up in the cellar under Poco's papa's saloon, and as long as they never messed with the old man's beer barrels or raised too much hell, he let them alone. Now Alberto had a mansion on Long Island, where his alcoholic wife lived in luxury and despair over the demise of Sal and the lack of visits from their married daughter, who had publicly disowned them, and the lawyer son who had put a continent between him and the family whose money had paid for his deluxe schooling. And Alberto was only around on the occasional weekend.

Weekdays, Alberto worked and relaxed in his comfortable Y and S Club suite, which included a small kitchen and a modest office with no staff, since he was retired, after all. Various of his business interests around the greater metropolitan area did have larger office setups and all kinds of staff.

But old Alberto *was* retired. Just puttering these days. Right?

The Y and S, by the way, stood for the Yelling and Spitting Club. Little of that was done here now, except maybe the punks on the first floor.

This, at least, had been the arrangement of the club when I had last been there, over a year ago, when I had asked for and received a sit-down with Alberto Bonetti in his suite.

I had tried to reason with the old man, requesting that he get a handle on his son Sal, whose ruthless loan-sharking activities had been causing a client of mine grief. Alberto had listened politely, thrown up his hands, and said, "What can a father do? Kids these days."

I had been up late, dealing with the aftermath of the intruder at the Commodore, and Pat had made me wait until the photographers and lab boys were through and the stiff had been rubber-bagged and hauled out before allowing me to gather my things and move to my new room. The gigantic bed in the Honeymoon Suite, with its *Every Day Is Valentine's Day* decor, had a pillowy mattress that was perfect for everything but sleeping.

So I wound up camping out on the damn couch, where I finally dropped off, and it was ten A.M. before I woke up. I went over to Bing's for a workout, took a swim at the hotel pool, then skipped breakfast and went straight for lunch. I had a steak sandwich at the Commodore's café, passing on the salad and barely touching the fries. I needed some protein but didn't care to haul anything heavy along.

Because I was going to drop in on an old friend—the kind of old friend capable of the brand of warm welcome that made a bulletproof vest and three extra .45 clips in my sport-jacket pocket the minimal precautions.

When I had closed the MEMBERS ONLY door behind me, I

planted myself over the threshold and waited. Lots of young faces at pool tables and at booths turned my way — narrow, bony faces; round, acned faces, lots more hair than you used to see on this type of punk, including muttonchops like those sported by my late intruder last night.

This floor hadn't been Frankie Cerone's likely hangout, though — at his age, and with his standing, Frankie had probably been eligible for the second floor with the curved bar and the Rat Pack music.

So the pale-faced punks peeking at me from booths and glowering at me over pool cues were not necessarily pals of Cerone. They'd probably heard that one of their own bought the farm last night, six feet of acreage straight down with grass for a crop and I don't mean marijuana. They'd probably even heard it was thanks to a guy name of Hammer.

But I was just a tough-looking older dude they didn't recognize, who might be a cop. Nobody stepped forward to question my presence. This was a clubhouse without a leader. No Leo Gorcey, just a bunch of homicidal Huntz Halls.

Any thought that I'd be patted down and have to justify carrying the .45 in the sling into their den of budding thieves didn't even come up. I just walked along between the two pool tables and the row of vending machines and such, the boys in the booths on the other side of the room eyeballing me like monkeys in cages frustrated that the zoo patrons weren't getting close enough to hurl feces at.

I just kept nodding and smiling at the curious dopes, my hands in my pockets, very unthreatening, loping along like I belonged nowhere else but here and knew exactly what I was doing, no big deal, fellas, no big deal.

I got all the way to the second-floor landing without a hitch.

Somebody had called from downstairs, though, because from the fancy club room, a big guy stepped out into the bland little reception area to meet me. He was about thirty-five with short, dark, military-cut hair and dark, no-nonsense eyes, and wore the black suit with matching bow tie of those who attended the members. He would have a revolver on his hip. Probably a cross-draw affair like lots of cops were wearing these days.

"I know you," he said. Nothing intimidating about it. Matter of fact. Then: "Mr. Hammer, you've been here before. But surely you know this is a private club."

"Yeah. I was hoping Mr. Bonetti might see me."

"If you had an appointment, I'd know."

"I don't have an appointment. A guy named Frankie Cerone, who may be familiar to you, tried to kill me in my hotel room last night, also without an appointment. I'm here to talk to Mr. Bonetti about that. On his turf. I'm here on peaceful terms, requesting a sit-down."

That was a lot to absorb, but he got it right away.

"I need to check with Mr. Bonetti," he said.

Good—the old boy was in.

"But, Mr. Hammer, before I do that, you'll have to stand for a frisk."

"No need." I opened my jacket and let him see the .45 in the sling.

His frown was like a father's to an untrained child. "You expect to wear that in to see Mr. Bonetti?"

"You can tell him I'm armed. I saw fifteen guys downstairs. You probably have another twelve members, anyway, in that fancy club room. And I'll bet there are guards in the hall upstairs, outside the suites."

The big guy said nothing.

"I keep the gun," I said, "or Mr. Bonetti can come to see me on my turf, on my terms. *He* can bring a gun. Because I sure as hell will."

He was thinking.

"Another option is you can try to take it away," I said.

That he didn't think about at all, just nodded, said, "Take a seat," and slipped back in the club room.

I did not take a seat, though a couch and several comfortable chairs were available. The paintings out here weren't of the pinup variety—they were landscapes. Probably Sicilian landscapes, but who the hell knew? Trees are trees.

The big guy returned and said, "Mr. Bonetti will see you. He is unconcerned that you are armed. He understands that you are vastly outnumbered and outgunned."

"Yeah, that was my point."

"We'll take the elevator."

"It's just a flight up. I don't get winded that easy."

He shook his head. "The elevator is private. It opens up inside Mr. Bonetti's suite."

"Ah. Okay."

I followed him over, he used a key on a metal panel, and we stepped inside the elevator, which was about the size of a refrigerator carton. I had my coat unbuttoned and my hands casually on my hips. It looked natural enough but the point was, if the elevator opened up on a bunch of guns, I would have easy access to mine.

But it didn't open on anything except another little receiving area. My escort stayed inside the elevator, and the doors shut him in as tiny slapping slippered footsteps from the nearby hallway announced my host.

Alberto Bonetti, in a pale green sweater, yellow button-down shirt, and the kind of tan slacks old people garden in, came trotting up and offered his hand for me to shake.

I did. It was a soft handshake, but my hunch was it was soft on purpose.

In the equally soft face—where under the slicked-back gray hair sharp young eyes hid out in the seventy-year-old oval of flesh—a smile blossomed, friendly but with the faintest hint of shark. Old shark, but shark.

"You walk an interesting line, Mr. Hammer."

"What line is that, Mr. Bonetti?"

"The line between hero and fool, between brave and reckless." He gestured vaguely back toward his suite. "There's coffee. We'll sit in the kitchen."

I followed him, but I already knew the way from my previous visit. Off the hallway on the left was his small office, a cluttered desk, file cabinets, photos hanging crookedly depicting him with political and show biz figures. Soon the hall opened out and a living room yawned off to the left, with a small, warm kitchen—modern but with wooden cabinets—at right.

The place had surprisingly little personality. It was a nicely appointed modern condo, like many older people retired to, but with none of the Renaissance bric-a-brac some old dons affected. The only distinctive aspect was the lack of windows. Even prison cells had windows, but old Alberto had once been shot at through the living room window of a summer home down in Florida, and ever since he'd had an aversion to anybody outside blowing him a kiss.

So we sat in the kitchen of this bunker at a nice round wooden table drinking coffee that he served me himself. He also had a little plate of hard white biscuits sprinkled with sugar. There was cream for my coffee and Sweet'n Low. He was a good host. On the counter behind him were shiny new appliances, including a big glass-fronted microwave.

Alberto sipped his coffee, which was black, and said, "I suppose this is about Frank Cerone."

"Yeah."

"My people tell me you cut him open and handed him his entrails."

"I cut him open. I didn't have to hand him anything—he caught what he could of them, before he went down. He didn't suffer much, but he didn't go out on a happy note."

This seemed to amuse him. He set his coffee down on a paper place mat. He'd provided me one, too. "I have the feeling you would have liked to make him suffer, given the opportunity."

"Oh, I had the opportunity. I'm just getting soft in my middle age."

"Wait till you're *my* age . . . if you get there." He nibbled a cookie. So did I. "We both know I sent him. Do you understand *why* I sent him, Mr. Hammer?"

I told him my theory—that he'd been given undue credit for Doolan's faked suicide, and for the failed hit-and-run attempt on me, and that he'd seen an opportunity to raise his standing among his fellows by *really* having me whacked.

He sipped more coffee. "Astutely reasoned. You are right, of course. But I failed. And I'm going to suggest that you coming here today in good faith—and me receiving you the same way—indicates that this temporary truce can be maintained. Can become a *permanent* one, so much as anything is permanent in this life."

"Yeah, it can slip through your fingers." I grinned at him. "Just ask Frankie Cerone."

He chuckled silently, then shook his head. "I never know whether you're grandstanding with such remarks, Mr. Hammer, or if you really, truly have that sick a sense of humor."

"Beats me. Why would you want us to strike a truce, Alberto?"

He smiled more with his eyes than his mouth; the bland softness of his face was only lightly creased with old age. "I might ask you the same thing . . . Mike."

I had another cookie. "I don't see that I have any argument with you. Or anyway I didn't until last night. I settled my score with Sal and his crew a long time ago. You knew damn well that your boy was a twisted piece of work, and in a weird way I figure I did you a favor, ridding the world of him. Ridding you of him."

Alberto said nothing, but his eyes seemed to confirm my assertion. He sipped more coffee, glancing at his watch.

"After I took Sal out," I said, "you must have decided, at some point, that killing me to save face just wasn't worth it. With Sal and half a dozen of his best boys dead on that dock, the cops waded in and put the squeeze on your family, and you were lucky not to do hard time. You retired, or pretended to, and had to just sit back and watch while somebody else stepped in and took over the drug trade in this town. In this country."

"*Somebody,*" he said, and sneered a little. "Do you know who that somebody is?"

"Yeah. It's Little Tony Tret. He's sold this Club 52 bill of goods to the public and the politicians, where doing coke is just acceptable behavior for the beautiful people. And the cops and maybe even the feds can't imagine Anthony would be bold enough to take advantage of all the slack he's being cut to use the place as a front for major trafficking."

The dark eyes flared. "But he did. He has. He is."

"And more than that, he's opening Club 52 spots all around the country—a conduit for coke and every other controlled substance, getting a free ride from starstruck local politicians. Plus payoffs when necessary. The kind of money he's generating, that's just the price of doing business."

Alberto brushed cookie crumbs off his sweater. "Then you must know, Mike, that I am the last person on earth who would ever have arranged for your friend Bill Doolan to die. Doolan was investigating Club 52 and hoping to bring Little Tony down, an effort I can only applaud."

"You weren't actively helping Doolan . . . ?"

"No! No, that hard-ass old copper would have been too proud, not to say suspicious, to accept the benefit of my counsel, much less help. I may have fed certain information to him through contacts, but that's all."

I frowned. "Why sic Cerone on me right when I'm closing in on Little Tony?"

The don shrugged. "It seemed the right card to play. You know nothing personal was intended. But I believe I have lost my moment. Even the police are knowledgeable enough to connect the late Mr. Cerone to me and my affairs, and that will require . . . pulling in my head and playing turtle again."

"But you're not a turtle. You're a different animal altogether."

Half a smile dug a groove in a smooth if gently lined cheek. "I'm aware that Assistant District Attorney Marshall also has her shrewd eye on Anthony Tretriano. And I hear interesting whispers that the D.E.A. and the I.R.S. are about to look into his activities as well. No, Mr. Hammer, I felt I could afford taking you out of the game to enhance my standing. But, as I say . . . I failed." He glanced at his watch again. "Can we agree to move on?"

I grunted a laugh. "It's just business, right? Even when your own kid dies, you do all the calculations and decide whether or not to go after the guy responsible. Christ, Alberto—I killed your *son*. *That's* the reason to take me out. Not fucking business."

He shrugged. "That's why you are a small businessman, Mike . . . and I am, shall we say, a captain of industry. More coffee?"

"No thanks. You up for answering a couple more questions, Alberto?"

"Ask and we'll see."

"What do you know about gems being used for payoff purposes?"

He frowned. Blinked. "Why, nothing."

Was he that good an actor?

"Did you have anything to do with the murder of a seaman named Joseph Fidello?"

He shook his head. "Never heard of him."

"Fidello had his throat cut. A kill with a knife, the same goddamn day that your boy Cerone comes calling on me with a blade."

Leaning on an elbow, he cupped his chin and got a thoughtful look. Something gently mocking danced in his voice. "I wonder how many knifings there are in New York on any given date?"

"Yeah, okay. But what about Ginnie Mathes?"

"What about who?"

I shifted in the chair. "You really aren't part of this, Alberto? There have been four murders — Doolan, the Mathes girl, a hooker named Dulcie Thorpe, and now Joseph Fidello. And none of them are names that mean anything to you?"

His shrug was elaborate. "Only Doolan. The others, no. If you want to know where I stand in this — or rather where I *sit* — it's on the sidelines, watching Anthony Tretriano's world crumble. His father was a minor player, not a nobody, but a very small somebody. Big Tony owed his loyalty to me. Which means his son owed me the same." His eyes flashed, an edge came to his voice. "But instead, Little Tony became a big shot, went to great lengths to rehabilitate his reputation while behind the scenes he sought to usurp what is rightfully mine."

The lion behind the lamb was revealing itself.

"So," I said, "when Little Tony and his Club 52 scheme go down, *you* rise back up."

The eyes said shark, too — hard and dark and cold. "Why? Did you really think I was a harmless retiree, Mr. Hammer, ready to move to Florida and clip coupons? *You* can move back to Florida, if you like. You have my word I won't send anyone to kill you, ever again, as long as you stay out of New York."

"What's the plan, Alberto?"

"Would I just . . . *tell* you, Mike?"

"You've told me a lot already. Why not?"

He shrugged. Chuckled. "Why not indeed? Some of us who are written off as over the hill are still very much able to play the game. Don Giraldi. Pierluigi. When Anthony crashes in a cloud of coke dust, we will rise up. Our distribution system is already in place."

"What, Sonata Imports?"

That got his attention, the shark eyes flaring. Then he eased back into his soft-spoken host's role. He glanced at his watch again. "You are remarkably well informed for an outsider, Mike."

"Am I keeping you, Alberto? Got another appointment?"

"No. Not at all. I find your company interesting. Even illuminating."

I studied him. The back of my neck was tingling. "I have an idea, Alberto."

"Oh?"

"Yeah. I have an idea that before I got off that elevator, you sent down word to rally the troops. You probably had some of the older fellas sent safely away, and everybody else you advised to arm themselves and get ready. Maybe you even had phone calls made, while you were stalling me up here, to bring in more troops. What kind of army will I be facing when I leave your condo, Alberto? Will they kill me here, or will they put a bag on my head, toss me in a car trunk, and drive me somewhere to make an example out of me?"

Alberto Bonetti couldn't hold back the smile. He couldn't stop that upper lip from pulling back over white teeth, which were no less sharklike for being store-bought.

"Why don't you ask *them?*" he said and began to laugh, softly.

I saw the two men reflected in the glass of the microwave door—the big guy who'd come up with me on the elevator and another of the club-room attendants, both with revolvers in hand. "Reinforcements have arrived, huh?"

Alberto raised a hand as if in benediction, but actually to pause the pair of gunmen behind me. They had entered through a door into the living room, the soft carpeting cushioning their steps. They weren't right behind me—maybe ten feet. . . .

"Outgunned and outnumbered, Mr. Hammer," Alberto said, and his eyes were hard and his smile was a sneer. All business or not, the old don truly hated me. I could see that now. Maybe vengeance was part of his agenda after all, which at least made him more human.

"Lousy odds," I said.

"Terrible."

"Better than yours."

The .45 came into my hand of its own volition and I blew his brains out all over the reflection of his boys. Fast as it had been, he'd had time to be surprised, and now stared in shock at the ceiling as blood and brains spilled from his shattered skull like awful jelly onto his otherwise spotless kitchen floor.

This I noticed only in a peripheral way as I was busy tipping that table over on its edge and giving myself cover, an action accomplished in the startled second shared by the pair that shooting their boss had bought. From behind the wooden wheel, I ripped off two shots so fast neither man had the chance to react before my .45 slugs took root in their heads and blossomed red. They made as little sound falling to that soft carpet as they had creeping up on me.

I grabbed the dead don by his shirt collar and dragged him down the hall, leaving a sluglike trail of scarlet slime on the tile floor. I had to keep looking fore and aft, fore and aft, because I didn't know whether more guns would come spilling in through the living-room entry, or maybe beat me to the elevator.

And I was almost to the elevator—no key was needed on the boss's end—when I heard the rush of footsteps and the grunt of breath from guys not used to running. Two more of the armed and dangerous club-room waiters came barreling at me from the living room, shooting, but wildly. I dropped their dead boss to the floor and stood sideways, making as narrow a target as possible, and picked them off one at a time. The first one was another head shot and he went back in a tangle of legs leaving a blood-mist cloud, but the other one slipped in his boss's blood trail and was already careening back when the shot meant for his head caught him under the chin, dropping him in a pathetic pile as he clutched his red-spurting throat and bubbled blood. It was an even bet he'd drown on the stuff before the wound killed him.

I grabbed dead Alberto by the shirt collar and held him up like a meat shield as I hit the elevator button. If somebody below, hearing the shit hit the fan, had summoned the elevator, then sent it back up, there could be guns poised in that car to blast me to ribbons.

But the car was empty, and Alberto and I stepped on. *Which button should I push?* They would expect the ground floor. I hit the second. Firepower would be waiting but not as heavy as downstairs. Holding the late Alberto in front of me, my left fist clutching his collar right behind his shattered head, I was getting blood and other ooze on me, but it couldn't be helped. The elevator wasn't big enough to hide to either side, so I stayed more or less dead center, and when the door slid open, a guy in a green leisure suit with a big mustache and a head of curly hair let rip with a grease gun, a vintage M3, and the bullets *bup bup bup*ped right across and through the dead don and thudded against me, slowed down by the cadaver and just tapping the bulletproof vest.

I shot Leisure Suit in the left eye, which got a surprised expression out of the right one, and before the big guy tumbled to the floor of the little receiving area, I dumped the don on the threshold of the elevator, to keep the door from closing, stranding the car, and bent down to grab the grease gun from limp fingers. I had it in my left hand and the .45 in my right as I moved into the club room.

It appeared empty. Abandoned. I checked behind the long bar and a bartender and waiter were crouched there. The waiter thrust a .38 snout my way, and I shot him between the eyes, not that tough at close range. The bartender, unarmed, had his hands up — he was about fifty and balding and was crying, looking away. Apparently just a bartender. He'd pissed himself, you could see it and smell it.

Keeping his eyes off me, so as not to see his own death or maybe to tell me he wouldn't be able to I.D. my ass, he was begging for his life and I told him to shut the fuck up.

"I know there are ways out of here," I said. "Any from *this* room?"

"No! No. Please . . . *please* don't. . . ."

"*Where* then?"

A finger pointed at the ceiling. "The end suite upstairs — parking lot side. The fake fireplace swings open, there's stairs down to the cellar."

"How do you get out of the cellar?"

"I don't know!"

Shit.

I could hear a lot of hustling and hollering above me. I had no desire to go back upstairs. Maybe I could go out the front way just as easy. Back out in the reception area, I checked the late Leisure Suit—he had a pair of thirty-round magazines for the M3 in a jacket pocket. I collected these and shoved a fresh one in. I would have rather had a Thompson than an M3, but at least the thing was light. Even with ammo in, it was only ten pounds.

When I went down the stairs, two punks in muscle shirts with handguns and dumb expressions were coming up. I panned the grease gun across and wiped the stupidity off their faces and the guns tumbled from dead fingers and they served no further purpose now other than giving me obstacles to step around. Halfway down, the room presented itself, and there was more of the young crowd down there, a confused, excited swarm with guns in hand—I counted twelve, and mixed in were half a dozen older Bonetti hitters, who were jockeying for position, so many bodies down there that they were in danger of shooting each other. Bullets were flying around me, chewing up the wooden stairs and the banisters, and a couple thunked into the bulletproof vest, hurting like hell, like Marciano was working over my midsection, but I passed the grease gun across the sea of faces and turned them scarlet and screaming then moved the spitting, smoking snout in a half circle, chewing up not just flesh but the green felt of the pool tables and shattering the jukebox glass and punching holes in the pop machines and tearing the wooden booths apart, pausing only briefly to toss the empty clip and jam the second one in and give them more, even more, *and I was in the jungle again, sweating in the steam with my Thompson chopping up exotic plants and hacking limbs off trees and snipers as screaming Japanese tried to swim through the sky only to belly flop on the ground, and somebody was laughing, and it was me.*

The grease gun was empty.

And I had no more clips. I got out the .45 but down below was nothing but silence and the smell of cordite and bodies flung haphazardly in various awkward postures of death with the pools and smears and streaks of blood glimmering under fluorescent lighting that had taken not a single hit.

Nobody was alive down there, or if they were, they were faking it well enough to deserve a pass. Still, something told me not to go out that front door. That was where reinforcements had entered, and more would be waiting.

So I went back up the stairs, slamming a fresh clip into the .45, and nobody was waiting in the second-floor reception area, nobody alive anyway. I took the fire stairs up and came into an empty hallway. I moved slowly down the carpeted pathway, waiting for somebody to pop out of the doors to the suites on either side, like a real-life Hogan's Alley.

But nobody did.

The door to the suite at the far end was locked. I shot the knob off and shouldered in, sweeping the .45 around a living room decorated tacky bachelor pad–style. The fake fireplace was already ajar. Somebody had used it as an exit.

I went down the narrow, unlighted stairs with the .45 ready. When I found myself in the cellar, where a lot of empty boxes were piled up, I heard somebody whimpering. A small, pale figure was huddled in a corner, hugging its legs, trying to turn into a mouse. It was a girl in panties and no bra, maybe twenty, with a lot of makeup that had run with tears, and lots of permed blonde hair.

"Please don't kill me," she said, her raccoon eyes pleading. Basement dirt smudged her slender little shape like bruises.

Somebody's mistress or hooker of the day or whatever. Poor kid. Like Ginnie Mathes or Dulcie Thorpe, she was just another victim of thoughtless, selfish assholes. I didn't want to be one of them.

"Shush, baby," I said, putting my coat around her shoulders. "It's all right. Nobody's gonna hurt you. I'm a cop."

Not a complete lie.

I helped her to her feet and she hugged me.

"Do you know the way out of here?" I asked.

She swallowed and nodded and pointed. Beyond some stacked boxes, an arched doorway opened onto a brick tunnel, an escape route for the Bonettis in case something bad went down. Hadn't been much help today. It was just big enough for the kid and me to go holding hands as we moved down. My other hand held the .45, though.

The tunnel came out in another basement, which had steps up to old-fashioned storm-cellar doors leading onto a gravel parking lot. A padlock had a key waiting in it for quick escapes, and I used it. We were half a block down from the Y and S Club, standing under an overcast sky on a spring afternoon that had turned chilly.

She gazed up at me, got her first real good look at my face. I assume there were streaks and spatters of blood on it, and even under the best of conditions, that mug wouldn't instill much confidence in any sane human. Her eyes, which were big and blue, saucered, and her mouth made an O, and she ran away from me on bare feet, the sport jacket slipping off her shoulders onto the gravel.

I picked up the jacket, put it on over the now-holstered .45, and started walking. I was maybe twelve blocks from Cummings's office, where I could hole up. The sky growled at me and I couldn't blame it. A lot of men had died this afternoon, some very young, as young as they'd been stupid. I felt nothing for them. I had given old man Bonetti a chance to make peace and he chose war.

Bad choice.

If the family had been crippled by the shoot-out on the pier a year ago, it was decimated now. Over. History.

I limped off, the two hits I'd taken on the bulletproof vest burning, making each breath I took a clutching, clawing thing. One of the hits had punched very near that hot spot under my ribs, turning bad into worse.

But I was still alive, and when the rain began to fall, I welcomed it. It would wash off the blood and save me the trouble.

Chapter 12

SOMEHOW I GOT UP the stairs to the little landing outside the ancient office, the weathered wood under my shoes wheezing as bad as me. I worked the key in the lock, stepped inside, didn't bother hitting the light switch. I got out of the wet sport jacket and let it drop to the old wood-slat floor like a sodden little corpse.

With some effort—the painful places from where bullets had pounded the bulletproof vest were prodding me like sadistic children with a helpless pet—I climbed out of the speed rig and flung it somewhere, retaining the .45, which I tossed onto the old leather couch.

Wracked by a hurt that threatened my consciousness, I wriggled in the dark as rain clawed at the windows and got out of my shirt and the bulletproof vest, kicked out of my shoes, and stepped out of my drenched trousers, just dropping things in damp clumps wherever they chose to fall. Then I stumbled in my T-shirt and shorts, which were moist not wet, to the supply closet where on a high shelf I'd seen an old folded-up blanket. I dragged that behind me like a squaw's papoose over to the leather couch. The .45 I moved to the floor where I could reach it—the wood-and-pebbled-glass door was to the right of the file cabinets, and I had a decent enough view of it.

The blinds behind Cummings's desk, a vague blobby shape over to my far right, were shut, but there was no daylight out there to get in. On my walk here, I'd seen the afternoon give way to night, hours early, thanks to the thunderstorm and black clouds that rolled and roiled like a black tidal wave in the sky, shot through with crackling veins of white.

After reclining in slow motion, I settled on the couch, on my right side, the plump armrest my pillow. Soon I got to like the driving sound of the storm. The thunder had let up, mostly, its roar reduced to an occasional halfhearted murmur. Now there was just downpour, cleansing the gray collection of steel and glass and concrete that New York had become, or giving it a good goddamn try.

I didn't dare go back to the Commodore, not right now. Too many people knew I was staying there. And too much temptation for me to return to those pill bottles, the magic vials that quelled the hurt and beat my subconscious into submission and mellowed me out when that was the last damn thing I needed.

But the temptation remained, as the pains in my side and my midsection throbbed and burned and traded spasms like they were in competition for my attention. They had it, all right.

The saving grace was how tired I was, the energy I'd burned in the jungle of that three-story brownstone, followed by a wind-whipped, rain-lashed twelve-block walk, had left me spent, empty, and it didn't take long for sleep to roll in like fog and fill me up.

* * *

The sound of the key in the door lock was small and scratchy and subtle, and if the rain hadn't reduced itself to drizzle that merely pattered at the windows, I might not have heard it.

I came awake at once, but moved not at all. The dream I'd been lost in had been intense and dramatic and was gone now, a tiny vivid life snuffed out by the reality of someone entering the office.

A woman.

Framed there in the doorway, enough light making its way from the street to the little landing two floors up to give me the shape of her, tall, with a shoulder-length helmet of hair, blonde, a raincoat, the hand holding the key going into a purse and coming back with something small and flat.

A gun.

A little automatic.

I held my breath. She hadn't gone for the light switch, either. She was moving toward Cummings's desk, and my hand was snaking silently through the darkness to the floor by the couch where the .45 lay.

The shape of her against the windows was indistinct but again I knew she was tall, and well built, and it might have been Angela Marshall.

Had she come looking for me?

Her head was lowered when she clicked on the little desk lamp and all I could see was the top of her head, the blonde hair.

Was it Chrome? How had *she* known to come here?

As she went through papers on the desk, the file folders I'd been going through still there, the little automatic remained clutched in her right hand. Meantime, my fingers touched the cold oily metal of the .45, and then found the familiar walnut grips, and the weapon was in my hand when I said, "You want to lay that little automatic down gently, doll. Nice and easy."

The blonde looked up at me, startled, but the hand with the gun neither released nor pointed it. The ash blonde hair curled around a lovely face whose deep brown eyes searched through the darkness, a lush, red, moist mouth open in surprise but not dismay.

"Mike . . . ?"

". . . *Velda?*"

She let the nasty little hammerless .32 drop to the desk and came around quickly, and I was off the couch, the .45 plopping on a sofa cushion as she rushed over and I took her in my arms, every aching muscle and bone in my body not giving a damn about discomfort, because the wonder and joy and delight of seeing her again, of having her in my arms once more, overrode all else.

She was a woman in a sopping raincoat and I was a mess in damp underwear with a mouth full of thick sleep and neither of us cared, the kiss of hello making up for the goodbye kiss that never happened, any recriminations, any frustrations, any irritations gone in one fast embrace.

Her face was buried in my neck, where she murmured my name again and again.

"Velda," I said. I felt like a man who'd been crawling across a desert and had seen an oasis and crawled and crawled some more and *thank you God* it was no mirage, it was real, so very real. "Velda."

"Oh Mike . . . oh *Mike* . . . coming in from the airport, I heard about that slaughter at the social club." She brought her eyes around to meet mine. "Was that you, Mike? Did you do that?"

"What do you think?"

"The cops are speculating it was two mob factions mixing it up. The only survivor is a bartender who said he didn't see anything. They say twenty-four are dead."

"Sounds about right, kitten." My legs went rubbery, and I groaned.

Alarm colored her voice: "Were you wounded?"

"I had a vest on. I took a couple in the midsection."

She was shaking her head, the ash blonde arcs swinging like scythes. "Jesus, Mike, you can die, getting shot up in a vest. You might have internal bleeding."

"I'm . . . I'm all right, baby. Now that I see you, I'm all right."

But she wasn't hearing any of it. She put me back on the couch, switched on a standing lamp nearby, and headed for the little john in the rear corner. She came back with a cool cloth and sat beside me and soothed my brow and cleaned my face. And my hands.

"Blood all over you, Mike."

"But not mine."

"You need something for the pain?"

"I'm off the meds."

"Aspirin at least. I have some in my purse."

She fed me half a dozen that I washed down with a Miller from Cummings's little fridge. Then I was stretched out on my back again. She perched beside me and looked down at me with so much love I could hardly take it.

"I'm sorry, baby," I said. I felt my eyes fill up. Goddamn sissy.

She shook her head. "We were both fools. That's all the discussion we need."

"Okay. So . . ." I gave her my slyest grin. ". . . You been in Colombia, huh?"

Her eyes widened, like a pinup girl whose skirt blew up in a convenient gust of wind. "How much do you know?"

"I know that Doolan didn't kill himself."

She frowned, shook her head. "He would never do that. Never. I wanted to come back right away, as soon as I heard, but I had things to do first. You made it for the funeral?"

I nodded. "Saw to it that that gun he gave Pat got buried with him."

"Good." She swallowed. "That's good."

233

"You were the mystery woman everybody thought was Doolan's girl."

"Is that what they thought? Well, I guess we wanted them to. All he ever talked about was how I should stop being so goddamn stubborn and go find you and get back with you. He said without me in your life, you would be lost. And without you in my life, I'd never be whole again."

"Doolan wasn't wrong. What *was* your relationship?"

She sighed, smiled a little. Hard to get used to her as a blonde. "He came to me for help, Mike. You weren't around, and I had a P.I. ticket. And anyway, I could go undercover better than somebody as well known as you."

"When was this?"

"Four, five months ago." She cocked her head and her eyes narrowed as she regarded me. "We need to tell each other our stories, Mike. You want to go first?"

I did.

I told her how Doolan had been found in his apartment with the night latches undone. How whoever killed him was close to him, a girlfriend maybe. How a young would-be dancer got herself mugged and killed in a war zone near McCormick's Funeral Home the night we gave Doolan his send-off. How the dancer's apartment had been searched, and how a boyfriend of hers had been killed. And when I mentioned Basil's pebble, her eyes flared and her nostrils, too.

"You know something about that, baby?"

"I do. But go on, Mike."

I told her about Dulcie Thorpe getting run down because some amateur got sloppy making a try for me. I told her about Assistant D.A. Angela Marshall's interest in the case, but did leave a few details out — why spoil a great homecoming? I explained how Anthony Tretriano wasn't really deserving of his reputation for going straight, and how his Club 52 was a degenerate's Disneyland that was about to go the big-time franchise route, like McDonald's. Cocaine with that?

I told her everything. Almost.

"Okay, doll. Tell me about *your* spring break vacation."

There was something wistful in her half smile. "I have to give you credit, Mike. You came back to the city and in a few days gathered enough information to come to the same conclusions that Doolan and I had worked for over many months. But we had gone the second step—we had a strong lead on who and where Little Tony's coke connection was."

"In Colombia."

She nodded. "Let me dispense with one false assumption you made—those fabled stones of Basil, that unpolished pebble of yours? There are no others. It's the last one."

"The last? Why?"

"Because despite the legend, Basil did not escape the Holocaust, not really. He was betrayed by a high-level Nazi who had agreed to help smuggle Basil into Switzerland in exchange for the stones as well as a handful of precious gems already cut and set in rings and other jewelry. The exchange was made, all right, and the Nazi got the pouch of pebbles . . . but Basil escaped the gas chamber only in the sense that he died under a gun."

"Why has a stone turned up now?"

"After the war, a small cadre of Nazis hiding out in South America used the gems to build their new lives. This included the predictable cover stories and lavish estates, not to mention top-notch tutors to teach them a new language and culture . . . but eventually the need to create a new, ongoing income became imperative. This group of Nazis—three of them, two ranked just below Goebbels, the other was two notches under Himmler—used the stones and cut gems over the years . . . parceling them out to discreet, wealthy, very private collectors . . . to become the masters of the Colombian drug cartel."

"Gems were a perfect way to fund their activities," I said.

"Yes—your theory about the mob using them for money laundering was essentially correct, only it wasn't the mob. It was the cartel."

I was nodding. "And Doolan sold two valuable paintings, which he neglected to remove from his will, to fund your South American trip. What the hell did you do down there, doll?"

Her chin went up, proud of herself. "I landed a job as the executive secretary to one of the three masters of the cartel. They have also built up legitimate businesses over the years, in part for cover and money laundering, but some are very successful in their own right."

"How did you and Doolan swing getting you in that close to the top guys?"

Her smile had an impish quality, which in such a big sleek cat of a woman should have been silly, but wasn't. "I have contacts that even Doolan doesn't have . . . that even *you* don't have, Mike. You know I worked for Military Intelligence during the war."

"And did a C.I.A. stint in the Cold War. Which I could hardly forget. So they helped you with a cover story?"

"They call it a 'legend' these days, Mike. See? You're not the *only* legend in this partnership." She stroked my cheek. "Through those contacts, I got tight with some D.E.A. agents. They are anxious for this information."

"Bet they are. So your federal friends paved the way?"

"Yes."

"So what did you learn?"

"Plenty. I have microfilm of financial records and extensive photographs of all three former Third Reich bigwigs—they have been discreet over the years about having their pictures taken, as you might imagine. And I have confirmed their relationship with Anthony Tretriano. He'll be taken down by the D.E.A. and I.R.S. within days."

Old Alberto had been right—he'd had contacts, too.

"Doll, what was the photography bit? Why did Doolan want those pictures of Chrome, and where does she fit in? He wasn't *really* shooting photos for some L.A.-based reporter, was he?"

She laughed lightly. "Doolan was no photographer, Mike. You knew that."

"That was *you* taking the shots of him posing with Chrome, right?"

"Right. And as for Chrome, I don't know where or even *if* she fits in, Mike. She's an entertainer, and a very rich, successful one, and apparently Tony Tret really is crazy about her. Which surprises me, because I always thought he leaned the other way. But these days, you never know. The pictures weren't of her, anyway."

"Sure they were—I *saw* them. They were in Doolan's files."

"Well, she's *in* the photos. But we were after shots of the three guys in her band."

"Her band?"

"Yeah. So-called band. They're phonies. My friends in the D.E.A. suspected those three might be connected to the Colombian bunch, and they are. They're not musicians, not really—they're bodyguards with a long association with the cartel."

I snapped my fingers. "I *knew* they weren't playing those instruments on stage. Chrome was singing to a prerecorded track—they were just faking it, miming it."

Velda shrugged. "It may be as simple as Chrome needs protection. She's a big star in South America, and the word is that she's primed for superstardom here as well. Those three bodyguards are the only direct connection between her and the cartel."

"So who was the pebble for?"

She frowned. "What do you mean, Mike?"

"I mean that kid Ginnie Mathes—she was an innocent, manipulated into being a delivery girl. Somebody mugged and killed her before the handoff was made. Who was supposed to get that last stone of Basil's?"

Velda shook her head. "No clue. But it sounds like you think the mugging really *was* a mugging. . . ."

"I can't prove it, but I can tell you what makes sense to me. I think Ginnie Mathes got back together with Joseph Fidello, maybe not steady again but just saw him a few times when he was between cruise-ship gigs. And I think sailor-boy Fidello, who had been around, saw that unpolished gemstone and knew what it was. Knew that his dumb little ex-girlfriend had temporary possession of an object of untold value."

"So he mugged her?"

I nodded. "But Ginnie wasn't as dumb as Fidello thought—the pebble wasn't in her purse, it was tucked in the sleeve of her blouse."

"Then who killed Fidello?"

"Whoever sent Ginnie to make that delivery. That's who went to Ginnie's apartment looking for the stone, and that's who went to Fidello's apartment to look for it there."

She was nodding slowly, following right along. "*And* to tie him off as a loose end, when the stone wasn't found in his flop . . . or when Fidello claimed he never had it."

"Right. The problem with this case, doll, is that I have been viewing a whole scattering of puzzle pieces and trying to make one picture out of them. This is not one puzzle. It's two or three or even four puzzles, and each one is simple."

"Unless its pieces are mixed in with all those others."

"Bingo, baby."

"So what now?"

"Now I think I'd like to get cleaned up."

"I think I'd like to see you cleaned up."

I gave her a funny look. "I don't know, though—I can't quite buy you as a blonde."

She pretended to take offense. "Really? I was a blonde when we met."

"Yeah, you were an undercover policewoman and I damn near ruined everything trying to save your pretty behind."

"I didn't mind. That guy needed killing anyway."

Memories.

"So," she shrugged, "maybe blondes don't have more fun."

And she grabbed at the scalp of the ash blonde hair and yanked it off. She tossed the wig with the rest of the odds and ends scattered around the office floor, and unpinned all that black, auburn-highlighted hair and shook it and shook it and shook it some more . . . then smoothed it some.

Then there she was—Velda.

With that timeless pageboy and those beautiful brown eyes and a mouth that fed your hunger even as it encouraged you to sup some more.

"Baby . . . ," I said, and was reaching for her.

"First you get cleaned up," she said. She shook a finger at me. "And maybe buy a girl a meal. You don't think I'm easy, do you?"

She had left a suitcase out on the landing, and we collected that and caught a cab to the Commodore. When I took her up to my room, and she saw that it was the Honeymoon Suite, she started laughing, but managed to blurt, "You gotta be kidding me!"

"Hey, you know I'm a sensual slob."

She gave me a narrow-eyed look, hands on her raincoated hips. "Have you been having fun while I was away?"

I ignored that and pointed. "There's a hot tub in there. Big enough for two. You had a long plane trip. Maybe we could . . . wash away each other's sins?"

She came over and wrapped her arms around me and gave me a short but sweet kiss. "I don't think they have enough soap for that. But it's not a bad idea."

That was when the goddamn phone rang.

Velda said, "A buck says it's Pat."

"No bet."

It was Pat.

"Mike, where were you this afternoon?"

"At Cummings's office going through more files. Why?"

"Have you heard about the raid on the Y and S social club?"

"Yeah. Who'd have thought in this day and age those guineas would go back to the mattresses."

"Mike . . . we found a lot of .45 shells there."

"No kidding."

"No kidding. I put a rush through ballistics on them. Some came from an old grease gun, World War II era. Strictly illegal weapon. The others came from a Colt .45."

"Do tell."

"I thought sure it would match up with yours on file. But it didn't."

"I could have told you that."

"Somehow I think you could. It did match up to another weapon on file. The .45 used at the Y and S Club belonged to Bill Doolan. Somebody in that shoot-out was using Bill Doolan's piece, Mike. Who do you think that could have been?"

"Probably not Doolan."

His sigh was inevitable. "If the forensics guys didn't say that massacre likely involved an invading force of around ten, I would haul your ass to Centre Street."

"If elephants had wings, hats would get popular again. Where are you calling from? Are you outside?"

"Yeah, this is a public phone. I'm around the corner from Club 52. You might want to get over here and have a look. I think you'll be interested."

"Why?"

"Somebody just killed Tony Tret."

We had to postpone the hot tub, but I did take a quick shower and Velda laid out clean clothes for me. I switched back to my own .45 for the shoulder sling, and told Velda to go downstairs after I left and put Doolan's gun — which I'd borrowed from his private stash in the old desk at his apartment — in a manila envelope and have it stowed in the hotel safe.

"I'm not going with you?" she asked.

"No. I want a better sense of who's doing the shooting before I risk putting you back on the firing line."

"If you say so. But I am a big girl."

"And in all the right places. Do keep that little .32 of yours handy. People have been dropping in on me at this hotel with more in mind than leaving a mint on my pillow."

"Got it."

So I was in the trench coat and my dry-cleaned suit with my hat only mildly spattered with remnants of my afternoon at the Y and S. I would get a new porkpie soon enough. Right now I had a cab to catch.

The rain was gone but its memory endured in the slick black patent-leather look of the sidewalks and streets. I grabbed a cab and fifteen minutes later got dropped at where yellow police sawhorses cut off Club 52's block. The only crowd in front of the art deco marquee tonight was police-oriented — an ambulance, four black-and-whites, Pat's unmarked Ford—and the only people playing dress-up were uniformed cops and E.M.T.s.

They were loading the long, lumpy rubber bag into the ambulance when I strolled up to where Pat was watching the procedure. "Do I need a look at him?"

Pat shook his head. "Not much to see." He pointed across the way at an office building. "It was a rifle shot from the fourth window over, on the tenth floor."

"He got shot right here, out on the street, in front of the club?"

The Homicide captain nodded. "While he was picking out tonight's lucky customers from the crowd." His eyes went to the office building again. "We've already been up there. Empty office space."

"Night watchmen?"

"Six empty floors get a cursory inspection, twice a night. Whoever did this had a little eagle's nest setup. Regular Oswald routine. We found nothing but the three spent shells."

"Three?"

"Yeah, took the shooter three tries. The third one went in small and came out big, splattered a security guy pretty good." Pat sighed. "They were lucky it was a rainy night, and the crowd unusually small. Otherwise, those other two shots might have taken out a clubber or two."

"Have you released the crowd?"

"Yeah. We took names. I didn't see any need for holding them here. They saw nothing."

"What about the security guys?"

"They're still inside."

"Mind if I step in there?"

"What for?"

"Maybe I want to pick up a souvenir swizzle stick."

He grabbed my arm—not hard, not exactly friendly. "Mike— what's going on? I'm trying to tell myself you had nothing to do with that slaughter this afternoon. But even without that, the body count is getting out of hand. What kind of war *is* this?"

"I'm not sure yet."

"Mike. . . ."

"Pat, you'll be the first to know."

"Will I?"

"Okay—the second." I grinned at him.

He couldn't help it—he grinned back. Where would he be without me to do his dirty work?

The lights were up inside Club 52 and its magical world was revealed as the old theater it had once been, all its renovations designed only to work in the near dark. The club was a blowsy woman wearing a lot of flashy makeup, hoping to get picked up before last call and the lights coming on.

Chrome was on stage.

Not performing, sitting backward on a white caneback chair, like Marlene Dietrich in *The Blue Angel.* She was in an electric blue version of that midriff-baring outfit she'd done her disco thing in the other night—the blue against her naturally tan skin made a stark contrast. Nobody was up there with her. The drum kit on its riser, the synthesizer, a guitar on a stand, a few amps. But her Colombian "musicians" were M.I.A.

I walked across the plexiglass dance floor where a pair of bare- chested bartenders were sweeping up, a strangely pitiful sight. Normally the stairs at the far side of the stage were blocked by se- curity staff, but not now. I was able to go right up there.

"Hi, honey," I said, depositing myself before her.

She looked up. Her makeup had run, and the big brown al- mond-shaped eyes had the same raccoon look as that little, mostly naked kid in the cellar at the Y and S. The platinum mane was in disarray. "Mike. Oh, Mike, what a terrible night is this."

Stress had not robbed the Latin lilt of its musicality.

"Any idea who might want to kill Little Tony?"

Her chin quivered. "He like to be called Anthony."

"I know. No offense to the dead. You're taking it hard, kid. Wasn't he just a guy you worked for?"

"I love him, Mike. He love me."

"I thought you weren't anybody's girl."

She swallowed. Tears were streaming. She was a wreck. "If he here, if he were alive . . . I would be his. Only his."

"Sorry. Look, Chrome—Anthony's murder is the latest sour note in a pretty sorry symphony. That nice man Doolan got killed, and so did a little hooker named Dulcie Thorpe."

"Doolan, he kill himself, the papers say."

"They say wrong. And there was a girl you knew who was mugged and murdered."

She nodded, swallowed, trying to be brave. Her face was a shambles within the unruly platinum frame, but the long legs on either side of the chair were as smoothly appealing as ever.

"Ginnie," she said. "My young friend, Ginnie Mathes. We were in dance class together. She was good. I wanted her to join my new act."

"Didn't know you used backup dancers."

"The new act, it will. Both boys and girls. It would have mean the whole new life for Ginnie. It is sad. Very sad."

"Did you know Joseph Fidello?"

Her scowl was underscored by those smeary, runny cosmetics. "Ginnie's ex? He was a bad person. He knew her a long time ago and he . . . what is the word? Try to worm his way back in her life. I told her, he is the bad . . . what is the word? Influence. I do not think she was seeing him anymore, when she . . . when we lose her."

"Okay. Look, I'm sorry to bug you right now. I can tell this is rough for you."

"You come see me, Mike. You come see Chrome later. I will have myself put together." She smiled bravely. "You will like what you see. I promise."

Her smile was a quavering thing, and I nodded and smiled, and left her alone.

Alone in the middle of the stage of the hottest club in Manhattan, which tonight—and perhaps on any future night—was as dead as Little Tony Tret.

Chapter 13

THE CLOUDS OVER the city were as gray as industrial smoke, and you could smell the rain up there. But whether the stuff would get dumped on us again was hard to say. The gentle mist barely registered, a little thunder grumbled, and I had a feeling the worst was over.

Or soon would be.

A pity, in a way—when a heavy rain came, city sounds were overwhelmed by nature, traffic thinning, pedestrians driven indoors and leaving the sidewalks to those who liked walking in the rain. Velda and I had gone out in it often enough, grinning into the wind and spray like sailors riding the bow through choppy stuff, and if it caught up with us today, we wouldn't mind at all.

Still, we were prepared—I was in the trench coat and she in her raincoat when we stepped from the cab in front of the East Side address of the turn-of-the-century former residence that housed the Enfilade gun club. It was pushing noon. I had skipped the Bing's workout and didn't swim either, because I got my exercise yesterday at the Y and S Club.

And in the Honeymoon Suite. Our reunion had been a loving, gentle affair, as I was recovering from that pummeling my midsection had taken under the bulletproof vest. Bruises blossomed overnight like exotic purple and black flowers. At breakfast—where we sat and talked and worked at putting the remaining puzzle pieces together—Velda had fed me more aspirin.

There had been no effort by her to get me back on the prescribed meds. Just the opposite. She had looked at the vials, reading over their contents, and her dark eyes flashed at me as I stood nearby shaving.

She said, "Do you *know* what you've been *taking?*" I said no, and she just shook her head . . . *and* shook the contents from the bottles into the toilet and flushed them all away.

Gerald, the dignified grayed guardian of the Enfilade gates, was at his nicely carved antique desk as usual. Velda smiled a little at the formality of his manner and his funeral director garb. He rose and bowed to her, which was pretty goddamn cute, I have to admit, then we stood before him like employees reporting to a benevolent boss.

"Mr. Hammer," Gerald said. "You are welcome to bring your lovely guest along this morning. But you must both sign in . . ."

He pushed the book toward me when I held up a hand. "We're just here with a couple of questions, Gerald."

"Oh? Detective business?"

"Gathering background."

"Nothing regarding our members, I hope."

"Well, frankly I'm investigating Inspector Doolan's death. It may not have been a suicide."

Gerald frowned thoughtfully. "He did seem an unlikely candidate for such, so vital an individual. How may I be of service?"

"I've never been an Enfilade regular, Gerry, so I'm not sure about certain procedures. Do members store their weapons here? I find it difficult to believe they hop out of a cab, or walk over from their parked cars, lugging firearms."

His smile was gentle, as if he were dealing with a child. "Some, like yourself, Mr. Hammer, have permits to carry." He nodded toward my left shoulder, indicating he could again tell I was packing. "Of course, there *are* firearms in use at the Enfilade, some of them vintage weapons, which would be difficult to transport in that fashion."

"The range downstairs—I've only seen handguns in use. Do any of the members keep rifles here?"

"A number do. Yes."

Velda was looking at the book that Gerald had pushed our way. Her eyes came up sharply to mine. "You need to see this, Mike. A couple of interesting entries. . . ."

I checked them out, and said, "I see that Congressman Jaynor is downstairs."

"Yes he is. This is not a busy time—he's one of a handful using the facility. Your friend Mr. Webb is here again, and a few other members. Would you like to go down?"

After asking Gerald a few additional pointed questions, we did, passing the framed photos on that celebrity wall. Velda paused to look at several where Doolan posed with a group that included Anthony Tretriano and Alex Jaynor. We could make out the very muffled sounds of gunfire from the enclosed target range, but found Alex in the lounge area, seated with Smith & Wesson's resident champ, Chuck Webb. Two Wall Street boys sat with them in the midst of friendly conversation.

Introductions were made, with everybody standing to smile and nod at Velda, all of them taking in her beauty with open but not offensive admiration. I helped her out of her raincoat and she showed them what a real woman could do with a simple white blouse and black skirt.

I draped my trench coat over the back of a chair, and the Wall Street pair — in running clothes — excused themselves to go into the range. Chuck, in another polo shirt with the S & W logo, followed them in, throwing me a secret look and head wag, in back of Velda, letting me know what a lucky stiff he thought I was.

The sandy-haired, brown-as-a-berry politician was apparently not here to shoot. Alex was in a well-tailored black suit with white pinstripes and had enough bulk that I could tell a bulletproof vest was a part of his ensemble. When you get shot at from the street often enough, that kind of vest can become a necessary fashion accessory.

"So this is Velda," Alex said in the smooth, resonant voice that had served him well on television and in the political arena. "Doolan spoke of you warmly. He said you were the brains in the Hammer agency."

She shrugged and smiled.

I said, "Making me the beauty, I guess."

The light blue eyes in the narrow handsome face turned alertly serious. "Are you getting anywhere with your investigation into Doolan's death, Mike?"

"I've wrapped it up," I said, "as much as possible. In a case as complicated as this, not every loose end gets connected."

"Does this Tretriano killing factor in?"

I nodded. "At least in a peripheral way — Doolan was closing in on Little Tony. I believe the old boy was able to get close to

'Anthony,' and even scored an all-access pass to Club 52, thanks to their shared membership here."

Alex's expression grew thoughtful. "Well now, Mike—they weren't exactly close friends. Of course, all of the members here are sociable, and I suppose that *did* provide a certain common ground. . . ."

"It must have. Doolan was fairly regular at Club 52 for a while, and he amassed evidence that connects Tony and his club to drug trafficking. These new clubs Little Tony's opening—or anyway *was* opening—would have expanded that operation nationwide."

The politician's expression combined alarm and disgust. "My God. Why didn't Doolan share this with me? I would have helped!"

"He was a sneaky old coot. He compartmentalized. You were close to him and shared his concern about illegal drugs in the city. And yet Doolan kept you unaware that Velda here had been working for him for nearly six months, the last two in South America, gathering intel on the cocaine cartel itself."

"Remarkable," he said, looking at Velda through new eyes.

I said, "This is far-reaching, Alex. Where all of the tendrils will finally reach remains to be seen . . . but you can bet they'll be gathered up by federal investigators better equipped for the job than an old-time private dick like me."

Alex sat forward, his gaze going from me to Velda and back. "Was it the Bonetti bunch? The news is full of that shoot-out at that Mafia social club. If Doolan really *was* murdered, they make a good candidate for instigator. The Bonettis, remember, are the family behind the drug operation that Doolan and I ran out of his neighborhood."

"Hard to say," I said with a shrug. "If Little Tony got wind of what Doolan was up to, he might have been behind that fake suicide. And old Alberto Bonetti had his own reasons to get rid of Doolan, too. We'll probably never know."

Alex squinted at me, like he was trying to get me in focus. "You're not just going to walk away, are you, Mike?"

"Why not? It's over. That sniper who took Tony Tret out was almost certainly a survivor from the Y and S Club melee."

"A reprisal?"

"What else? When the rival mob families trying to control the narcotics racket are both in shot-to-shit disarray, what's left for me to do?"

Now he shrugged. "I guess . . . nothing."

"Well," I said absently, "there is one thing. There's a very valuable item I came across, early on in this mess. I haven't even told Pat about it."

"What is it?"

"Can't say, or anyway shouldn't. You'll read about it eventually. Let's just say it's priceless and is nothing I should be holding on to. Frankly, it probably belongs in the estate of a poor dead kid named Ginnie Mathes."

With an alarmed glance, Velda said, "Mike, this 'item'—is it somewhere safe?"

"Oh yeah. I hid it where nobody will find it." I grinned at Alex. "You'll love this. It's stashed in Doolan's apartment. Little hiding place that only he and I knew about. Fitting, huh?"

I exchanged casual smiles with Velda, and we got up, shook hands with the politician, and excused ourselves.

"Mike," Alex said, "if you think of anything . . . if there's *anything* I can do . . ."

"You'll have plenty to do," I said. "When the feds come in and mop up after me, you'll be in a position to keep the drug racket at bay in this town for a goddamn change."

I put the hat on, grabbed my coat, nodded at him, and followed the nice view Velda provided up the stairs.

Out on the street, she said, "Think he took the bait?"

"Oh yeah." My grin felt like it might burst my face. "Oh yeah. . . ."

This was where it had started.

And started long before I'd returned from Florida, this quiet neighborhood that had gone from fashionable to rundown only to be rebuilt and reinvigorated before finally fading into a low-key, livable area where its many older residents felt comfortable and secure—like a certain Bill Doolan, who had been through fifty-two years of changes. Then a peaceful, even dull way of life had been threatened by the intrusion of a criminal element that the old retired cop had risen up on his haunches to help drive out like the plague-carrying rats they were.

So once again I went up the sandstone steps into the small vestibule with its old-time ornamented brass mailboxes. This time the inner door was locked, and when I hit a random buzzer—not Doolan's—no one asked before buzzing me through.

The door behind me closed of its own will, shutting out street sounds and replacing them with the stillness of the lonely life the old building's residents endured. I went up the two flights of stairs and down the hallway to the door of Doolan's apartment. I still had Pat's key for the padlock that had been affixed to the damaged door of the crime scene, but I didn't need it.

Someone had forced it off, hasp and all.

The lock lay on the floor, sleeping on a small bed of sawdust and splinters. Wouldn't have been much of a job, even with just a screwdriver, any noise minimal. Even as watchful as older tenants could be, the hearing-aid crowd would not likely be alerted by this break-in at Doolan's lonely, dimly lit end of the corridor.

The trench coat was unbuttoned and my hand slipped easily under it and the sport jacket to bring out the .45 from its snug home under my left arm.

Could the trap I'd set have been turned around on me? Had I been so obvious that the drama I'd staged would wind up starring me as its tragic hero? Was a cold-blooded killer waiting on the other side of that door with his own gun?

But when I walked into the old, slightly musty space—no lights on but enough of the gray day seeping from windows deeper in the place to help me navigate—no one greeted me with a gun or otherwise. I moved through the well-decorated, tidy quarters that still bore the signs of the cops who'd been here—print powder, cigarette butts—past the master bedroom and bath and on into Doolan's office/den.

The antique desk that faced a window, adjacent to the wall that held the old man's beloved stereo system and books and mementoes, had its swivel chair pushed away to give the intruder better access to the hidden button that opened a side panel.

Alex Jaynor had emptied the hideaway of the four guns stowed there, and they lay on the blotter of the desk like a courtroom exhibit. He had a hand stuffed in the compartment, feeling around, searching, obviously frustrated.

From my trench coat pocket, my left hand withdrew the rough pebble with the shiny little window. I had it poised between thumb and middle finger, held up to window light, before I said, "Is this what you're looking for, Alex?"

He whirled. That hard-edged, handsome face had a new wildness, the eyes wide and bright with something feral, the sandy hair not so perfect, three or four lacquered strands sticking out this way and that, like springs liberated from a threadbare couch. Only his pinstriped suit retained its dignity.

"It was never in there," I said.

I slipped the stone back in my pocket. What the hell—I put the .45 back in its sling, too.

He swallowed, straightened himself, smoothed his suitcoat, though it didn't need smoothing. His head went back, and only the stray manic strands of hair betrayed him. Those and a seldom-blinking intensity of the sky-blue eyes.

"That little stone is worth a lot of money," he said.

"Yeah. The last of Basil's crop. Maybe you felt honored, being the final 'honest' man bought off with one of them. A lot of corruption flowed from a simple pouch of pebbles over the years. Enough money generated to make Nazis into good South American citizens, and to keep Colombian officials at arm's length while a cartel developed cocaine into the country's leading cash crop."

His words were tight, bit off, with an undercurrent of indignant hysteria. "Haven't you heard, Hammer? You can't legislate morality. Look at how eager the mayor and every politician in this town were to rub shoulders with celebrities at Club 52. No one cares about drugs. No one cares about anything anymore."

I wasn't here to talk philosophy or social mores. "You were supposed to get that gemstone handed off to you by Ginnie Mathes. That out-of-the-way location was chosen because it was close to where you'd be that evening, and yet was an area no one would associate with you. Only you didn't get to her in time—her sailor boy Joe Fidello mugged his own girlfriend for it, and when she saw it was him, he panicked and killed her."

"*He* killed her, Hammer. Not me."

"But Fidello missed the stone. He got her purse, but she'd tucked the little beauty away in her sleeve, and it fell out onto the street where, as fate would have it, I ran across the thing. Ain't kismet a bitch?"

"Hammer, that stone is immensely valuable. If you deliver it to me, and forget any of this happened, then—"

"You mean forget you tried to run me down with a stolen car? Forget that a young woman named Dulcie Thorpe got splashed on the pavement because you weren't up to the job? What I'm wondering is, why such a big payoff? You're just a local politician. But then I thought about it—you're young, good-looking, personable, with TV experience. Your roving reporter background gives you contacts here and in Canada. You're a natural conduit to get cash to other bent politicos, plus down the road, you'll make an ideal candidate for governor or maybe U.S. senator. Who was it that said someday the Mafia will own the man in the White House, and he won't even know it? That's almost right. *You'd* know it."

He was shaking his head, desperation in his tone. "All right. All right. I admit I panicked and I stole that car and . . . but you weren't killed, you were barely injured." Hope leapt into his eyes. "So we can still do business."

"Dulcie Thorpe can't do business anymore."

That remark astounded him. "A hooker? A filthy little street tramp, and you pretend to care? I made a mistake, Hammer, and now you can take advantage of it, and me. You can go back to Florida and retire out of the New York rat race with an ongoing pension the likes of which you never dreamed."

"Okay, Alex. Let's shrug off Dulcie Thorpe's life and death. In her game, her life expectancy was a big question mark anyway, right? But how do you justify Bill Doolan? Your mentor! A man who valued you and your friendship, encouraged you, but who you only got close to for your own aggrandizement, and to keep an eye on the enemy. No *wonder* the Bonetti family tried to hit you in those drive-bys! You helped run them out of the neighborhood at the very same time you were partnered with Little Tony Tret!"

He had been shaking his head ever since I mentioned Doolan, and now he got a word in: "I cop to the hooker, but not Doolan. I didn't kill him, I would never kill him, I loved that old guy!"

"Maybe. I don't think so, but maybe. I know for sure you killed Tony Tret. I can sell it to Captain Chambers, too. I saw your name in the Enfilade book—you were there yesterday in the late afternoon, picking up a rifle from your locker. The little guy on the door, Gerald, saw you leave with a zippered carrying bag. And he saw you bring it back this morning. Ballistics will take about five minutes to make a match with the shell casings from that office window. You left a kind of funny signature—you have a rep at the Enfilade for not being much of a shot. And it took you three tries to nail Tony."

Jaynor was smiling now. Still nervous, but smiling. "All right, Hammer. Am I supposed to believe you take any offense at me getting rid of a mob lowlife like Anthony Tretriano? There are some people saying that what happened at the Y and S Club yesterday *wasn't* two warring mob factions—that it was just you, a one-man army, who did it all. You're a murderer yourself, Hammer. Where the hell do you get your moral indignation? Your sickening self-righteous attitude?"

"I like to think of myself as the guy who puts those extra little weights on the scale . . . to make things balance out. But maybe I'm as evil a shit as you. I don't think so, though. Because there's still Doolan, isn't there? There's still Doolan."

"I told you, I had nothing to do with that!" Jaynor pointed at the chair. "He sat *right there* and thought about the protracted death sentence he was facing and took the easy way out. He was an old man, and you can't blame him."

"I don't blame him. I blame you. I'm guessing you spent the evening with him, and drugged his coffee or his beer—there'd be no toxicology screen on a gunshot suicide victim. I figure you had a key to the place, to lock up after—you and Doolan were that tight. Just like you were tight enough to know about his secret stash of handguns in the desk. You selected one, and when he fell asleep in that chair, you pressed one of his prize guns in his hand and helped the unconscious old man pull the trigger. And burst his heart. At least he slept through it. Had he been awake, you'd have broken it before you exploded it."

"I had no reason to do that."

"Sure you did. I think Doolan finally told you about Velda and the work he and she did, investigating Little Tony and 52, and how she'd been in Colombia for months gathering intel that would be shared with the feds. You knew that Doolan was getting close — that he'd be onto you very soon. I'm guessing you figured you would find documents in his desk, not knowing he kept his work-related files with Peter Cummings, the P.I. he sometimes worked for. Even then, even before the handoff of Basil's pebble was botched, you were in damage-control mode. And you have been in that mode ever since, panicking. Killing Doolan. Trying to kill me. Shooting Tret. An amateur, just floundering around, trying to save his ass."

He grabbed the nearest of the guns, one of the matched German P38s. He pointed it at me and it clicked and clicked.

"If you really knew anything about guns," I said, "you'd have noticed the weight was off. I unloaded all of those. You can keep trying if you like."

He looked down aghast at the other weapons on the blotter that were just useless hunks of metal without their little messengers.

I didn't fool around, since he might have another rod on him, one that did have ammunition, and whipped the .45 out and squeezed off a round, hitting him right in the heart.

It rocked him back a little, against the desk — the .45 had considerable recoil. He winced. It hurt. He braced himself on the lip of the desk with the heels of his hands.

"That's where you shot Doolan," I said, gesturing with the .45 at his chest. "Of course, he wasn't wearing a bulletproof vest."

"You . . . you made your point, Hammer. Call your friend Chambers. I want a lawyer. We'll see . . . see how much evidence you really have."

"That's a good one," I said with a chuckle, and shot him in the stomach. "Like I give a shit about evidence."

He was bent over clutching his belly, his mouth open, the air knocked out of him. The next shot was in the sternum and I heard the splintering crack of bone. He made a gargling sound and went down, hard, across the chalk outline of where the chair had been, where Doolan had been found.

"It's like getting punched by Joe Frazier, huh?"

I put one in his rib cage and he squirmed like a bug on its back. "I could unload a dozen clips into you, and this standard army cap-and-ball ammo would never penetrate that vest of yours. These are just nice soft lead slugs that will tenderize your muscle tissue and puree your organs and break every goddamn bone in their path. Hard to say how long it will take you to die, Alex, but you should have time to work up a good speech for Saint Peter. Kind of think you're heading south, though, no matter how glib you are."

I had four more in the clip and I spread them around evenly, two for Dulcie Thorpe, two more for Doolan, and a free pass on Tony Tret, and he just took them, shuddering under the impact, not even screaming because the soupy insides of him couldn't make it happen, all he could summon was bloody bubbly froth.

"I have another clip here," I said conversationally, "but now I think I *have* made my point. When I leave, the door will be open. Maybe you can crawl out of here. Maybe you can get help."

He was crying, but when a sob came, it hurt too much and he forced it back.

"There's one last touch I think you'll enjoy," I said. "Smart guy like you, you might savor the irony."

I bent over and showed him the .45.

"This is Doolan's gun," I said. "When the cops check out these shell casings, that's where it will lead them. Same gun was used at the Y and S shoot-out, which will tie you to a mob hit. Anyway, my point is—in a way, it's like Doolan himself killed you."

I holstered the gun. He was on the floor, crawling. He hadn't made much progress when I exited the room, but I left the door open for him. He probably couldn't make it down to the street alive, but I liked the idea that he'd die trying.

Chapter 14

MIDAFTERNOON, VELDA and I sat in a booth at Cohen's Deli. I had my namesake corned beef and pastrami sandwich, having worked up an appetite, and my secretary behaved herself with a little bowl of chicken soup. What a beautiful woman puts up with to stay that way.

I dabbed my mouth with a paper napkin, then reached over and dug in the left-hand pocket of my trench coat, which was wadded up next to me.

I held the marble-size stone up to the light. It didn't look like much of anything. Basil had died for this and other stones, and they had funded new lives for inhuman beasts and franchised human weakness into even more wealth.

"That," she said, "might make a nice engagement ring."

"Here's what we're going to do with it," I said, and handed it to her. "You're going to take it to David Gross at the diamond exchange."

"I am?"

"Yeah. I have my own last errand to run. But I want you to get copies made of every photograph you have of those south-of-the-border Nazi bastards, and all the evidence that you've gathered with the feds in mind."

"Okay. What for?"

"You give the stone to David, and the packet of evidence and photos. You tell him to quietly sell the diamond, and to keep a finder's fee according to his own conscience. But the proceeds — like the packet — are to go to some people he knows."

"What kind of . . . ? Oh. Nazi hunters?"

"Yeah."

"To bring these monsters to trial?"

"No."

Took her half a second to process that, then she just sat there staring at the innocent pebble in her palm. Finally she said, "Fine. What's *your* errand?"

"Some things you're better off not knowing about."

"In case I'm questioned? Or because it involves a beautiful woman?"

I grinned at her. "Right. We'll meet back at my room at the Commodore."

"The Honeymoon Suite, you mean."

"Yup. Then we'll paint the town red."

"Haven't you done enough of that already?"

That made me laugh. "Well, I am back in a New York state of mind. But tomorrow, we'll catch a plane down to Florida. I'll teach you how to catch snook."

"Do I want to know how to catch snook?"

"It's not optional."

"Are we moving there? If we're going to retire while we're still young, maybe we should hang on to half of what this diamond's worth."

"No, it's a vacation. I got a car down there. We'll drive it home."

"Home?"

"Yeah. I'm not kidding anybody."

I glanced out the window at a street where people were moving, staying out of each other's way without acknowledging each other's existence. A gray sky loomed, threatening rain but not doing anything about it. The buildings had a terrible interchangeable blankness. Cabs were honking at cars whose drivers were screaming at the cabbies. A Puerto Rican hooker in a miniskirt and black mesh stockings and a cheap blonde wig was watching out for potential johns with one eye and the beat cop with the other. A legless beggar on a wheeled board was having success with the occasional tourist and nobody else.

I shrugged. "This is where I live."

The towering apartment building on Park Avenue had been there forever, exuding a quiet splendor that passersby were welcome to glimpse but only the wealthy could afford. The intimidating doorman in gold-braided blue moved to cut off my entry, then recognized me.

"Mr. Hammer," he said, and nodded.

We'd never met. He just read the papers.

"You happen to know if Miss Chrome is in?" I grinned at him, shoved the hat back on my head. "Hey, I know that sounds dumb—I never got her last name."

"She's never shared it with us, either," he said, in a good-natured growl. "But, yeah, I believe she's in. Guy in the lobby will call up for you. That's a lot of woman, Mr. Hammer."

"I met women before."

He laughed, tipped his braided hat. "That's what I hear."

Getting past the lobby was easy. The guy there confirmed "Miss Chrome" was in, and called up to see if she'd receive me, and she would.

So when I knocked on the door in a gold-scrolled marble vestibule about the size of your average SoHo flat, I half expected a butler to respond. But all I got was the platinum blonde disco doll her own self, in a fluid silver silken dressing gown with a rope belt. White open-toed shoes revealed red nails against tan flesh. The contrast between the stark white hair and the very brown flesh was ever startling.

The hand she extended for me to take was similarly scarlet nailed.

"So nice, Mike, that you accept my invitation," she said, the Latin accent a sensual purr. Nothing showed of last night's sorrow, not even in her eyes, which were bereft of spidery red.

I took my hat off—I'd left the trench coat with Velda. "I know I should have called. Forgive me?"

"There is nothing to forgive," she said, gesturing me inside. "The invitation, it was open. I was in a bad place last night. I am embarrassed for you to see me so."

"You lost somebody dear to you."

I had figured on brilliant splashes of primary color in the pad, the fiesta rainbow cliché gringos always expect. This was more like old Hollywood, a snowstorm of a living room with the kind of modern white furnishings and carpet you might expect from Jean Harlow or Marilyn Monroe, with walls and ceiling to match. Still, many tones were on display—ivory, cream, off-white, interrupted by a handful of large black-and-white glamour photographs of herself. Well, she knew what she liked.

The blizzard was relieved by a big picture window with a view all the way to Central Park, a postcard-worthy vista. The sun had finally cut through the clouds and smog, and the sky over the geometric shapes of the city wore the bright blues and whites of a perfect spring afternoon.

Strangely, her first move was to go to that window and close the cream-color curtain, blotting out that lovely view, as if Act One was over and this was intermission.

"Too bright for a night person," she said, with a little laugh. The only light now came from a single lamp on a white-lacquer end table. "Something to drink?"

"Maybe later. I want to talk first."

"Then we will talk. Suddenly you sound so serious, Mike. Is it about Tony's death? Are you investigating it? You *are* a detective."

She settled in an overstuffed white leather club chair, tan arms slipping from loose silk sleeves to rest regally along the chair's elevated sides as she crossed her long, lush legs.

I sat opposite her on a low-slung couch assembled from intersecting rectangles, as hard and uncomfortable as a doctor's examination table and about the same color. Between us squatted a glass-and-metal coffee table, not unlike the one at Club 52 with the coke mirror. I tossed my hat there.

"I've been working on something complicated," I said. "But I couldn't get anywhere, because I was operating from a faulty premise."

She frowned, as if my English was too dense for her to wade through, though she didn't ask for clarification.

"I was looking at four murders—Bill Doolan, Ginnie Mathes, Dulcie Thorpe, and Joseph Fidello—and then last night, a fifth, Anthony Tretriano. This is further complicated by the Mathes girl's murder rising out of a mugging, which involved the theft of a valuable gemstone."

The widening of her eyes was almost imperceptible. Her chin went up a little, too.

"Wrongly, I assumed one killer was behind it all," I said. "I didn't stop to think that in a criminal enterprise, motives for murder are cheap, and motivations among those involved often run counter."

She cocked her head and one side of her hair fell like a silver curtain. "You are saying . . . there were *two* murderers?"

"Three." I sat forward. "Alex Jaynor, the politician, staged the suicide of Bill Doolan. He also tried to run me down in a car, which makes the death of Dulcie Thorpe a homicide, too. And the police are running ballistics on Jaynor's rifle, which should tie him to the sniper shooting of Anthony Tretriano."

"They will arrest him?"

"No. Jaynor was found dead about an hour ago on the sidewalk outside the old apartment building where Doolan lived."

She frowned. "How did he die?"

"Slow and painfully. That bother you? He did kill your friend Anthony."

"He was more than a friend—my Anthony." She swallowed. Rose slowly, a queen from her throne, those legs seemingly endless, only one hidden by the glistening silver fabric. "I would like a drink. May I serve you?"

"Sure. Rye and ginger. Rocks."

Chrome moved to the padded white leather bar off to the right. She got behind it and poured herself a martini from an already made pitcher.

I leaned against the other side of the bar as she built my drink.

"If you're wondering why I'm here," I said, "it's as a sort of courtesy."

"I had hoped you were here, Mike, because there was a . . . spark? A spark between us, that first night at 52?"

"You're a handsome woman. And you've done nothing to cause me harm that I'm aware of. So I'm giving you the benefit of the doubt."

With the bar still between us, I could see my reflection in the mirrors over the row of bottles.

Her expression was quizzical. "Benefit of the doubt, Mike—the benefit of the doubt for what?"

"I don't have any hard proof that you are anything but a pawn in this. I think it's likely that you were directly involved, but the police—and the D.E.A. and the I.R.S., not to mention Immigration—will be moving in soon enough to sort it out. So my opinion is beside the point."

Her forehead tensed, her dark eyes bore into me. "I *assure* you, Mike, I knew *nothing* of Jaynor and Anthony's scheme. . . ."

"I don't remember mentioning their scheme. Whether you know it or not, you touring your act, opening all the new Club 52 locations, was the conduit through which Little Tony and the Colombian cartel planned to move their coke and other fun powders. You have your own Lear jet, and you go back home between gigs—meaning separate shipments for each club opening. You travel with a band that isn't a band at all—they are drug mules and bodyguards who mime playing instruments while you sing to a canned track. Yet you travel with all sorts of gear, instruments in flight cases, hard-shell drum cases, trunks of electrical this and electronic that—none of it needed. And probably not functional, gutted, to make room for packing fat packets of what the D.E.A. likes to call controlled substances."

She had been holding the cocktail glass, without taking a single sip, and now she set it down, hard. It sloshed and spilled a little.

"Mike, just because the new Club 52 locales will not come to pass, that does not mean I cannot still tour your America—I am the number-one star in South America and have a big record contract here, and I do the TV and . . ." She leaned across and her mouth was a moist red invitation. ". . . and if you keep your suspicions to yourself, you could take Anthony's place, in my business . . . and in my heart."

"Yeah, well, tempting as that is, and I do dig those long legs of yours, I have to say any tour you mount is gonna get looked at very hard by that alphabet soup of government agencies I mentioned."

I finished the rye and ginger and thanked her for it. She was still behind the bar when I walked back toward the coffee table where my hat waited. I glanced back and saw her reach under the bar for something, something she tucked behind her, and the mirror gave me just enough of a silver metallic flash to know it was a nickel revolver.

She came around from behind the bar slowly, smiling just a little, almost as catlike as Velda, and said, "What can I do to convince you not to make trouble for Chrome, Mike?"

I shook my head. "This is all you get. Just a little head start. See, I do kind of blame you, in part anyway, for the Mathes kid's death. She admired you, trusted you, and you got her involved in playing messenger in a very dangerous game."

She took two measured steps my way. Her red-nailed toes in the white shoes were all but buried in the plush ivory carpeting. Her eyes were wide and a weird excitement glittered there. Something about our confrontation had excited her—sexually. Or was that just an act?

"I do not mean, ever, to do Ginnie no harm," she said. The double negative was unintentionally telling. ". . . In fact I mean only to do very *good* by her."

"How about Joseph Fidello?" I asked. "Him I *know* you meant to do harm. In fact, he's the odd murder out, isn't he? You're the third murderer. *You* killed Fidello, Chrome, trying to find that uncut stone. Well, that stone is on its way now to help bring your Nazi cohorts some good old-fashioned Old Testament justice. About time Basil's gems funded something positive."

Her expression was of astonished confusion. "Why should you care about Fidello? *He* is the one who kill that stupid girl. You might have kill him yourself, had you the chance!"

"Yeah, probably. It's a matter of motivation. I would have taken him out for the low-life murderer he was. You were just removing somebody who might cause you trouble. Somebody who knew just a little too much about you and Ginnie . . . and that uncut gem."

Her mouth and eyes promised unknown pleasures. The sexual heat was damn near shimmering off her—*she liked this.*

"I am a very famous woman in my country, Mike. I can return to my home, where I am a very, *very* rich woman. We can go there together and leave your ugly city and your so very stupid and selfish country behind. There would be nothing bad, nothing criminal in our life together, the whole foolish scheme of Alex and Tony, it would be as if it never happen."

"It *did* happen. And an old man with a great heart was murdered because of it."

"Not by me . . . not by *me.* . . ."

"But maybe you're not just a pawn," I said. "Maybe *you're* the top man in the Colombian cartel."

She overplayed her quizzical expression.

You'd have to call my smile a sneer. "Tell me, Chrome—how was it two gay men were so attracted to you? Is there something under that gown you're hiding from me?"

Her smile held no sneer at all; it was the whitest thing in this white room, radiant and self-possessed. "Was I born a *man*, Mike? Or maybe . . . *both* the man and the woman? An extra chromosome—is that the little joke of my name, Mike?"

"I was thinking maybe a surgeon had more to do with you than God."

"Or the devil? So old-fashioned are you, Mike. Such ancient notions of sexuality."

"I get by."

"You cannot deny you enjoyed me, Mike. I was on my knees before you — remember?" A graceful hand with tapering fingers gestured toward the lovely body. "All of us, Mike, even *you,* we have our female side, and our male. Men like Tony . . . like Sal . . . you killed Sal, did you not, Mike?"

"I killed him."

Something nasty flashed through her dark eyes. "Chrome, she was one woman they could accept. And I could accept their love *like* a man . . . you understand?"

"Spare me the diagrams."

She prowled toward me, one hand still casually behind her, and with the other she undid the rope at her waist and the dressing gown dropped in a silken puddle at her red-nailed feet and exposed her golden goddess form with thrusting breasts and narrow waist and flaring hips that flowed into the long, long legs, as muscular as a man's. But nothing else about her suggested anything but woman, as beautiful a specimen of the sex as I had ever seen.

The mouth was as wet and red and lush as ever, the dark eyes hooded, chin up, a red-nailed hand cupping a perfect breast — too perfect.

"Mike . . . Mike. I am a sexual being — you said it yourself."

She was almost in my arms and that hand was coming ever so surreptitiously from behind her back to blow me a .38-caliber kiss. . . .

"No, Mike, I am *all* woman. I was born a woman."

My .45 came up and the tongue of flame from its muzzle licked her belly where the bullet had punched a new hole.

As she staggered on those magnificent legs, Chrome's eyes were wide and wild, and before they filmed over, and she could go down in an ungainly pile to stain that soft, thick white carpet scarlet, I got one last shot in, not from the .45.

"Die any way you like," I said.

About the Authors

MICKEY SPILLANE and MAX ALLAN COLLINS collaborated on numerous projects, including twelve anthologies, two films, and the *Mike Danger* comic-book series.

Spillane was the best-selling American mystery writer of the twentieth century. He introduced Mike Hammer in *I, the Jury* (1947), which sold in the millions, as did the six tough mysteries that soon followed. The controversial P.I. has been the subject of a radio show, comic strip, and two television series; numerous gritty movies have been made from Spillane novels, notably director Robert Aldrich's seminal film noir, *Kiss Me, Deadly* (1955), and *The Girl Hunters* (1963), in which the writer played his famous hero.

Collins has earned an unprecedented sixteen Private Eye Writers of America Shamus nominations, winning for *True Detective* (1983) and *Stolen Away* (1993) in his Nathan Heller series, which includes the recent *Bye Bye, Baby*. His graphic novel *Road to Perdi-*

tion is the basis of the Academy Award–winning film. A filmmaker in the Midwest, he has had half a dozen feature screenplays produced, including *The Last Lullaby* (2008), based on his innovative Quarry series.

Both Spillane (who died in 2006) and Collins received the Private Eye Writers life achievement award, the Eye.